Dear Reader,

When I wrote A New World, I'd recently enjoyed a family reunion in Gloucester, Massachusetts. Now I've just returned from another one. The family's bigger and even more far-flung, but Gloucester remains special to us. Good Harbor Beach, Dog Bar Breakwater, Rocky Neck—these are the landmarks of childhood stories about my ancestors who left Ireland and immigrated to Gloucester.

Perhaps they were whispering in my ear when Cahill McCrea first strode onto a page—a charmer and a dreamer, who especially dreams of building a life in America...and of practical New Englander Eleanor Thalston.

Come dig your toes into the sand or watch the fishing boats come into harbor, and see Cahill and Eleanor discover their new world together.

Patricia McLinn

PATRICIA McLINN

finds great satisfaction in transferring the characters crowded in her head onto paper to be enjoyed by readers. "Writing," she says, "is the hardest work I'd never give up." Writing has brought her new experiences, places and friends—especially friends. After degrees from Northwestern University, newspaper jobs have taken her from Illinois to North Carolina to Washington, D.C. Patricia now lives in Virginia, in a house that grows piles of paper, books and dog hair at an alarming rate. The paper and books are her own fault, but the dog hair comes from a charismatic collie who helps put things in perspective when neighborhood kids refer to Patricia as "the lady who lives in Riley's house." Friends, family, books, travel, gardening and sitting on her porch are among her joys. She would love to hear from readers at P.O. Box 7052, Arlington, VA 22207.

Books by Patricia McLinn

Silhouette Special Edition

Hoops #587
A New World #641
*Prelude to a Wedding #712
*Wedding Party #718
*Grady's Wedding #813
Not a Family Man #864
Rodeo Nights #904
A Stranger in the Family #959
A Stranger to Love #1098
The Rancher Meets His Match #1164
†Lost-and-Found Groom #1344
†At the Heart's Command #1350
†Hidden in a Heartbeat #1355

*Wedding Series
†A Place Called Home

Harlequin Historicals

Widow Woman #417

babies
& BACHELORS USA

Patricia McLinn
A New World

Silhouette Books

Published by Silhouette Books
America's Publisher of Contemporary Romance

To Dad, for his stories of Gloucester and Ireland.
To Mom, for her insight to the human heart.
To both, in honor of fifty years of marriage, family and romance.

ACKNOWLEDGMENT
The author extends her gratitude to Séamus,
Mary and Andy Costello and Lori McKeever
for sharing their experiences and expertise.

 SILHOUETTE BOOKS

ISBN 0-373-82269-3

A NEW WORLD

Printed in U.S.A.

Chapter One

"Look at him, Ellie—the perfect man."

Eleanor Thalston grimaced at her cousin. Not that it would do any good. You might as well hope that every driver in Boston would use turn signals as hope Valerie would watch what she said, even in a public place.

"I mean, there he is. Just what we need. He's the perfect man for us."

The red-bearded man to their left was actively eavesdropping, Eleanor decided. If she hadn't already suspected it, his stillness and the way he averted his eyes, thus putting his right ear directly in the path of Val's voice, would have convinced her. Of course, it didn't require much effort to pick up what Val said. It wouldn't be so bad if she mumbled. But since her multitude of jobs had included six months as a public radio announcer, Val's enunciation was flawless. No Boston accent for her.

"Cahill McCrea. He's perfect for us and you know it, El."

"Val—"

"Just look at him. And listen. That's all I asked—that you come and listen to him sing. That's all I want." Val's mobile face shifted to an expression of supplication, wide brown eyes limpid as a waif's.

Eleanor almost laughed out loud. Valerie Trimarco hadn't *asked* her to come to this small South Boston pub at all. She'd badgered until, knowing how long the barrage could go on, Eleanor promised to drive in from Cape Ann through a cold March rain teetering on the edge of sleet.

So here she was on a Saturday night, at O'Herlihy's Saloon, where the bartender did a steady business, where everyone seemed on a first-name basis except them, where decades of elbows kept the wooden bar polished smooth and where the cumulative effect of curious eyes was like a searchlight trained on the scarred table she and Val shared.

And the only way to escape with some sanity was to do what Val wanted. She knew that; she'd known it since they'd shared a playpen as toddlers. For sixteen years—as teenagers and adults—they'd hardly seen each other, but in the past year as Val's partner in The Fishwife, she'd learned just how little her cousin had changed from the days when they'd scrambled over Dog Bar Breakwater as children.

A sigh slipped through her lips. Sometimes she felt as old and weary as the only grown-up shepherding second-graders through a glass factory.

"All right, Val. I'll look. And I'll listen. But that's all."

"That's all I ask."

The thrum of a guitar announced a song, and Eleanor hitched her chair around for a clearer view of this man her cousin wanted her to weigh against perfection.

A guitar slung easily over his broad shoulder, he sat ten feet away. He had a hip on one stool and a foot propped on the rung of another. The second stool held a tin whistle, a harmonica and a beer mug freshened through the good graces of his audience.

Cahill McCrea. The name suited him. He was more ruggedly interesting than handsome. But attractive, definitely attractive.

A stiff sea breeze could have tousled his thick dark hair off his forehead that way. But not even the strongest gale seemed likely to make an impression on the prominent bones of brows and cheeks that, under the makeshift spotlight of O'Herlihy's Saloon, shadowed his eyes.

He turned for a sip from the mug, and Eleanor considered a profile that dropped in a nearly straight line from his high, wide forehead to a bump midway down his nose. A memento of a fight? With the thrusting lines of that stubborn jaw, she didn't doubt it for a minute.

Considering the muscle and sinew of forearms revealed by the rolled-back sleeves of his faded blue shirt, she wondered what had happened to the other fellow. The broad shoulders and wide chest stopped just this side of burly, and jeans worn to a powder blue encased powerful thighs.

A quiet note from the guitar pulled her attention back to his face. Without seeing them, she sensed his shadowed eyes resting on her as his comfortable baritone began to sing of his love with the ribbon in her hair. Her heart gave a startled jerk.

She felt familiar, despised heat push up her cheeks. She thought she'd overcome that weakness. How ridiculous! A woman of thirty-one blushing. Blushing was for silly, giggling schoolgirls, not for competent businesswomen. Especially not just because a stranger caught her staring at him.

Looking at him, she amended.

And she had every reason to look at him, she reminded herself during the second chorus. He was an entertainer, after all, and it was as an entertainer she assessed him. That was the reason Val had insisted she drive more than an hour from Gloucester to this working-class bar in South Boston.

She frowned at her own thoughts.

Entertainer? Somehow the tag didn't fit. If she'd seen him on the street, she'd never have picked him as an entertainer. Even now, sitting and listening to his songs, she sensed an incongruity in the picture. Oh, his voice and his instruments blended pleasantly enough, but she had the odd feeling he wasn't really performing. Her frown deepened as she tried to pin down the elusive impression. He didn't sell his music the way other performers did. Maybe that was it. He just sent the songs out there to be accepted or not, and whichever happened wouldn't affect him.

"Well?" Val demanded simultaneously with the last sad, clear note.

"I'm not sure that Irish music—"

Val waved the objection way. "He does other things, too. That's just for here, although Irish music is awfully popular. Besides, it's not just his music," she said with a fervor Eleanor recognized all too well.

Another of Val's enthusiasms. Eleanor glanced at the bent head of the man testing his guitar's tuning. Could a man like Cahill McCrea be hurt because the fire of Val's interest burned bright and high, but never burned long? Her surge of concern was probably totally irrational.

"Look at how good he is with the people," Val continued. "He really gives this place an atmosphere. And that's what we need at The Fishwife."

That was true. With Val planning the menu and her directing the business, they gave customers a delicious meal and efficient service. But if they didn't find a way to give them something more, The Fishwife wouldn't last another season. Perhaps not even half a season if they had as many bad-luck expenses as they'd had a year ago. To cover the bill the second time the air conditioner broke down, they'd had to ask the employees to wait three days for their wages.

She didn't voice the admission, though, because Cahill McCrea began his song just then—a stirring tune that had her tapping her fingers against the table while more demonstrative listeners clapped.

Maybe Val was right. Maybe this man, with his voice as smooth and potent as the oldest Irish whiskey and his careless smiles, could draw in the summer customers and keep The Fishwife afloat another year.

The song came to a rousing climax with the audience joining in on the last chorus and cheering the finish. One male voice, heavy with beer, rose over the calls of appreciation and demanded the singing of "I'll Take You Home Again, Kathleen."

"No!" The negative chorus seemed near unanimous.

Looking past the bulk of the red-bearded man at the next table, Eleanor picked out the requester from among the crowd at the bar. He had to be at least half a foot shorter than her own five foot eight and easily a decade past retirement age. He wore a tweed cap, flanked by feathery white tufts above his ears.

"'I'll Take You Home Again, Kathleen'!" he insisted above the protests. "And I'll fight each and every one of you who doesn't want it, do you hear?"

The idea of the little man fighting anyone seemed laughable, but she felt no urge to laugh. Someone in the room wasn't laughing at all. She sensed tension.

She scanned the faces around the wizened, pugnacious man at the bar and saw expressions ranging from good-natured smiles to mildly irritated frowns. None produced the uneasiness she felt. But somewhere—

"I'll fight you, Cahill McCrea, if you're thinking you won't sing it. Fight you to the death. Do you hear that, Cahill McCrea?" The man's challenge drew stifled chuckles.

Eleanor's search ended at the next table. The red-bearded stranger—it was his tension she felt. The tight line of the beefy back and broad shoulders straining his white shirt communicated it as clearly as words. How strange. How could the little man at the bar possibly cause this bear of a man a moment's concern? He wasn't even looking in that direction. Instead, she realized as she followed his frown, he focused on Cahill McCrea.

The singer still rested at ease on the stool, although his smile appeared oddly tight. But that could have been an effect of the lights.

"Can't you just imagine that?" Valerie gleefully murmured in Eleanor's ear. "It's like Mickey Rooney challenging Muhammad Ali."

Eleanor didn't answer and didn't take her eyes off the red-bearded man and McCrea. She had the feeling a drama was being acted out that only she could see.

Cahill McCrea ducked under the guitar strap, further shadowing his face, but his voice held only easy confidence when he called out, "I'll sing you 'Brennan on the Moor' next set, Michael. Will that be doing you?"

She held her breath. Ridiculous. Nothing's going to happen. But still she didn't breathe. Warily, she watched the elderly man addressed as Michael slide off his stool. The red-bearded man seemed to coil, as if preparing to spring. McCrea held totally still, his face unreadable.

But Michael only doffed his tweed cap to McCrea with great ceremony before returning it to the nest of white tufts and resuming his seat.

Air rushed out of her lungs, letting relief in. *Relief over what, for heaven's sake?*

McCrea responded with a brief salute, then turned to rearrange his instruments on the stools. Eleanor considered his back for a puzzled moment, but it told her nothing. Nor did the now relaxed profile of the solitary red-bearded man at the next table. Had she imagined the whole thing?

She turned, studying again the faces at the bar. Certainly no one there seemed to consider that anything out of the way had occurred, least of all Michael. The little man sipped from his beer mug between emphatic comments to companions on either side of him, nodding approval or thumping an adamant fist on the bar.

Nothing.

"What's the matter with 'I'll Take you Home Again, Kathleen'?" came Valerie's voice.

Why on earth would her cousin ask her? How would she know? She started to turn to ask Val that very reasonable question, but never said the words. Val hadn't asked her; she'd asked Cahill McCrea.

He stood not three feet away, looking down at her and smiling. With only the scarred wooden table separating them, he appeared even more powerful, his shoulders wider, his chest broader, his arms thicker. And, tilting her head back, she added taller to the list.

Experiencing his smile from close range gave her a new understanding of Val's enthusiasm for the man.

He split a grin between her and Val as he dropped into the chair opposite them and answered the question.

"It's just that Michael cries every time he hears it."

"Is it sad?" asked Val.

"Indeed. It's the story of a man promising to take his wife back to Ireland where her heart's grieving for, but he never does till it's to take her home to bury. It tears Michael up. He gets terrible maudlin, he does, though no one knows why." He paused and looked from Eleanor to Val and back. "His wife's name's Mary Margaret and she's likely to live another twenty years."

Eleanor and Val joined his laugh.

"Then he must have liked that last song. It sounded upbeat," offered Val.

He turned to Eleanor, with the quirk of an eyebrow making her his accomplice in whatever he was about to say. "Did you listen to the words, Valerie?"

"No," Val admitted.

"That 'upbeat' song's about a man going to be hung."

"That's terrible," breathed Eleanor.

"Not a'tall," he contradicted, grinning. "He was hung a hero. There's a saying that Ireland's a land of sad love songs and happy war songs. That's one of the happy war songs. Now, what'll I be getting you ladies at the bar before we have our talk?"

Val's voice cut in before Eleanor had the chance to reply. "El will have wine—white wine, the driest they've got. And I'll take red."

He nodded cheerfully and set off, his progress impeded by handshakes and snippets of conversation at nearly every table.

"So you've already talked to him," commented Eleanor

evenly, noticing that the red-bearded man joined McCrea by the bar.

"Oh, a little."

She turned to look at her cousin. "Val, what have you told him?"

"Told him? I don't know why you think—" Val shifted her thin frame on the wooden chair seat. Occasionally, Eleanor recognized that her lush build had advantages over Val's spare wiriness. Advantages like a shade less discomfort from sitting on a hard chair. Right this moment, though, she had every intention of adding to the discomfort of her cousin's conscience.

"I don't think. I know. I know you and it's obvious the man expects to talk about more than the lyrics of Irish folks songs."

"Well, I did talk to him some, El," admitted Val in a burst of candor. "Oh, not to negotiate. I'll leave that up to you, of course. But just to feel him out. I didn't want to ask you to make the trip in here on a weekend if he wasn't interested at all in coming to Cape Ann."

"How considerate of you," Eleanor said dryly. "What exactly did you say, Val?"

"We talked about his singing and how he's traveled all over the United States. He's been coming here as often as he could since he was a teenager—on vacations, visiting family and sometimes singing. He's picked up lots of songs that way, you know. American folk songs, too."

"Val—"

"And of course we talked about Ireland. He's from County Donegal, way up at the northern tip of the whole island, but it's not part of Northern Ireland and—"

"Val." This time Eleanor made sure her no-nonsense voice couldn't be ignored. "Did you offer him a job?"

"I told him we'd love to have him come sing at The Fishwife," said Val. Her brown eyes, dominating her thin face under the volume of dark hair, met Eleanor's. One thing about Val, once you convinced her she had to face the music, she always faced it squarely.

"Did you also tell him we can afford to pay him next to nothing, and that's on the good days?"

"I told you, we didn't negotiate at all. I know you're the wizard at business, El."

"Wizard?" Exasperated, Eleanor scoffed. "I'm going to have to be a wizard *and* a magician to figure out a way to pay this man anything. If the firm hadn't brought me back to do this temporary accounting work during tax season and you weren't teaching cooking and photography at that junior college, we wouldn't have the money to open this season at all. Not at all, Val."

"We'll open this season if I have to stand in front of Faneuil Hall begging for quarters." Eleanor recognized bone-deep determination mixed with the humor in Val's voice. "Franklin Britt won't have the satisfaction of driving us out of business—ever."

"I don't care for him any more than you do, Val, but we can't close our eyes to the facts. Don't you realize how close we are to having to give up?"

Val put her hand on Eleanor's arm and squeezed it. "That's why we need Cahill McCrea. I just know he'll give The Fishwife what it needs to be a success."

Eleanor looked at Val and knew she was lost. Just like when they were kids. Val, for all her intelligence, had never cultivated more than a nodding acquaintance with reality. Twenty years ago, when Val wanted to see Gloucester from the top of the lighthouse, she hadn't bothered her head with how they might accomplish the feat. She'd left it to Eleanor to convince the caretaker they needed to climb to the top for a school assignment. Now Val's imagination was set on making a success of The Fishwife, and she left it to Eleanor to come up with the ways and means.

"As long as Cahill McCrea doesn't expect The Fishwife to give him anything he might need, like a salary," she said grimly.

"I'm sure it will work out, El. Just wait and see. You always worry too much."

"It's impossible to worry *too* much in this family. I could spend all my time worrying and still be behind." She heard the echo of sharpness in her own voice, but Val chuckled and she felt an answering smile tug at the corners of her mouth.

"You just have to look on the bright side more, Ellie. With your attitude and your surroundings. Even with your clothes. Take today, for example."

Cahill McCrea arrived at the table just then with their drinks and a fresh mug of beer for himself. Eleanor's smile lingered as she looked up to thank him, and found his eyes on her. He held the look as he dropped into a chair. The shadows cast across his face lifted for the first time, and she stared into eyes of pale green framed by thick black lashes. Lashes that dark and that dense should have overwhelmed the soft color, but Eleanor felt certain nothing could overwhelm the vibrancy of those eyes.

With a slight smile fanning lines at their corners, his eyes seemed friendly and calm, like the ocean on a peaceful day. And like the ocean, she thought with unaccustomed fancifulness, these eyes could change in an instant to something powerful, intense and frightening.

She shook her head free of such thoughts.

"I think that wonderful rose sweater-dress from the boutique would have been perfect for tonight," Valerie continued.

Eleanor pulled her attention back to the topic Val had pursued while her mind had wandered to eyes and oceans. "First of all, I don't own that rose sweater-dress."

"I told you to buy it."

"And second, even if I did own it, that dress would hardly be appropriate for this weather. Cashmere doesn't mix well with spring mud and rain."

Or with me, she thought. She'd looked in the boutique's mirror when she'd tried on that dress, and seen hips that flared too widely, a stomach no one would call washboard flat and breasts too lush. The color suited her sandy brown hair and fair skin, but she preferred clothes that didn't advertise quite so clearly that she didn't have the slim, straight figure of her cousin.

Val could talk all she wanted about envying her "sexy" figure, but Eleanor would trade in her curves for fashionable thinness in a minute. And, as long as she indulged in some useless wishing, she'd take full, pouting lips over her wide, straight mouth. She'd seen too many candid photographs not to know that the combination of a very slight overbite and the habit of pulling her lower lip in when she concentrated could make her look like a child aspiring to solemnity. Her eyes were large enough, but gray—a color likened not to oceans but to dreary skies that produced the kind of cold rain pounding outside, she thought with a mental shrug.

"That's very practical of you," said McCrea with amusement seeping into his voice.

It *was* practical of her; she was a practical person. She'd noted the weather and dressed for it with a loose-fitting pale gray sweater and charcoal wool slacks that would hide any errant spots of mud. Leave the red bolero jacket and winter-white skirt to Val, who could carry it off. So why did she resent his amusement?

He chuckled, blatantly inviting her to join in. He was probably the kind who found amusement in everything, the type who laughed off flat tires, unpaid rent and failing businesses.

"Yes, very practical," she said, and watched his eyes change at her cool tone. The laughter didn't fade, but it was complicated by the immediate recognition of her reserve and a spark of curiosity.

"Oh, yes," said Val, glumly contemplating the ruby liquid in her glass. "Eleanor is the practical one. Sometimes I think if she'd been Cinderella, she'd have told the Fairy Godmother the coach was entirely too glitzy and she'd just take the bus."

Cahill's laughter cracked out, fading into a cozy rumble. This time Eleanor, a little to her own surprise, did join in. Val was probably right.

Val looked up with the wide-eyed stare of someone who hadn't realized she'd said anything funny, then started chuckling, too. After that, when Val pointedly said that Eleanor's practicality was the reason she'd wanted her to talk to Cahill about singing at The Fishwife, no awkwardness lingered as the conversation smoothly shifted gears.

Eleanor's questions drew out details on the sketch of his background Val had given her—he was Aidan Padraic Cahill McCrea, age thirty-two, from near Lough Swilly in County Donegal and a veteran of five trips to the United States, mostly to visit numerous aunts, uncles and cousins spread around the country. She also discovered that he had a mother and seventeen-year-old brother in Ireland and he was unmarried.

"What do you do in Ireland, Mr. McCrea?"

"At the moment I don't do anything, Miss Thalston, since I'm not there a'tall."

"C'mon, El. What difference does it make?" asked Val, her patience with the job interview obviously past. "And for Pete's sake stop calling each other Mr. And Miss. It's Cahill and Eleanor."

Eleanor wasn't entirely sure she could say what difference it made what he'd done in Ireland, except that it had something to do with his reluctance to talk about it, something to do with her earlier thoughts about him as an entertainer, and something to do with the challenge implicit in the slight tilt of his right eyebrow.

"What did you do in Ireland before you left? Last October, wasn't it?"

"October, yes."

Eleanor waited for more; he said nothing. "What did you do?"

He looked into her eyes a moment, then over at Val, answering her sympathetic frown with a grin. Finally, he looked back at Eleanor and shrugged. "I worked in a small hotel, Eleanor. More of an inn, really. I often sang in the evenings there, and in the days I did...a bit of everything." He dropped his chin, and again shadows masked his green eyes.

"But...then you won't be able to stay...." The realization brought a sharp disappointment. A disappointment, of course, that resulted simply from her very justifiable irritation that all this had been one of Val's wild-goose chases.

"I've gotten one extension. There'll be more," he said with confidence.

"But your hotel will want you back for the summer season, won't they? That's the busy time in Ireland, too, isn't it?"

"The hotel?" His puzzled frown cleared in an instant. "We're talking at cross-purposes, Eleanor. I thought it was of your Immigration Service you were talking."

"The INS? Is there a problem with your visa?"

"Not a bit of it. It's just a matter of going back for extensions now and again so they don't feel entirely useless in this world."

Val chuckled, but Eleanor looked at him with a frown. Cahill McCrea's casual attitude didn't seem realistic.

But his next words drove that thought from her mind.

"As to the hotel, there's no cause to be going back there. I quit."

"You quit? But I thought jobs in Ireland were so hard to find. I read unemployment—"

"Is very bad indeed," he finished, perfectly cheerful. "It is. But no McCreas are on the dole yet, Eleanor. My mother and brother are taken care of and I...I get by here with my singing and a bit of help from my friends and relations."

His smile widened, warm and charming. Oh, yes, with that charm and that smile and that brogue, she could well imagine he "got by." Some people didn't need to be practical and realistic to get by; they did it with charm and good looks. Or they tried to. She'd been raised by one; her family was dotted with them. So, Cahill McCrea was one more.

At least this charmer was no responsibility of hers. It was no concern of hers that his voice could make any name sound like an endearment. That his smile would never fail to soften a heart. That his hair would always look as if a sea breeze— or a woman—had just tousled it. In bed with Cahill McCrea it would be impossible to resist sliding your fingers through those dark waves.

Eleanor's fingers slipped off the stem of her wineglass.

In bed with Cahill McCrea...sliding fingers through his hair...? She never indulged in thoughts like that about a man, especially not a perfect stranger. What had gotten into her?

Only Cahill's quick-diving recovery of the glass prevented the slop of wine on the table from becoming a flood. Heat crept up Eleanor's throat. If only her discomfort didn't translate into raw color for all the world to read.

"El, what's the matter?" Count on Val to call attention to her state.

Eleanor willed the heat and color to disappear.

"Nothing's wrong. I just was clumsy, that's all. Now, Mr. McCrea—"

"Cahill," he corrected.

"Cahill," she conceded. "I hope you understand that my cousin and I are running The Fishwife on a very narrow margin. We're hoping to begin renting out a meeting room for parties this summer, but in the meantime we have only a small dining room with the bar in the same room and, in good weather, outdoor seating on a deck. This will be only our second season and getting established is difficult. Our salary offer is very limited." She named a figure and waited for him to turn it down. She could come up with a few dollars more a week, but even that would barely be a living wage. He'd say no, and that would be the end of Val's brainstorm to have Cahill McCrea sing at The Fishwife.

He looked at her with the pale green of his eyes just a vague impression of lightness beneath his strong brow bone. He didn't say anything.

"You'd work every night except Tuesdays, plus lunchtime on Fridays, Saturdays, Sundays and holiday Mondays."

Still, he said nothing.

"Well?" she finally demanded.

"I wouldn't go so far as to say it was 'well,'" he said judiciously, "but it'll do."

Eleanor heard Val let out a sigh of relief, and was surprised by her own breath being released. She hadn't been aware of holding her breath.

"If…" he added, and paused again.

Instantly wary, Eleanor prompted him with a neutrally even tone. "If?"

"If I'll be keeping any tips from the generous hearted."

"Of course."

He nodded acknowledgment of her agreement and added, "And if I can take my meals with you there."

She looked over his large frame consideringly. It would be no small matter feeding him. Still, there had always been leftovers last season. Surely this year there would be more than enough to feed the staff, even with him added.

"All right," she said, meeting his smiling eyes. She knew he'd read her thoughts.

"I'll not eat you into bankruptcy."

She couldn't help but smile back at him.

"Then it's a deal." Automatically she put out her hand and he met it firmly.

She'd never considered her hand—long-fingered and strong—particularly delicate, but it nearly felt that way, engulfed in his strong grip. He brought his other hand up to cover the back of her hand. Warmth seeped into her from the tips of her fingers to her wrist, where his fingers brushed against the skin just below her sleeve. She felt the slight scrape of calluses on the pads of his fingers against her sensitive skin. From the guitar, she thought, trying to block the sensations. The nerves all along her arm quivered like guitar strings from the touch.

She retracted her hand without meeting his eyes. Really, she was acting so strangely tonight.

"This is great. I just know you'll be perfect for The Fishwife," enthused Val as she shook his hand in turn. "I can't wait. We'll be open for weekends starting the end of next month. There aren't many customers then, but it'll give us a chance to get everything settled in before Memorial Day weekend. And, of course, you'll want to come out before that. What are you doing, El?"

She finished pulling on her coat before answering. "Our business is done, so there's no sense in my staying. It's a long drive home."

"You could stay to hear another song or two," suggested Cahill, and Eleanor thought she caught a chuckle just below the surface of his voice. "You might want to know you're not buying a pig in a poke."

Eleanor was saved from having to answer that by Val. "Oh, stay a while longer. You don't have to work tomorrow morning. Although—hey, that's right. You know, you have a point there, El." Eleanor saw from his expression that Cahill shared her confusion at Val's apparent shift to another topic. But she knew her cousin would eventually provide a connection. "That's going to be quite a commute for you, Cahill. It's more than an hour, and you'd be driving late at night. You better look for some place on Cape Ann. That'd be a lot easier on you."

"It'll be a bit of a drive, but it's hard to beat the price of my present accommodations," he said. "My mother's cousin won't let me pay a penny, just my share for food."

"You sure couldn't find a deal that good on Cape Ann," agreed Val. "Especially during the season, with the summer tourists, the rents can really be—oh, wait! What am I thinking of, you can stay in the room above The Fishwife! It's not fancy, but there's a bathroom and bed and a great view. You look over the rocks right onto the ocean. And your meals are already taken care of. It's perfect."

"Val, I don't think—"

"It's a great idea." Valerie's enthusiasm flooded Eleanor's effort to stem the proposal. "With Cahill there, I bet we won't have any of that vandalism we had last year, either. It helps him and it helps us. What could be better?"

Before Eleanor could find a polite way to say that she could think of at least half a hundred things better than having Cahill McCrea in proximity twenty-four hours a day all summer long, he'd accepted.

His solemnity was complete—and totally failed to convince

Eleanor—as he added, "It seems a most practical scheme, doesn't it, now?"

Cahill McCrea sang the tale of a brave highwayman that he'd promised old Michael, and considered the cousins who'd be his employers for the summer.

If you could call it employment, he thought with a slight smile. Certainly not the kind of employment he'd come to America seeking, nor the kind he'd left behind in Ireland. But that kind of job wasn't his yet. He knew his abilities and he knew the value of his résumé. But too many potential employers didn't look at either. They looked at his passport, and they saw potential hassles. He'd fought long and hard to overcome that. Now, if he could bide his time until next spring...

In those moments right after Eleanor Thalston had named his trifling wage, he'd thought of all that. And of the mixture of concern and determination he'd seen in both women's eyes. He'd decided that he could afford a summer's poor pay, a summer by the water perhaps helping to ease that burden of concern, a summer to store up strength for another attack on the dream he'd inherited from his father.

Still, he thought with a wry inner grimace, he'd best hope for generous tippers, indeed.

He hadn't been paid such a small wage since he'd carried bags at the Inishowen Hotel after school, in the days when Kiernan was so small their mother couldn't work, those first dark days after Dad and Patsy... He shut the memory off, even as his voice slid into the second chorus of the familiar song. His mother had ordered him to stay in school, even when better-paying jobs beckoned, and she'd insisted he accept the scholarship to university. She'd been right; the hard times had paid off. Hard times, hard work and hard choices had created a comfortable life for the three of them.

Comfortable, but not what he truly wanted. Not what he and his father had talked of so often. So, here he was, in this land where so many of his countrymen over so many decades had sought their futures, hoping he had a future here, too.

For the next few months his future would certainly be linked to the two young women sitting a dozen feet away. An odd pair, they were. Valerie Trimarco, with her energy and enthusiasm, and Eleanor Thalston, with her practicality and calm.

He'd liked Valerie from the moment nearly two weeks ago that she'd come up and told him about the pub she and her cousin owned on Cape Ann. He enjoyed her vivid looks and animated expression, but he found his eyes following her cousin as they prepared to leave.

Eleanor Thalston held up practicality like a regiment's standard. Yet the load she clearly carried on her shoulders hadn't squeezed all the humor out of her. She even retained the ability to laugh at herself. He admired those qualities.

Admiration, indeed. He could practically hear his mother laughing at that. What he'd felt when he'd caught Eleanor Thalston's hand between both of his had been something a mite more elemental. He knew he'd disconcerted her. He'd seen the same reaction earlier, when she'd knocked her glass, although he hadn't an idea what the cause had been then.

It certainly wasn't her cousin. She took Val's waywardness in stride like a veteran. No, Eleanor Thalston seemed more likely disconcerted by her own thoughts than by anything someone else might do.

That intrigued him. She intrigued him.

He liked her quick competence, and the suggestion of more beneath.

He returned Valerie's farewell wave as he launched into the final refrain. Eleanor nodded once, then turned away before he could respond. But at the door, as his song finished with the poor highwayman cruelly betrayed by a falsehearted woman, she hesitated a moment and smiled back at him.

It could be a most interesting summer.

Chapter Two

Sunday nights were the worst at The Fishwife.

The weekends were either a rush, or a worry that they weren't a rush. By closing time Sunday night heads ached, backs nagged and feet throbbed.

Then, after the flood of weekenders retreated to the city, after the week-long visitors repaired to their sand-laden accommodations and after the permanent residents went to bed to dream of the relative peace of the next four days, Eleanor went to work.

Most days she chipped away at the books a bit at a time. But the weekends kept her much too busy for that, so she set aside Sunday night for catching up and getting everything in order for the coming week. Only this week Monday night was the worst because Memorial Day had added to the weekend toils.

So far this season, she thought as her fingers performed a tap dance on the calculator keys, the weekends had happier conclusions than a year ago. She worked steadily in a pool of brightness cast by a solitary light over the back booth. Beyond her, The Fishwife's dining room formed a shadowy landscape of tables topped by upside-down chairs. But Eleanor could have found her way blindfold around the booths that rimmed two walls, the bar stretched along a third wall, the archway to the front door, the doors to the deck and the fireplace corner where Cahill McCrea played his songs and plied his charm.

A tall glass of something liquid would do wonders for her parched throat right now. But she was nearly finished. She'd just complete this, then she'd treat herself to an iced tea or lemonade before she closed up and headed home.

She copied a figure from the calculator's screen to the neat pad by her side and allowed herself a small smile.

"Now there's a sight we don't see often enough."

Cahill McCrea's soft voice just by her left shoulder made her jump.

"Lord! You startled me. I thought you'd gone up an hour ago."

He set a glass of iced tea in front of her—how had he known?—and another before himself as he sat down next to her.

"And here I thought you'd grown accustomed to my face," he lamented.

She smiled again, but didn't bother to reply beyond raising her iced-tea glass to him in salute. Greedily, she poured the cool liquid down her throat.

The odd thing was, she *had* grown accustomed to his face. It wasn't even a week into his full-time occupation of the room above The Fishwife, and already he seemed very much a part of the place. Maybe the four weekends he'd worked before that had let everyone grow accustomed to each other.

She'd come to enjoy the sound of his songs blending with the noise of The Fishwife, to appreciate his good humor, to respect his ease with the staff and customers. In short, she liked him.

There had certainly been no evidence so far of any grounds for her concerns about personal feelings interfering with how he and Val worked together. Their conduct at The Fishwife was strictly that of friends. Almost buddies.

Eleanor took another long swallow. In fact, unless Val had suddenly developed a talent for deviousness, they weren't seeing each other away from work, either. Since they shared the house they'd jointly inherited two years ago from Great-Aunt Susan along with The Fishwife, she couldn't help knowing if Val dated somebody.

Hard as it might be to imagine, Val seemed to be leading with her head instead of her heart this time. Not that her cousin gave her heart lightly. Still, anyone who'd ever heard that Valerie Trimarco's middle name was Prudence had gotten a good laugh.

"I can grow accustomed to anyone who brings me iced tea when my throat feels like a salted cod. Thank you. I can also grow accustomed to anyone who brings in business the way you have," Eleanor told Cahill with a pleased tap of her finger on the pad.

There was no question he'd contributed to The Fishwife's improved business. From the first weekend, he'd done just what Val had predicted—he'd given The Fishwife an atmosphere. He charmed everyone who came in with his songs and his easy smile.

He leaned over for a closer look, bringing his right side in contact with her left. "It's good, is it?" He phrased it like a question, but she had the feeling he already knew the answer.

Eleanor took another gulp of iced tea before answering. "It's better," she amended. "We've come out a little ahead on each of my projections for the other weekends, but this weekend was considerably ahead."

"Well, that's grand," he said, and she couldn't help responding to the broad smile that softened the hard lines of his jaw. Still, she automatically preached caution.

"It's an improvement over our first year. That's not saying much, since we seemed to slip farther behind each week last summer on top of trying to pay back all the start-up costs. We still have a long way to go. Especially if Franklin Britt starts another promotion like the one he had last summer.''

''Franklin Britt?''

''He owns Sand Witches down at the other end of the beach. We started off fairly strong against them when we opened a year ago. Val's cooking was an instant hit.''

''What is it Sand Witches serves?''

''You have to ask?''

His chuckle rewarded her wry question. ''Indeed I don't. Are they no good at all?''

She shook her head. ''It's no lie to say fine food is not one of Franklin Britt's priorities at this Sand Witches or the one over by Annisquam or his high-priced seafood restaurant near Stage Fort Park called The Old Salt. In fact, I'd probably be safe saying that money is his only priority in anything. Just don't go telling anybody I said that,'' she ordered him with a mock scowl. ''I don't want to be sued for slander, even though I would have the perfect defense—the truth.''

''I swear it'll never get past these lips.'' He tapped a forefinger to his mouth. Eleanor's gaze followed the movement.

His mouth had bothered her for some time now. Not just the way it stretched wide in a ready smile, or formed the words for his songs. No. She was bothered by a nagging sense of familiarity whenever she looked at his mouth, as she did now. Precisely cut, the lines of his lips could be called harsh, except that, laughing, talking, singing, they had an animation far from harsh. Between his mouth and the jutting line of his chin rested a severe indentation that could have made his full bottom lip appear pouty. It didn't. It made it appear strong and sensual. As if it would be worth kissing.

She jerked her gaze away, grabbing her nearly empty iced-tea glass. Not two minutes ago, she'd mentally applauded Val for showing some sense. And what was she doing? Indulging in ludicrous thoughts about an employee, a near stranger.

''So if the food's better at The Fishwife, why be bothered at all about this other place?'' he asked.

She glanced at Cahill's face. Only a slight smile touched his lips now. His eyes were veiled as he looked down at the glass, which was nearly lost in his big hands. Could he really be so unaware of what she'd been thinking? She'd been told her gray eyes were calm and unemotional; maybe her thoughts hadn't been as transparent as they felt.

She let out a breath—partly of relief at having her indiscretion unobserved and partly of remembered frustration from the summer before. "Britt started a happy hour. Sometimes he practically gave drinks away. It was wildly successful. There's more parking at that end of the beach, so more people were there in the first place. Lots of people ended their day at the beach with drinks at Sand Witches. Few bothered to come back down the beach to eat here."

"Couldn't you have a happy hour?"

"We considered it, but Val and I decided we didn't want the emphasis at The Fishwife to be alcohol. We want to offer customers good food, comfortable surroundings and friendly service. We don't want them to leave here as a danger to themselves or anyone else on the road."

She sensed his approval though he hadn't spoken, and found she appreciated it more than she would have expected.

"And now it's a worry he'll do the same this year, is it?" he asked.

"No. There's been community pressure on him not to have happy hours this summer. Some said he'd been serving minors—not firm enough evidence to press charges, but enough that when the happy-hour issue came up at town meetings over the winter, some of the more irate citizens wanted to try to have his license pulled. That scared Britt into voluntarily promising to cancel happy hour this year."

"But he's still worrying you, is he?"

She nodded. "Franklin Britt doesn't give up a profit easily. The Fishwife's improved business—" she tapped the pad "—must be cutting into that profit. He won't sit idly by while that happens."

She shook her head. "But there's no sense worrying about the milk when it hasn't even spilled yet. Which reminds me..."

Pulling a loose paper from her pad, she added another item to a growing list. "You keep bringing more business in, so I keep having to increase our supplies. I'll have to pick up some extras myself on Friday."

A man's sudden appearance at the open kitchen door startled her, but when she recognized bartender Tom Hustine, she relaxed. "Oh, Tom, you scared me. What are you doing here?" With Cahill sitting so close, she felt the tightening of his arm and leg, but his face remained still.

"I didn't know you were still here, Eleanor," said Tom. He glanced at Cahill, but addressed only her. "I was straightening up in the cellar for next weekend."

"Thank you, Tom," she said gratefully. The Fishwife offered him only part-time employment; she appreciated his willingness to put in any extra effort. "Maybe you can check this list of supplies I wanted to get in for next weekend, and see if I've missed anything?"

After a slight hesitation, he came over to take the list.

Tom Hustine was new to The Fishwife. Val's older brother Anthony had scowled when he'd heard of his hiring, but the only objection he'd voiced was that Hustine had played dirty football for a rival high school. Val laughingly teased him about judging the world by what happened between the sidelines twenty years ago. Eleanor also laughed, then doublechecked Hustine's application.

From high school he'd gone into the army. Since then, steady employment had eluded him—or vice versa—but he was a good bartender.

"You could add Scotch. Keep the Irish whiskey about the same," Hustine said after considering her list. "As long as you keep the high-class customers you've got, you'll always be needing more Scotch than Irish whiskey."

She hoped he hadn't meant that as some sort of slap at the Irish; they didn't need that sort of thinking at The Fishwife. Giving him the benefit of her doubt, she pushed the conversation along.

"Fine. I'll add Scotch. I'd like you to come with me Friday morning to pick this up, Tom. We'll pay you for the time."

"I have plans that morning. Actually, the night before. But I expect to still be, uh, occupied in the morning." His slight hesitation seemed to be more a matter of emphasis than embarrassment.

Eleanor said nothing. She just looked at him and waited, a method she'd found very useful.

Tom glanced away, then gave in. "Oh, all right. When?"

"Nine."

"That's damn early when I'll be here till two the next morning," he complained. Again, she said nothing. Finally, he repeated that he'd be there, then said a terse good-night and left through the kitchen.

As she gathered together her papers, Cahill took their glasses to the kitchen. She heard him checking that the back door had locked after Tom. One less item for her to take care of before she left.

"Are you ready to be going home now?" She looked up to see Cahill's large frame propped against the kitchen doorjamb.

"Just about. No need for you to wait. I'll finish closing up before I leave. Good night."

"Good night, is it? Not yet, it's not good night. I'm walking you home."

"Thanks, but that's not necessary, Cahill. It's just down the beach—"

"A deserted beach and the darkest of the night."

She smiled, a little warmed by his scolding tone. "I walk it every night," she reminded him.

"But not alone."

True. She and Val usually left together, except the nights she did the weekly projections. "My cousin's great company, but I don't know how much protection she is, so I'm sure I'll be just as safe tonight," she said with a laugh.

"That's right, you will. But I'll be walking at your side tonight, instead of behind you," he agreed, cupping a hand under her elbow to guide her to the door. "I'll finish whatever needs finishing when you're safe in your bed."

They were already outside, with the front door locked behind them before she recovered. "You mean you've been following Val and me home every night?"

"Mmm-hmm," he said. He took her arm and tried to urge her toward the old concrete ramp-walk that led to the beach, but she stood firm.

"What on earth for?"

"Because you're two lovely young ladies who think you're so ready to take on the world, but you don't know any better than to let somebody be following you down the beach night after night," he said with exasperation, admiration and laughter braided in his voice.

"I don't know whether to be angry or grateful," she admitted at last.

"Well, if you're leaving the choice to me, I'd not pick angry. Now quit nattering about it and tell me about yourself."

She gave up and laughed. "What do you want to know?" she asked as they reached the beach, one of a series of sandy crescents divided by rocky points that marked this part of Cape Ann. She glanced back for a final check on The Fishwife. With its stone foundation, weathered gray siding and a roof that sloped and peaked with abandon around a central chimney, the building sat isolated. Resting on a knoll of solid rock, it overlooked a quarter mile of marshes behind it, Rock Beach to the left, Tide Beach to the right and, straight ahead, the Atlantic Ocean.

Walking just above the waterline of Tide Beach, Eleanor and Cahill headed toward Boulder Point, where Franklin Britt's Sand Witches stood and Harmony Beach began. Above a side-walk-topped seawall, Harmony Beach hosted a line of houses dating from the first two decades of the century. The house Eleanor and Val shared sat nearly in the middle.

"My great-aunt left us that house and The Fishwife," Eleanor told Cahill. "She had holdings in several companies and a good deal of stock, plus a house in town. All that, she left to her own children and grandchildren, but her will was quite vehement about leaving the beach houses to Val and me."

"I've no doubt I'm going to regret the asking of this, considering the light of deviltry I see in your eyes even in this gloom," said Cahill, with such a martyred sigh that Eleanor grinned at him, "but I'll give you the pleasure of answering—why did she want you and Valerie to have the houses?"

"She said in her will that having these two houses should remind us—her only unmarried female relations—that the way to avoid the misery of marriage is to keep your distance. You see, Great-Aunt Susan and Great-Uncle John had a very stormy marriage. After three years, Great-Uncle John built and took up solitary residence in the house he called The Fishwife, apparently naming it after Great-Aunt Susan."

Cahill laughed and Eleanor laughed with him. "Not very flattering to Great-Aunt Susan," he said.

"No, but she must have forgiven him, because they had seven more children after he moved out and he came back for Sunday dinner every week until he died."

"He must have been coming back for more than Sunday dinner then, for seven more children," commented Cahill. "Don't be telling me you and Valerie have it in mind to follow in Great-Aunt Susan's footsteps?"

Still laughing, Eleanor shook her head. "No. I think we're too conventional for that, even Val. But we used to love to come out here as children and sneak into The Fishwife. They boarded it up when Great-Uncle John died when we were still babies. We had a secret entrance and used it as our clubhouse."

"I'd always heard about the Puritan stock of Massachusetts, but after hearing about Great-Aunt Susan and Great-Uncle John, I'm not so sure."

"There's plenty of strict Puritan blood in the family tree, especially the Thalstons," she said, staring out at the dark, rolling mass of the ocean for a moment. "Val and I aren't really cousins. Second cousins, I think it is. My grandmother, her grandmother and Great-Aunt Susan were all sisters."

He held up three fingers. "I've heard the tale of Great Aunt Susan. What happened to the other two?"

"Val's grandmother was Elizabeth, the youngest and the rebel. She married a man who was Portuguese, Finnish, Italian and Irish, thoroughly scandalizing her family, much more so than Susan did. At least Susan had married someone from old Yankee stock," Eleanor said with mock primness.

"Should have married pure Irish. That was her mistake," advised Cahill.

"Actually, I don't think Elizabeth made a mistake at all. I remember her as a happy, loving woman, adored by her children, grandchildren and even great-grandchildren. Val's a lot like her."

She saw his thoughtful eyes on her face and looked out to the water again. "And you, Eleanor Thalston, are you like your grandmother?"

Her laugh didn't hold much amusement, but she tried to keep her tone light. "Some people say I am. Her name was Eleanor, too. She made the best marriage of the lot. Samuel Thalston was twenty-five years older and from an old Gloucester family. They had one child. Samuel died of heart failure when my father, Samuel Junior, was eight."

Eleanor wished she could turn the conversation back. Or jump it ahead, past the questions about her family he'd surely ask. If he decided he truly wanted to know, she didn't think he'd be satisfied with evasions.

But he didn't ask. And he didn't speak. As they crossed Boulder Point and started along Harmony Beach, she looked up at him. Indistinct in the distant glow of civilization and moonlight, his face consisted only of line and shadow.

He wasn't going to ask. But her certainty brought no satisfaction.

Silence, she knew, could be a tool, the kind she'd used on Tom Hustine a half hour before. But it could also be a weapon, to hold other people at a distance, or to hold yourself apart. Was he waiting for her to volunteer her history? Or had he turned the silence on himself?

"Val and I must have been up these beaches a thousand times as kids." He gave no sign that he heard her, but she kept talking, not sure what caused her urge to fill the silence. "We'd ride our bikes all over—down to Inner Harbor, out to Rocky Neck and the artists' colony, then on to the breakwater and lighthouse. We'd go to Rockport with all the little tourist shops and Val would ride up on the sidewalk, scattering tourists left and right. Sometimes we'd make it all the way to the other side of the Cape, to Folly Point and Lane's Cove. We had a special spot up by Halibut Point, too—our secret cove. But this was always our favorite. We'd come to Fishwife Point and hide out from the world."

Slowly, he turned to her. "Hellions, I'm sure, the pair of you," he said, and smiled.

This feeling of relief was ridiculous. She had no cause to believe that he'd somehow retreated to a painful solitude and that her inconsequential reminiscences had brought him back.

"Oh, and I suppose you were the most angelic little boy in Ireland."

"I was," he agreed, straight-faced before a grin broke out. "At least for half the year."

She lifted her eyebrows in inquiry, satisfied to hear the lilt in his voice. She'd imagined goblins in a silence that had been nothing more than silence.

"You see, in Ireland, the days end early in the winter. Some days the suns sets before four o'clock, and those are the good days, the days there's no gales. On the days with gales the sun never rises a'tall. So, a boy has all that time to store up his deviltry. And when the summer comes, there's energy to spare for the days that don't see twilight till ten o'clock or past."

"Did all that energy get you and your friends in real trouble?"

"You mean with the law, do you?"

"Mmm-hmm," she confirmed.

He shook his head, as if disappointed in her lack of faith. "There might have been a time or two that the gardai wanted a chat with us, but it never seemed to come about. You see we all were related, us boys, one to the other, and there's that one thing about blood relations—they'll not give you away. Of course, a time or two our mothers found we weren't the altar boys they'd hoped for. And then I'd have preferred to be talking to the gardai!''

"The gardai?"

"The police."

Skeptical, she looked up at him. He was kidding, wasn't he? "You can't really be telling me you preferred the police over being scolded by your mother," she said.

"Scolding, is it? If she'd scolded me, I'd not have minded a bit. No, she just let the laughter die from her eyes and she'd look like a baby who'd been disappointed at Christmas. It was enough to make me want to crawl. You can ask her cousin Eamon when he comes out from Boston on Thursday. He'll tell you how that look could weaken the knees of the most devil-bound boy."

She laughed at his rueful tone while recognizing the love in his voice and the stir of her own envy. "She sounds like a wonderful mother."

"She is, indeed."

He smiled down at her, but she turned away. A wonderful mother… As a girl, she used to lie in bed dreaming that she was really Aunt Lucy's daughter. Being Val's sister would have been nice, but more importantly, she would have had a different mother. A different mother…

"I'm thinking Eleanor doesn't suit you entirely."

She blinked as his abrupt statement pushed away her memories. "What?"

"Your name. Eleanor. It's only the one part of you."

"One part?" She felt she was trying to catch up with a conversation that had started without her.

"The woman of business. The part of you that sends these fingers flying over the calculator so efficiently." He squeezed her hand, and Eleanor realized for the first time that he held it. Had been holding it for some time, judging by the easy way it nestled in his.

She also had to assimilate the fact that his voice held honest appreciation for her ability. That surprised her.

In her experience, charmers and dreamers like Aidan Padraic Cahill McCrea relied on the business skill of people like her. Required it and expected it. But they didn't appreciate it. Dreamers and charmers, they turned to practical Eleanor to give their fantasy substance. And she tried. Lord, how she tried. Until practical Eleanor couldn't hold the illusion together any longer, and she was left with only the dust of the dreams and the wistful disappointment of her charmers.

"The name Eleanor's fine for that part, but that's only one part. There's the part of you that's not all business. And that part should have a name, too."

If he wanted to indulge in a bit of silliness, she'd cooperate. But first she eased her hand out of his. He made no effort to hold on to it.

"Ellie?" she offered.

"No." He shook his head decisively. "Ellie's a barefoot girl larking about. And not El. That's for Valerie to call you. For her, that's fine."

She felt the thud of her heart against her rib cage as she read the inference that *he* needed something special to call her. Ridiculous.

He stopped and turned her to face him. She'd indulge him, she thought, despite the slight prickling sensation in her upper arms.

He took his time studying her face.

"Nora," he said, seeming to test the sound of it against what he found in her face. He shook his head. "No. Noreen." His voice took on a new note, warmer and deeper. He nodded in approval. "Noreen. Little Nora."

He met her eyes, and she felt small and delicate and protected. Not helpless, as she might have thought, but helped, cared for, comforted. An odd sensation.

She'd always been the strong one, physically and mentally. She'd always been the one leaned on, never leaning herself. He tempted her to lean.

She stepped back from him and continued down the beach. Three steps away, she shook her head, trying to free it of unfamiliar whimsy, and faced the salt-tipped breeze coming in off the water.

She knew the exact moment he came up next to her. Be practical, Eleanor, she told herself. When you come down to it, beside him you *do* appear small and delicate. It's a physical fact.

And protected? Are you also protected when you stand beside him? Do you want to be?

She talked to shut out the questions. "With all those names, I'd feel like a criminal with a string of aliases," she said with a small laugh.

"No. Just a very complicated lady," he said evenly.

Complicated? She wasn't complicated. She was practical, realistic, organized Eleanor Thalston. Straightforward and levelheaded. There wasn't anything complicated about her.

Two steps onto the wooden bridge across the tidal creek at the far end of Harmony Beach, she stopped dead. They'd walked past Sand Witches's orange and white facade, all the way to the start of Long Beach, well past her house. She hadn't been aware how far they'd come. She hadn't been aware of anything but Cahill McCrea.

A small strangled sound came out of her.

"What is it?"

"We walked too far. So busy talking, we walked right past the house." What had gotten into her?

Briskly, she climbed the stairs that led up to the seawall, then down the lighted sidewalk. The light posts above her, the houses to her left, brought back reality. She trailed her fingers along the top of a wooden picket fence just to feel its roughness. She needed that badly to push back the ocean mists that seemed to have filtered into her head.

At the gate to the brown shake-sided house where a light burned over the door, Eleanor turned to Cahill with words of thanks for the escort home and a firm handshake. He told her she was quite welcome. The hint of a grin on his face suggested he didn't take her formal good-night entirely seriously. He started to say something more, but before he could, she moved up the short walk, across the deep porch and inside the house, then leaned against the door.

She shouldn't have put her hand in his. She was in danger of falling under his spell, just like all the customers who walked into The Fishwife. How many women had she already seen him charm? Even the men fell for his easy ways. He was easy with everybody. That was the crux of it. He loved everybody, and everybody loved him.

It was just his manner. Not that there was anything wrong with it, it just didn't suit her. He could charm, all right. Look at tonight. It wasn't as if he'd even really flirted with her, but she'd become so absorbed by him that she'd walked right past her own house.

She welcomed the business he pulled in, of course. And she liked him. She just realized, now that she'd seen him in operation, one-on-one so to speak, that he was one of those men who treated every woman as if she were somebody special. Her mistake had been—had nearly been—reading too much into it.

His attention was all very nice and, for all she knew, he meant well; but his attention wasn't to be relied on. In that way he was a lot like Val. How many guys had she seen misinterpret Val's enthusiasm and end up being hurt?

For that matter, he and Val were a lot alike in other ways, too. He could match her cousin, charm for charm, zest for zest. Maybe Cahill McCrea was the perfect man—for Val.

Chapter Three

No one had ever accused the Irish of being an unimaginative people. But while eating lunch with Val in The Fishwife's kitchen Wednesday, Cahill decided imagination had nothing to do with his belief that Eleanor was avoiding him.

She'd disappeared from her front gate like a genie Monday night. One second there, the next gone and the door closed behind her. He'd shrugged it off.

Tuesday he saw her only briefly as she darted in and out of The Fishwife like an errand-running dervish. He'd begun to wonder about that when Eleanor volunteered to go into town for some special cooking oil for Valerie. "Do you think she's sick?" Valerie had asked Manuela Ruiz, a petite woman nearing fifty with great dark eyes and a numerous extended family. The Fishwife's first employee, she apparently knew both her bosses well enough to laugh. But the comment made Cahill believe there'd been more behind Eleanor's eagerness to run the errand. He'd given up thoughts of asking her to spend his evening off with him, and had gone for a long, solitary exploration of the nearby beaches.

This morning, he'd started to feel that whenever he walked into a room, some invisible pole pushed Eleanor out of it. He caught only glimpses of her, always as she was leaving.

Whatever had gotten into her, he didn't know. And she made it abundantly clear she had no intention of lighting long enough to let him ask. Finally, to give the woman a rest from this jack-in-the-box imitation, he'd settled in the kitchen with Valerie.

Everyone else cleared out after the lunch rush. While Val started preparations for dinner, and between her comments on the week's menu and where the recipes had come from, he gathered more pieces of his employers' family history.

"My grandmother made the best rhubarb relish on the Cape. When I managed a gift shop in Gloucester, I made up some in little jars and the store sold them. I still sold the relish, even when I moved to the radio station. Then I went to the PR firm." She stared into space for a moment. "No, it wasn't the PR firm next, it was the photography studio. Then the freelance photography, *then* the PR firm."

"So relish gave you your experience with the culinary business before you and your cousin started this restaurant?"

"Oh, no. I've worked in the kitchens of three, no, four restaurants. That's what took me down to D.C. I was chef at a very tiny, very posh restaurant there. New England-style, of course. That's how I got the job on Capitol Hill."

Cahill considered delving into the jump from cuisine to politics but decided to save that for another day. First things first.

"And Eleanor?"

"Oh, Eleanor stayed with the same Boston accounting firm from the day she graduated from college until the day she quit when we started The Fishwife. She worked her way up very steadily and took classes at night to get her M.B.A." Valerie supplied the information offhandedly, but her brown eyes narrowed to a shrewd line.

"I didn't see much of her in those days, even when I lived here. More, of course, than when she moved away with Aunt

Connie and her second husband when Eleanor was 12. But when she came back to Boston she kept awfully busy with work and going to school. And I had kind of an erratic schedule. Plus, there was her grandmother.''

Valerie's voice implied that Eleanor's grandmother fell into the same category as death or taxes—unavoidable but regrettable.

"What about her grandmother?"

"El stayed away from the Cape because of her grandmother. I know she did. After Mrs. Thalston died about four years ago, we started seeing more of her. She hadn't wanted to risk coming to Gloucester and being pinned to a wall by that Medusa stare. Even Mom says Mrs. Thalston deliberately scared Aunt Connie. See, that's the kind of woman she was. Even my mother called her own aunt Mrs. Thalston.''

"Eleanor's mother didn't get along with her mother?''

"Mother-in-law. Aunt Connie was left with a six-year-old daughter and a gorgon for a mother-in-law when Uncle Samuel died of cancer. She might not have made the wisest choices, but I always figured Aunt Connie was driven to it by that old woman.''

Valerie stopped abruptly, tipping her head as if to better catch voices from the dining room. Cahill had heard and classified the voices already. He didn't recognize the male voice, but as long as Eleanor's maintained that distant coolness, the man's identity didn't matter to him.

Valerie obviously disagreed. With a sound in her throat like an irate kitten's growl, she marched out the swinging kitchen door. Cahill followed more slowly.

"Valerie, how nice to see you, too,'' the man's voice said as Cahill stopped just inside the doorway. He was around fifty with a shiny moon face and a body with the spread of a melting snowman. Giving the stranger the benefit of the doubt, Cahill figured he could be forgiven for slicking his graying blond hair so ruthlessly—with a thinning crop like that you'd want to make sure none escaped. But there was no excuse for his sharp eyes.

"I was just telling Eleanor how badly I feel that I haven't had a chance to come by before to say hello," the man continued in a voice as soft and round as his body. "We've been so busy at the Sand Witches and, of course, in town at The Old Salt, that I've neglected to be neighborly."

So this was Franklin Britt. Cahill shifted his weight for a better view of Eleanor's face. She looked like someone braced to clean out a clogged kitchen drain, no matter how unpleasant the task.

"And I hope Eleanor was telling you to get lost," replied Valerie.

Franklin Britt's chuckle echoed without humor. "Valerie, you have to learn the art of friendly rivalry, to separate business from your personal feelings. You'll never succeed unless you do." From patronizing, his manner switched to something less admirable. Cahill felt the muscles across the back of his shoulders tighten. "I find you and Eleanor very attractive, very lovely young ladies. But that doesn't stop me from wanting to drive you both out of business."

Turning his smile from Valerie to Eleanor, Franklin Britt apparently caught sight of Cahill for the first time. His smile faltered, then turned up a notch.

"Ah, the secret to the ladies' success, I believe. I'm Franklin Britt, and you must be the singer I've heard so much about. Someday soon, I'd like to get together to talk to you about coming to work for me. I'm sure neither of these lovely young ladies would begrudge you such a beneficial career move. A definite step up, I can assure you."

Cahill didn't bother to glance at the extended hand. He kept his eyes on Britt's. He heard Val sputter in indignation, but the only crack in his concentration came when Eleanor turned toward him. She quickly looked back at Britt, and Cahill continued to stare at the man.

"I think you'd better leave, Franklin." Eleanor seemed as untroubled as Valerie had been riled. "Surely you agree friendly rivalries are best maintained from a distance."

"Of course, and my negotiations with Mr. McCrea could

best be handled in private." Britt smiled at each of them before pivoting on his heel and walking out.

The most audible sigh came from Valerie. "Good. Now I feel like I can breathe again. You were great, El. I always want to punch that guy, even though it would take a hell of a wallop to get through all that padding, but you're always so calm.

"And, Cahill," she continued, "that was terrific, just staring at him like that. I bet Franklin Britt hasn't had anybody treat him like that since he drove his first competitor out of business on the lemonade-stand circuit. Offering you another job like that right under our noses."

Valerie punctuated her words with agitated swipes at the counter with a cloth. But Cahill was more attuned to Eleanor's stillness. She was too still. She wasn't as unconcerned by Franklin Britt's arrival as she'd pretended.

"And I don't care what you say, El. I still think he arranged for all those things last year—the vandalism and the air conditioner breaking twice, and the oil drained from my car."

"Val—"

"That's just too much coincidence. And the vandals spelled too darn well to be kids."

"You know what the police said."

"Yeah, and I know what I think."

"So does everybody else, Val. You've said it often enough. You could get in trouble saying it, too, without proof." Eleanor held one palm up to stop Valerie's predictable retort. "What we have to worry about now is getting ready to open tonight. We have a lot to do."

She resumed sliding glassware into slots above the bar.

"Okay," Val said with a shrug, and passed Cahill to push through the kitchen door. "C'mon, Cahill. You can get some stuff from the top shelf in the pantry for me."

He followed, but not before he gave Eleanor's back a long, appraising look. He considered three things. She hadn't said she didn't believe Britt was behind last year's problems, just that she couldn't prove it. She hadn't reacted to his presence. She definitely was avoiding him.

* * *

Cahill's mother's cousin, Eamon Dougherty, arrived Thursday afternoon and revealed himself as the red-bearded stranger Eleanor had noticed at O'Herlihy's the night she and Val hired Cahill. In fact, he owned O'Herlihy's.

Eleanor shook hands with him from behind the bar where she prepared for the evening's business. She always filled the jobs of hostess and cashier. In addition, on weeknights she shared bartending duties with Manuela Ruiz, who also assisted Val with the cooking.

"How do you do, Eamon. Welcome to The Fishwife. We hope you'll be able to come visit often during the summer."

"I'd like to do that. With everyone raring to get out of the city, business is as quiet as a church, so I can slip away now and again. And keep an eye on this rapscallion relative of mine."

"You're Irish?" Val asked with tongue firmly in cheek. Not as tall as Cahill and round where his relative was broad, Eamon Dougherty made Eleanor think of a Santa Claus in training. He was only in his mid-forties and his hair and beard were still blazing red, but the jolliness was already in place. "I never would have guessed it."

"Are you blind, girl?" asked Cahill with elaborate disgust before Eamon could answer. "Can't you see the map all over his face."

"Map?" Val's wide-eyed question could have won her a spot as the straight man for any comic.

"The map of Ireland, of course." Cahill stared at Eamon's face a moment, before a puzzled frown drew down his eyebrows. "No, it's not Ireland. It's...it's a map of Boston. He's been in the city so long, his face looks like a map of the place. You'd think he'd get out and see this grand country he's a citizen of, now wouldn't you, Valerie?"

"And doesn't he?" she prompted.

"Not a'tall. I'd wager this is the farthest he's ever been out of the city. He sits in Boston, in his place of business, and counts up his profits."

Eamon turned a long-suffering face to Eleanor, but she didn't miss the twinkle in his blue eyes. "I can see you're a reasonable woman and with a fine business here. Let me warn you that this relative of mine will have no regard for how hard you work for your business. He'll want you to go off and dance in the surf just for the fun of it, and that's when he's not eating you out of house and home."

"Ah, I'm wounded," declaimed Cahill with a hand to his heart. "Do you hear what the man says of me?"

Eamon looked from Eleanor to Valerie and back. "Can you imagine, I actually told the United States government that I wanted this scoundrel in the country, that I sincerely petitioned them to make him a citizen?"

"And a lot of good it did. You've no pull with the government at all," said Cahill with a snort of disgust.

Everyone laughed, but Eleanor noticed that some of the twinkle went out of Eamon's eyes.

She and Val excused themselves to check supplies for the weekend's menu. But before the kitchen door closed behind her, she heard Eamon ask, "Have you had any word yet?" and Cahill answer in a clear voice: "No, but don't be worrying about it. I've yet to try the full measure of McCrea charm."

Cahill knew that answer would not satisfy Eamon, and now that they were alone, the older man asked, "What are you doing here, Cahill?"

"Just what it appears, Eamon—meeting some people, walking some beaches, singing some songs."

The red head shook in exasperated bewilderment. "You ran your own hotel in Donegal, for heaven's sake."

"More of an overgrown inn," demurred Cahill. "And I own as much of it now as when I worked there twenty-six hours a day."

"But this is getting you no further. You're wasting your training and experience singing here. You want a position managing a hotel—or an overgrown inn, if that's what you want to call them. If you haven't heard about another extension by now, you might not get one this time. If you get a petition from an established employer, you could get your status switched from temporary visa to immigrant, and not have to worry about extensions.''

''Do you think I don't know that's the way of it?'' Cahill snapped, then pushed back his impatience. Of all the people in the world not to take his frustration out on, Eamon ranked up there with his mother and brother.

''I know, Cahill. And I know what a good opportunity that resort in Rhode Island would be, but with the construction delays...'' The job he'd secured after a long and careful search, the job that was supposed to have been his three months ago, had been delayed a year. The developer couldn't sponsor him for a work visa when there was not yet a resort to manage.

''Maybe one of the other places that was interested in hiring you...''

Cahill shook his head. He'd thought all this out time and again. ''You know how many letters I sent off, how many hotel owners I talked to before I found the right one. Most don't want foreigners. They're afraid of the penalties if they hire me and I turn out to be an illegal, and they don't want to be bothered with the paperwork to be sure I'm legal. And why should they? They've their pick of American applicants. There's no need to be bothered with the others. And then there're the ones who'll take a foreigner, no questions asked, for a good bit less money.''

''But there were others besides that Rhode Island developer who offered a decent living.''

''Yes. But if one sponsored me for the work visa, I'd be tied there. Not free to take that job in Rhode Island when the construction is finished.''

Eamon sighed. ''I know, Cahill, and I understood when you took a break and filled in your time singing at my place. You deserved some time off. But this—''

''This is another kind of break. Don't you think I'm entitled to a summer in the sun, Eamon?''

Actually, he'd considered contributing his training and experience here at The Fishwife. It hadn't taken him many days to see that what he'd learned from running the Inishowen could help here, especially in easing some of Eleanor's burden. But with her withdrawal the past few days, she didn't seem to be wanting anything to do with him, much less take his help. So, if he contributed it would have to be very quietly.

Cahill saw that his careless shrug didn't ease Eamon's frown. "If you sold your share of the Inishowen Hotel, you could buy your own place here. Foreign investors can immigrate—"

"That's security for my mother and brother. You know I won't sell."

"I know." Eamon exhaled a long breath. "But I also know how long you've wanted to come to America for good, Cahill. I remember you and your father talking about it, urging me. If I could do something. If they'd accepted my petition…"

"What you can do for me now, Eamon, is not be mentioning this to my new employers. And let me enjoy my bit of summer by the water."

For the hour Eleanor spent in the kitchen and cellar, she found her thoughts on the question of what word Cahill McCrea waited for and Eamon Dougherty seemed so anxious about. So anxious, in fact, that she thought she detected worry still in his eyes when she returned to the dining room.

Eamon sat on a bar stool watching Cahill adjust the microphone of the small amplifier system he'd brought with him to The Fishwife. Slipping behind the bar, she asked Eamon if she could get him anything to drink.

"I do have a bit of a thirst," he acknowledged as Cahill left the microphone and came to the bar.

"We have fresh-made lemonade," Eleanor offered.

Cahill laughed at Eamon's look of dismay and moved to stand next to her. He was too big. Too close. Too hot.

"When an Irishman says he has a bit of a thirst, it's not the type you'd be satisfying with lemonade," Cahill said as he reached behind her for a mug, then across her to depress the tap. He set the filled mug on the counter.

In the small space behind the bar each of his movements missed becoming a caress by a hairbreadth.

"Thank you, Cousin Cahill," said Eamon fervently.

Eleanor jerked herself out of immobility, picking up a cloth and polishing an already clean glass.

"Well, why didn't you just say that?" she demanded of Cahill without looking at him. "I would have been happy to pour him a beer myself."

"Ah, that's my practical Eleanor."

She heard the smile in his voice so she didn't need to look. She polished harder, trying to wipe away the impossible warmth of such a simple possessive. It was just his way with people, she reminded herself. Spread The Charm Thick And Spread The Charm Wide—that could be his motto.

"We take a bit of understanding, we Irish do," Eamon said as he regarded the golden liquid in his glass with solemn admiration.

"You certainly do," she agreed emphatically. She threw down the cloth and turned, prepared to slip past Cahill. But he blocked her way. Against her better judgment, she met his eyes.

"Not only the Irish," he said evenly.

She saw quite clearly that her withdrawal the past few days confused him. She thought he hadn't noticed, but she saw now that he had. A current, perhaps of understanding, passed between them. At least that was what she called it. It consisted mostly of the mutual recognition that they were being a little silly. They were, after all, grown-up, reasonable adults, not given to making mountains out of molehills.

She watched the light of laughter spill into his green eyes, but she laughed out loud first. It felt good. It felt even better when he joined her.

Avoiding him, even for just over two days, had made her miss his jokes, his teasing, his charm. Avoiding him had also been decidedly awkward in the small confines of The Fishwife.

Their laughter sounded friendly and easy. The uneasiness between them had nearly disappeared. She was glad. They'd be friends again. As for the sliver of tension that did linger, well, that would fade with time.

"Did you just become a citizen, Eamon?" she asked when their laughter had mellowed to smiles.

"Oh, no. I've been a citizen of the United States near twelve years and lived here more than sixteen."

"But you talk with more of an accent—would you call it a brogue?—than Cahill."

Cahill gave a derisive snort. "It's not a brogue at all. It's a mishmash anyone born in County Donegal should be ashamed to claim. He could be taken for an Englishman."

Elaborately ignoring the jab, Eamon addressed Eleanor. "I take care to preserve my accent as a legacy of my homeland."

Cahill winked at her. "Then there must be something in it for him."

"There is," agreed his cousin with no trace of sheepishness, perhaps even a bit of self-admiration for his resourcefulness. "American women love it. And when you're not a handsome young devil like Cahill here, who needs no such advantages, you cultivate your selling points."

"Do you miss Ireland?" she asked. She didn't intend to let this conversation develop into a discussion of Cahill McCrea's success with women.

"Ireland'll always have some part of my heart, but this is my home now," said Eamon. He put a beefy hand on Cahill's shoulder. "I love this country, just the way he said I would when he convinced me to emigrate all those years ago. I wouldn't have done it if it hadn't been for him. And that makes it all the more a shame—"

"Enough."

Cahill's voice, with no hint of anger, stopped Eamon.

Eleanor glanced at Cahill, but his bent head seemed to be contemplating the nearly empty glass between his hands. Why hadn't he wanted more said? Eamon had been telling her Cahill convinced him to emigrate to America sixteen years ago, when Cahill was only sixteen years old himself.

"Ireland's greatest export has always been its youth," said

Eamon. "For five hundred years there've been pressures pushing the young away from Ireland—famines and rebellions and poverty and politics. For a long time it was punishable by death for the Irish people to speak their language, follow their religion, educate their children. Their land was stolen from them. And if any of the people brought from other countries to try to rule them were foolish enough to be kind to the Irish or intermarry with them, they could be killed by law."

"I didn't know that," said Eleanor softly.

Eamon nodded. "So Ireland loaded the immigrant ships, and the convict ships, and gave the New World its youth."

Perhaps, she thought, she better understood why so many of Cahill's Irish songs spoke of rebellion. Maybe the surprise was that any of them were happy.

A swallow lowered the level of Eamon's drink.

"Of course, that's not all Ireland's given the world," came Cahill's voice. "It's a sad fact that so few know the full extent of Ireland's contributions to society."

He looked up and, like his tone, his face betrayed nothing. He met her gaze with solemn eyes and a straight mouth. Not a twitch, not a move gave him away, but Eleanor felt her own lips form a smile. Catching his mood was like catching a rainbow. "And just what is Ireland's contribution to society?"

"America, for one."

"America?"

He nodded with great dignity. "An Irish monk named Brendan sailed here a hundred years before that Columbus fellow set out from Spain."

"So it should really be Brendan, Ohio?"

"Indeed," he answered approvingly. Eleanor treasured the accomplishment of eliciting that telltale quirk of his mouth. "And of course the Irish really invented the bagpipe and whiskey."

Eamon shook his head. "Scotland tries to claim them, but all you have to do is study your history. In fact, the word *whiskey* is from the Irish—the Gaelic, that is," he explained for Eleanor's benefit. "It means 'the water of life.'"

He took a hearty sip of his own version of the water of life from his mug before continuing.

"And of course there's the potato and Irish stew and Irish setters and St. Patrick's Day and—"

When Eamon took a breath, Cahill took up the catalogue. "Irish coffee and Irish wolfhounds and—"

Eleanor, laughing, held up a hand. "And here I thought all Ireland had given the world was a good dose of malarkey."

Green eyes met hers, and held. There appeared something she couldn't define, something that went beyond the laughter.

"Sometimes that's what the world and its people need most," Cahill replied.

From a deep sleep, Cahill came instantly awake Friday.

There was no sound that should have awakened him—just the pounding of the ocean and the snoring of Eamon on the bed across the room.

Quietly, he pushed himself out of bed and went to the dormer window. Tide Beach spread out below. The sun began its battle against the morning mist, with a promise of good weather. That would mean a busy weekend for the beach, and good business for The Fishwife. But for now, the beach was empty except for a dog loping along the high-water mark behind two dark-haired little girls on their way to Harmony Beach, and a solitary figure crossing Boulder Point and heading this way.

Eleanor. He didn't need to look at his watch to know it must be a few minutes till nine. A quick shower and he'd be down before Tom Hustine arrived.

He couldn't put his finger on why the bartender raised his hackles so, and he didn't waste time trying. Ten years at the Inishowen Hotel, the last four as part owner, had honed his instincts for trouble, whether it came from customers or employees. Tom Hustine was trouble—from his free ways with the ladies regardless of wedding bands, or his habit of tending to the liquor supplies with no one else around, or his hand directly in the till. One way or another, the man was trouble.

But at least for now, Cahill told himself when he said good-morning to Eleanor in The Fishwife's kitchen, Hustine seemed to be trouble in absentia.

"Good morning," she responded with a surprised lift of her eyebrows. "You're up early."

"Thought I might take a drive with you into town. I've not seen much of Cape Ann beyond these beaches."

He watched guilt sweep into her gray eyes, and felt not the slightest compunction.

"I forget you don't have a car. It can be hard to get around without one. But anytime you want a ride…or if one of us is going into town on an errand…"

"I'd had a hope of seeing a bit of the town on Tuesday, but I never succeeded in catching up with you," he answered, and had the satisfaction of seeing her flush. Proof, if he'd needed it, that she had, indeed, been avoiding him. If she felt some guilt for it now, so much the better.

"Uh…Tuesday?" Her usually even voice stumbled. "There was a lot to do."

"Today will do as well," he said cheerfully, pleased that he'd neatly made it impossible for her to say no.

It took her only a second longer to apparently reach the same conclusion. "You're welcome to join Tom and me when we go into town for those supplies. But Eamon…"

"Will sleep till noon."

"Oh. Well, you're welcome, but Tom should be here any minute and you'd miss breakfast."

But Cahill had plenty of time for breakfast, because thirty-five minutes after nine, Hustine still hadn't arrived.

"We might as well go," she said at last. The muttered curse under Eleanor's breath amused him a little. She certainly didn't want to be alone with him. "There's no sense waiting. He isn't going to show up."

"I didn't know you were that fond of Hustine, to feel so badly at the lack of his company," he said innocently as they walked to her car. She and Valerie spent so much time at The

Fishwife, their cars were more convenient left here than at the Harmony Beach house.

She didn't rise to the bait; in fact she didn't seem to recognize it as bait. That pleased him. Eleanor attracted to Hustine would have been the worst kind of trouble.

"I feel badly over the lack of his strong back," she answered. "Several of these companies charge loading fees. I'd rather give the money to one of our employees."

"Keeping it in the family, in a manner of speaking?"

"Partly that," she agreed. Then a smile lifted her lips. "It's cheaper, too."

He laughed. "It's honest you are. I'll make you a deal, Eleanor Thalston. I'll load your supplies today for no fee if you'll give me a tour of Gloucester. I'd like to see this fisherman statue I've heard about."

"We have to get back—"

"A brief tour," he amended, more unwilling to let the idea go entirely than he would have expected.

She unlocked the passenger door. "There's a lot to load and—"

"A brief tour and I drive," he bargained. "And for that I'll load everything there is to load."

She tilted her head back to look at him. All he'd have to do was just lower his head, bend his neck and his mouth would be on hers....

"Okay," she said with an abruptness that made him wonder if she'd seen his thoughts in his eyes and made a decision— any decision—to break the moment. "Here." She put the keys into his hand and slid into the passenger seat, closing the door behind herself before he could move to help her.

He got in behind the wheel and confidently negotiated the road from the beach. It was so narrow the brush on either side touched the car. He enjoyed driving, even on the wrong side of the road as it seemed to him. He asked questions about the area, but Eleanor's answers became shorter and shorter.

Turning left on the main road, they swept through a pair of humpbacked curves that circumvented marshes, ponds and rises. After less than two miles, the close-packed buildings of the town hemmed in the road. Down a hill, he saw the inner harbor laid out to the left and the oldest part of Gloucester climbing the hills to their right.

With Eleanor talking in monosyllables, and those only to give directions, he contented himself with looking around. He'd have to come back to explore the streets that rose so steeply from the harbor that houses' bare backs showed above their next-street-down neighbors' roofs.

Main Street curved around toward the water, then a right turn brought them to the statue.

He shut off the engine and turned to her, realizing how much he liked having her at his side. Only this time, she looked a little pale and she held out an imperative hand.

"The keys," she said in a small, breathy voice. Obligingly, he dropped them into her palm. She clasped them like a lifeline.

"Next time," she said in a voice that seemed to bounce from laughter to anger to amazement, "I do the driving."

He was surprised but not hurt. He'd encountered enough American tourists on the roads of Ireland to know they could be a bit squeamish about driving. "I've never had an accident," he said with justifiable pride.

"Then you should contact whoever certifies miracles," she replied as she got out of the car. "Immediately."

He laughed. He couldn't help it. She didn't join in, but when he met her at the sidewalk he saw that her color was back and her eyes had humor in them.

She shook her head as she looked at the haphazard way he'd parked the car. "Next time, I do the parking, too," she added.

He shrugged as he followed her toward the statue. "There's not so much emphasis on neatness in Ireland," he said. "We don't so much park the cars as abandon them."

"I can believe it," she said.

"If I'm not going to be driving, that means the bargain's off, you know."

"Oh, no," she protested. "I'll just give you an IOU."

She must have read some of his ideas about what sort of

debt he'd like to collect, because she quickly added, "For a more complete tour, to compensate for your not getting to drive. Today's tour starts here with the Fisherman's Memorial, erected to honor all the Gloucester fishermen who never returned from the sea."

He followed her to the statue greened with age. A slicker-clad fisherman gripped a ship's wheel, his determined head lifted to face any storms that came in off the harbor. "'They that go down to the sea in ships, 1623 - 1923,''' he read the inscription. "It's a hard life, the sea."

At her murmured agreement, he turned to look at her. He liked the uncomplicated lines of her face, the curve of cheekbone, the straight nose. He liked the wide, straight mouth and the way she tucked her lower lip in between her teeth. It made her jaw jut out but it also gave her a vulnerable air. She was so real, so steady. Someone to hold on to against the storms of life. And to protect.

Seeming to feel his eyes on her, she turned to meet his gaze. Before she could move away, he hurried in with a question. "Do you come from a seafaring family?"

She appeared to relax some, nodding. "The Thalstons sailed from here since the 1600s. There was a sea captain and trader in the mid-nineteenth century. From what I've read, Jacob Thalston would've been a pirate if he'd been born a few decades earlier or a robber baron if he'd been born a few decades later. Rather amusing, really, that the Thalstons prided themselves on propriety, considering their origins."

"You don't like the Thalstons?"

She gave a stiff shrug accompanied by a forced smile as she turned and walked slowly across the semicircular paved area. "I'm really the only one left, other than some third or fourth cousins who live out of state, so that would be like saying I don't like myself."

"And your grandmother's people? What was Great-Aunt Susan before she met Great Uncle-John?"

"Great-Aunt Susan was a Barnes. Not as well-to-do as the Thalstons, but they've been here nearly as long." She leaned against the railing at the edge of the overlook and gazed across the water toward a jut of land studded with trees and buildings. "They've been just about everything—sailors, ministers, lawyers, engineers, laborers, even a criminal or two, especially of the horse-stealing variety."

He leaned against the railing, too, but faced her instead of the water. "Ah, I knew we had something in common. I've a number of convicts in my family tree, as well. There're one or two McCreas who found their way to Australia by way of Botany Bay."

"But since your branch of the family's still in Ireland, you're descended from law-abiding McCreas, right?"

He shook his head. "The ones too smart to get caught."

Her laugh floated across the water. "Ah, now I understand. I've wondered why you wanted to leave Ireland. The competition's so stiff because it's populated by so many smart descendants, right?"

She didn't understand, and suddenly he wanted her to understand. He considered his words long enough for the laugh to fade from her gray eyes.

"It's not that I want to leave Ireland, but that I want to come to the United States. Ever since I was a boy and heard tales of America from my father, I've felt it tugging at me. He never got to come to here a'tall. I've been here, and I want to make it mine. This country opens wide to hold so many things, so many possibilities. There's not a soul that couldn't find something to love here. It's not some wild-eyed dream about the streets being paved with gold I'm having when I think of staying here, but it's a dream all the same."

Caution slid across her eyes. He must have said it wrong. He didn't know how, but in some way, he must have said it wrong. Maybe he should have told her more, told her about his mother and Kiernan, about the hotel, about his father and Patsy. No. If he couldn't say this right, something so simple and clear to him, how could he tell her about something not simple, not clear at all?

"If we don't hurry up, you're not going to get even a brief

tour of America today.'' She slid a coin into the distance
viewer by her side and gestured for him to look through the
eyepiece. ''Just beyond the wharves to your left in Rocky
Neck. That's the oldest working art colony in the United
States.''

Her manner was brisk enough to remind him of winter
breezes off the ocean.

''It's a hard woman you are, Eleanor Thalston,'' he said
from the passenger seat nearly three hours later as they headed
back with supplies.

She looked at him, then away. She did that often. Too often.
It couldn't be his teasing tone that did it; she could answer that,
when it suited her, with more of the same. And he didn't think
it was his words. Maybe it was that she saw more in his eyes
than she wanted to.

He felt a clenching at the base of his stomach. He'd much
rather have her own feelings become more than she wanted.

''What do you mean?''

''That evil eye. The poor man never had a chance.'' He
chuckled to himself, remembering the hapless manager of the
liquor store who'd tried to say he didn't have her order because
someone from The Fishwife had called to cancel it. She'd informed the man in no uncertain terms that no such call had
been placed, and that she had to have these supplies now. Then
she'd just looked at him, until he came up with everything she
needed.

But Cahill noted her worried frown remained. Until he dis-
tracted her with talk of evil eyes.

''There is absolutely nothing evil about my eyes.''

''No, and that's a fact. They're the finest, softest gray, they
are.''

Clearly startled, she shot him a look, then turned away even
faster. ''They're just gray,'' she mumbled.

''Mmm-hmm,'' he agreed mildly.

This time she didn't even acknowledge him.

''Just ordinary gray. Plain and functional, like…like…''

"Like gray flannel," he supplied.

A quickly suppressed frown drew down her brows and the corners of her mouth, but her voice was even as she agreed. "Exactly like gray flannel. Plain and utilitarian."

"Some people like gray flannel," he commented to the world at large. "Or why'd they wear it day in and day out? In fact, some people like it so much, they want it around them all day *and* night."

They had reached The Fishwife, and she braked to a stop with more force than necessary, making the car rock forward. He pretended he didn't notice. "All night, every night," he said.

He got out but leaned down to speak through the open window. "In fact, you might be saying there are some people who have an outright fetish for gray flannel."

Cahill watched the man across the bar catch Eleanor's hand when she served him his drink. Why the hell didn't Hustine help her out? The bartender kept busy on hectic Saturday nights like this, but not so busy he could miss something happening not four feet from him.

The wiry man with the dark hair ran his free hand up Eleanor's arm and under the loose band of her short-sleeved blouse. Cutting "The Wild Colonial Boy" a chorus short, Cahill didn't bother announcing an unscheduled break.

"Let the lady alone," he said from behind the man, careful to keep his voice low and his hands off him.

The customer didn't even glance at him as he continued telling Eleanor what a good time they could have together. But Eleanor did.

"It's all right, Cahill," she said in her usual controlled tone. But her eyes told him she didn't like the feel of the man's fingers. Cahill wasn't entirely sure that if he'd read delight at the touch in her eyes he would have acted any differently.

The pressure of fury built up in him, tightening his muscles, drumming blood in his ears, narrowing his eyes.

"Take your hands away, mister."

He waited three seconds. His control wouldn't last much longer than that.

"Cahill—" He heard her protest and disregarded it.

"Now," he ordered.

The customer turned toward him with a loose grin on his lips, but still didn't remove his hand from Eleanor.

Cahill wrapped one big hand around the man's upper arm and half lifted him, half dragged him off the stool with minimal fuss. Three long strides took them to the kitchen door. He used the man's body to push open the door, then rammed him up against the wall just inside.

The whoosh of air from the man's lungs eased some of the anger tightly coiled in Cahill's gut. He became aware of Eleanor at his side, her hand resting lightly on the arm that still held the man pinned.

"Thank you, Cahill. You can let him go. I'm sure Mr. Mullen will leave now."

The moment he released the man, the customer scuttled to one side, muttering phrases about how was he supposed to know she was somebody's girl.

Cahill looked around and saw two waitresses, Manuela Ruiz and Henry, the dishwasher, staring in openmouthed surprise. Henry rarely said anything anyhow, but silence from the rest of them was almost eerie. Only Valerie, escorting Mr. Mullen through the back door with an extra-firm hand to his back, was still mobile.

The dining room door swung open, and Hustine stepped in. "Eleanor, I could use some help out here," he complained.

Fury surged through Cahill again, swift and powerful.

"Why the hell weren't you helping her when that bastard was mauling her out there, Hustine?"

"Go to hell, McCrea. You think you're God's gift, don't you?" Hustine's face twisted as he spat out an expletive. "Foreigners. Think you all have the right to come here and take over the country and try to tell Americans what to do. Well, get this straight, McCrea, you don't tell me what to do! I don't answer to you."

A deep growl tore at Cahill's throat. "You will answer to me!" He stepped toward Hustine, his hands curled into fists.

"No!" Eleanor stood between them. "Cahill, don't."

He could barely see her, but he stopped.

The echo of another rage, another voice saying "Cahill, don't" reverberated in his mind until he sickened with it.

She pushed Hustine back through the swinging door. "Get out of here, Tom. Go back to the bar. We'll talk about this later."

Then she turned back to him. But he didn't wait to see what her eyes held. He couldn't. It was the nearest he'd come to losing his temper in eighteen years. The nearest he'd come since his temper had cost the lives of his father and sister.

He spun on his heel and was out the back door.

Better she should know.... Better she should know....

The phrase was a rhythm pounded out by his feet. He ran barefoot, without knowing where he'd shed his shoes, without knowing where he headed. Running barefoot through shallow water and sand that slipped away from under him with each stride. Running from himself.

Chapter Four

When Eleanor arrived at The Fishwife on a Thursday morning in June, the building seemed eerily quiet. She'd never believed in auras and atmospheres, so she chided herself for being so jumpy.

An empty coffee cup in the sink explained the air of desertion. This was the day Cahill had said he had business in Boston and that he'd try to return in time to play for the early-dinner crowd. He hadn't explained what kind of business, and she'd quelled an uncharacteristic impulse to ask.

Good heavens, had she grown so accustomed to having him around that his absence made her nervous? The thought did nothing to improve her mood.

Neither did Val's arrival over an hour later with news that their usual source for produce had been totally bought out of strawberries and she'd had to drive around the Cape to four grocery stores before finding enough top-quality fruit for her special shortcake. At higher cost, of course.

That put them behind preparing for lunch. They operated

with barely enough staff, so everyone had to pick up the pace. Also, the daily beer delivery came late. The driver arrived as the frenzy started, saying he'd had a flat tire at his previous stop, and managed to be thoroughly in the way. Eleanor felt like a pinball, dashing from seating customers, to mixing drinks, to dealing with the deliveryman, to working the cash register.

Then, on the day's second load, the dishwasher broke.

The machine didn't even have the good grace to quietly sink into oblivion. Instead, it spewed a pond of hot soapy water across the kitchen floor that had the two waitresses caught in it squealing and high-stepping, and Eleanor, Val and Manuela diving for the water cutoff valve.

Val returned to the cooking, while Manuela directed the cleanup, and Eleanor tried to organize a system for washing dishes by hand. Henry usually helped out by chopping vegetables for salads and garnishes between stints of loading and unloading the dishwasher. Now he wouldn't be available for food-prep duty, and one person alone wouldn't be able to keep up with the dishes for this shift. They'd just have to improvise and hope they made it.

Eleanor took over the salads and garnishes along with tending the bar and the cash register. The waitresses pitched in. Billie seated people, Rae chopped carrot sticks whenever she could and Jean picked up extra tables. Henry rarely turned from the sink. Manuela plunged her hands into steaming hot water to clean the glassware. Val dried dishes just before she placed meals on them. At times they used dessert plates for hamburgers, wineglasses for milk and saucers for salads.

By two-forty-five, with the final late lunchers straggling out, they were down to two plates, three bowls and one glass tumbler. Dishes waiting to be washed had stacked up on the chopping block, the counter, the table and the small desk by the back door. Henry's shirt looked as if he'd plunged his whole body into the water instead of just his arms. Everyone walked with the slightly stiff-legged gait of exhaustion. But everyone except Rae, who had a dentist's appointment, agreed to help with the dishes before they left, in addition to their other cleanup duties.

When Billie called her to the telephone, Eleanor was already trying to imagine how they could survive the dinner rush. After the phone call, she knew they couldn't.

"Now what?" Val asked after one look at her face.

"That was Hillary and Sandy. Someone gave them free rock-concert tickets for tonight, and they're going."

"But they're scheduled to work tonight," Manuela sputtered. "They can't do that."

"They're going to," said Eleanor. "They said this concert's worth being fired for."

Manuela muttered a spate of Spanish that Eleanor found herself hoping was a curse on Hillary, Sandy and broken dishwashers. "Will you fire them?"

"I don't know. We'll worry about that tomorrow. First, we have to figure out how to get by tonight with two waitresses."

"I'll work tonight," said Billie.

"Me, too," said Jean.

"Thank heavens," breathed Val. "And thank you two, too. That's great."

Eleanor managed a smile of thanks, too, but added, "Then go home now and rest. We'll see you at the regular time."

"But the dishes—" started Jean.

Eleanor shook her head. "You'll both be dead on your feet tonight if you don't get some rest. That goes for you, too, Henry," she added, turning to the tall man with thinning brown hair. "Get a couple hours of rest."

It took a couple more minutes to convince them. She and Val both tried to tell Manuela the same thing, but she wouldn't listen.

"I was your very first employee. You think I'd run away now? You have been good bosses to me. I know how some employers treat their workers. I know how some bosses won't give jobs to people like me at all. You are good bosses. Now, let's wash dishes."

They washed dishes. And more dishes. And still more dishes.

An hour later, Eleanor's back ached, her feet felt as heavy as an old-fashioned iron, a muscle across her right shoulder threatened to cramp, and from fingertips to elbows, her skin had been washed raw by hot water and detergent. She looked at Manuela and Val and knew they felt exactly the same. And they were barely halfway done.

The back door opened, but she didn't turn from the sink until she heard the voice.

"A new game, is it?" Cahill asked. "Building a Leaning Tower of Pisa from dishes alone?"

Val and Manuela poured out the day's misadventures while Eleanor looked at him. Cahill McCrea in suit and tie was something to behold, even with the tie loosened and the top button of the shirt undone. Maybe especially that way.

She'd seen the thatch of dark hair that peeked from the opening of his collar every day. He never buttoned his shirts all the way. Every day when he helped out with loading and unloading supplies, teased the waitresses, greeted Henry, sang his songs, she saw those dark curls through the V'd opening of his collar. That was exactly what she saw now. But somehow it was different.

The raw power of his build suited the tight jeans and work shirts he usually wore. The suit did nothing to hide his strength, only adding a veneer that made him seem somehow less straightforward, and therefore more unpredictable, more dangerous. She could almost see him jerking loose the tie and yanking open the button as if they'd constricted him.

As Val's and Manuela's voices wound down he turned to her, and Eleanor saw his face fully. He was tired. In that instant, her imagination again saw him loosening his tie and opening his top button, this time not with the impatience of a man confined, but with the weariness of a man drained.

But why? What had he been doing in Boston, in suit and tie, that had worn down what she'd thought of as an inexhaustible supply of energy and good humor?

Then he blinked, and the vision disappeared, along with his vulnerability. Eleanor felt tightness behind her eyes, almost as if she wanted to cry. She didn't cry, ever, not even over the most miserable of days. Crying wasted time.

"So, when does the man come to repair this most inconsiderate piece of machinery?" Cahill asked.

In the deep and sudden silence that followed, Eleanor moved to the desk chair and dropped into it. Her elbows rested on a sliver of free space and she leaned her forehead against her fists. She hadn't called the repairman.

She heard Val and Manuela berating themselves for not thinking to call, but that was silly. Thinking of things like that was her job. How could she have forgotten to do something so basic?

She didn't realize she'd spoken the words until she heard Val's voice answering her. "How? Maybe because you were too busy sticking fingers in the dike, just like the rest of us. You can't expect yourself to be superwoman every day, you know, especially not on a day like this."

"I'll call now." Eleanor stood, then started to sway.

Cahill's strong hands wrapped around her upper arms.

"No repairman will come tonight. But if you drive down to Gloucester and talk to him in person, I'll wager he'll be here first thing in the morning. The drive'll do you good. You look to stand in need of a bit of fresh air."

"But the dishes—"

"I'll take care of the dishes."

"No. I could just call and—"

"A man could say no to you on the telephone, but no one could withstand those gray eyes of yours. But first..."

The sturdy warmth of Cahill's grip on her arms penetrated her senses, but she didn't try to shake it off. She'd let him guide her. She'd let responsibilities slide away. For a minute. For sixty restful seconds before she returned to reality.... Only she couldn't figure out why they were in the pantry.

That made no sense. Why would he bundle her into the pantry? But the oversize cans of tomato juice on the shelf in front of her eyes proved that was where she was, and Cahill's hands turning her around proved she wasn't alone.

His mouth, firm and sure, covered hers.

Confusion swirled across her brain. This couldn't be happening. Cahill McCrea couldn't be the man kissing her. Or she couldn't be the woman Cahill McCrea was kissing. Those weren't her lips that softened and warmed under his. Those weren't her hands resting at his waist. Couldn't be.

But it couldn't be anyone else.

She better understood that nagging familiarity when she looked at his mouth. His lips fit hers so right, so true. Some part of her had recognized that, anticipated it.

He lifted his mouth but only for an instant. She heard the short, deep rumble in his throat as if in comment on some discovery, then his mouth returned to hers. This time he wanted more.

Exhaustion cleared in a wave of sensation, as if she were taking a cold, cold shower. Only this surge over, around and through her body was pure heat. It also wiped away confusion, thought and practicality. Nothing was complicated, nothing was difficult. His lips on hers was very simple, very easy.

Too easy.

She felt her lower lip captured between his teeth with a gentle pull. The shivery trail of his tongue crossed her upper lip, her lower lip, her teeth. Her hands clung at his waist, his gripped her upper arms. She wasn't sure if he held her still, or held her up.

When he lifted his mouth this time, she had the sense to take a deep, steadying breath and a half step back.

He tipped his head a little, perhaps in acknowledgment of her withdrawal or maybe just to hide his eyes.

"So now it's in to town for you, and getting after the dishes for me," he said, nodding. Then he left her standing there.

Three deep breaths steadied her enough to walk out of the pantry with some degree of dignity. No one seemed to notice. Her purse and keys sat on the chair by the back door. She snatched them up and headed out with just one glance at the kitchen. Valerie carried a stack of dishes to the sink. Manuela swept a towel across a wet plate. And Cahill McCrea had his suit coat off, his sleeves rolled up to his elbows and his forearms in soapy water.

She welcomed the diversions of driving into town and convincing the repairman to come to The Fishwife first thing the next morning. At some level, she knew that all this constituted a mere distraction from the memory of Cahill's kiss. Perhaps she could be called cowardly, but she wasn't quite ready to face it yet.

Leaving the repair shop, she walked to the center of town, then turned uphill toward a section of old houses, a few dating from the Revolution but more the result of Gloucester's prosperity in the first half of the nineteenth century. She sat on a low wall and considered the house that had been built for Jacob Thalston.

The white frame house had gone out of the family just a few years ago when her grandmother died. She had no reason to regret the sale; she certainly had no sentimental attachment to the house. Nor to the last Thalston who had lived there.

Eleanor Barnes Thalston wouldn't have approved of her granddaughter running a restaurant. Eleanor could see the rigid back and hear the prim voice: "Thalstons have a position to uphold." But even the woman who had valued good sense second only to "position" would have approved of her methodical approach to the problems at The Fishwife.

Too many orders had been canceled. Too many necessary ingredients had been mysteriously sold out. Too many mechanical appliances had broken. Too many coincidences.

Last season, she and Val had talked to the police about the vandalism. They agreed to step up patrols, but said they required more than a hunch that the spray paint and broken air-conditioning system hadn't been the work of teenagers.

So she'd started accumulating proof. She followed up on every order gone astray, every ingredient sold out, every appliance broken. She asked questions, she noted dates, she took down names. Just now she'd asked the dishwasher repairman to keep an eye out for anything beyond normal wear.

Yes, her grandmother would approve. Eleanor's mouth twisted a little at the irony. She'd never wanted her grandmother's approval. She had the old woman's common sense, but that didn't mean she'd liked her.

Eleanor Barnes Thalston had valued only strength, not the softer traits of a dreamer. "Your mother's a fool, Eleanor." The harsh judgment had been voiced many times, but one day, twelve-year-old Eleanor hadn't denied it as she had before. She'd never forgiven her grandmother for forcing her to the tacit admission. Nor herself for the disloyalty. Nor her mother for being a woman she couldn't admire. *Yes, she is a fool.* She still remembered the words running in her head. *A fool of a dreamer.*

She stood up abruptly and kept walking. Away from thoughts of another dreamer. And his kiss.

"Eleanor, take the day off, for heaven's sake. You know how dead Tuesdays are."

Even if Val's exasperation hadn't vibrated in her voice, her use of her cousin's full name would have been a giveaway. She stood, hands on hips, in the center of the kitchen glaring at Eleanor, who was bringing the books up to date.

"I don't need a day off."

"Bull. Everybody's had at least one day off since we opened except you. And you're always the one talking about how people don't function properly when they're exhausted."

"I'm not exhausted. In fact, I'm fine."

"You may feel fine, but you look exhausted."

"Thanks a lot, Val."

"You must be tired, Eleanor," contributed Manuela, "to make a mistake like that yesterday on the bank deposit."

Eleanor winced. She'd misfigured the receipts by nearly five hundred dollars. The bank teller had caught it when Val made the deposit, but they'd had to call Eleanor to straighten out the mistake.

She didn't do things like that.

Val straightened suddenly. "Come here, Manuela," she said, leading the woman through the swinging door to the dining room.

Eleanor knew that tone of voice. Her cousin had an idea. And, Lord help her, she had no energy to worry about it. Maybe she did need a day off, she thought with a sigh as she punched a column of figures into the calculator for the third time. Her fingers didn't want to hit the right keys.

The door swung open behind her, but she didn't turn. If she just ignored them, Val and Manuela would go away.

Then her chair slid backward, and big hands lifted her up, pulling her forward until her nose practically bumped against Cahill's Adam's apple.

"Cahill, what—"

"Hush." He started tugging her toward the back door.

"Wait! What are you doing?" Digging her heels in slowed them some but didn't stop their progress.

"If you won't go to your day off on your own, Eleanor Thalston, I'll *take* you to your day off."

Manuela hurried after them, tucking Eleanor's purse and car keys into her free hand. Cahill winked a thank-you, and tossed a wave over his shoulder. "I've got my orders."

Eleanor twisted around to see Val grinning, as if she enjoyed seeing Cahill and Eleanor heading out the door. But she'd thought Val was interested in Cahill herself. If *she'd* cared about Cahill that way, she wouldn't stand there grinning while he walked out with anyone else.

But Val *would* coerce Cahill into spending his day off entertaining Eleanor.

As for that kiss in the pantry and the times Cahill had seemed to pay her extra attention, well, she'd finally figured that out. She'd read more into it than he'd meant. A kiss was a relative thing. To some people it meant hello, how are you. To others, it meant desire.

Cahill, with his easy charm, was probably of the first kind.

She'd discovered, a little to her distress, that she was the second kind.

So even if he was truly attracted in her, even if she forgot that her cousin and dearest friend was interested in the man, it was no good. They weren't the same kind.

"Shall I drive?" Cahill's question halted her musings. They stood by her car and he gestured to the keys dangling from her hand.

"Definitely not," she said, tightening her grip.

He laughed, seemingly uninsulted as she slid into the driver's seat and opened the other door for him.

"Where to? Gloucester?" she asked at the intersection with the main road.

He jerked a thumb to the right. "Rockport. This is a day for frivolity."

She raised her eyebrows a little at the notion of Gloucester as a more serious destination, but turned right.

As they roamed the sidewalks of Rockport among a steady stream of tourists, she couldn't argue that frivolity certainly was the mood of their day. Usually she limited her visits to Rockport to the off-season, and then she spent her time at the bookstores and art galleries. Today, she saw a different side of the town.

With Cahill's broad shoulders breaking through the crowds in the narrow roadway of Bearskin Neck and his hand tugging her along, she explored shops with wooden toys, Indian baskets, Christmas decorations and seashell novelties. Mostly, she followed docilely, but in front of one store window she tugged him back.

"Let's go in here," she said, not taking her eyes from the moody seascape that occupied the entire display area.

"Why?"

"I'd like to talk to the owner about arranging a display at The Fishwife for—"

"You're hopeless, Eleanor Thalston. You'll be doing that on your day off? Not when I have charge of your day off, you won't.'' He tightened his fingers around hers. "Now this is the sort of shop you should be enjoying on your day off."

She followed his gaze to the next window and encountered a display of skimpy swim wear and equally skimpy lingerie.

"Oh, no," she protested with false sternness. "If you won't let me indulge in art, I'm sure not going to let you indulge in this."

"But this is art. Of a sort," he said with that total solemnity that never failed to make her smile.

She damped the smile long enough to shake her head. "That's even worse. No seascapes for me, no nudes for you."

"All right, then. I know when I'm licked. We'll find something we can compromise on." He started down the road with her in tow.

They found their compromise in a bakery. They took their muffins, croissants, cider and coffee down to the end of Bearskin Neck. From a bench they had a view of Rockport Harbor with its multicolored dotting of pleasure boats and the red fishing shack dubbed Motif Number One because it had been the model for so many painters.

"That's actually a reproduction," Eleanor told Cahill. "The original got swept into the harbor in 1978, during one of the worst blizzards this area's ever had."

Cahill shifted on the bench so his light green eyes rested on her instead of the view. Under that assessing look, she wanted to walk away. Or run.

"What is it?"

He didn't answer for a full minute, then he shook his head. "Still too serious—talking of blizzards and landmarks. You're a hard case, Eleanor Thalston."

"Better give up, then," she suggested lightly.

"Never." This time she felt no urge to smile at his solemnity. "I'll just work harder."

She couldn't look away from those eyes. They were as fathomless as the ocean, and just as unreadable. What would those thick dark eyelashes be like to touch? She could practically feel them—they'd tickle the tips of her fingers. The same fingers that longed to trace the wirier texture of the straight, strong eyebrows. To skim across the faint lines that furrowed the wide brow, then follow the straight drop of his nose to that fascinating bump.

She tried to breathe, but it came out as a sigh that nearly slipped into a gasp. *Don't lose your head now, Eleanor Thalston. Not when you need it most.*

"C'mon, then," she urged heartily as she jumped up from the bench. "Let's get to work having fun. Did you run out of stores you want to explore? I could have sworn I saw you looking longingly at a stuffed lobster back there."

His expression remained serious, then a grin broke through. "Everyone should have a stuffed lobster."

Whether or not everyone should have a stuffed lobster, Eleanor was one person who *did* have one by the time they got back to her car. Cahill insisted on buying it for her, along with an inflatable clam, an oyster ashtray and a T-shirt with the legend Cape Ann Is A Hell Of A Woman. She retaliated by bestowing on him a cap with a stuffed crab riding its peak, a plastic cup that boasted one hundred tiny views of Motif Number One, and a seventy-five-cent gadget guaranteed to take the messiness out of peeling shrimp.

They were still amicably wrangling over whether that delicacy should rightly be called shrimp or prawn when Eleanor realized she'd automatically been following Cahill's directions out of Rockport, in the opposite direction from Gloucester and The Fishwife.

"Mind if I ask where we're going?"

"Not a'tall," he answered graciously, then said no more.

She gave a spurt of laughter. "All right, where are we going?"

"Valerie told me about a cove the two of you found as girls, someplace near the Halibut Point State Park."

"Oh. Yes." She remembered the spot with pleasure, and some pain.

"I haven't been back here since the day before we left Cape Ann," she said as they parked the car. Cahill grabbed the bag that held a midafternoon picnic they'd bought and an old bed-spread she kept in the trunk. "Val and I rode our bikes here that day. I guess it was our special goodbye."

She told him some of her funny memories of the spot, but in her mind's eye, she saw the young Eleanor, a girl of twelve, preparing to leave home. Not a perfect place, but the place she knew. The place where she had friends and relations who loved her. She'd tried to tell her mother all that. But Connie Thalston Garrett hadn't listened. She and Norman Garrett had been in the early throes of one of their sure-to-succeed schemes—Eleanor couldn't even remember now if it had been the new line of greeting cards or the three-wheeled bicycles for adults—and Eleanor had no say in being uprooted and transplanted to Arizona. Then it was Kansas City. Then Seattle and Dallas. Cincinnati and Tampa. Always with some fantasy bound to come true this time.

All mirages. Her mother and Norman fantasized; reality fell to Eleanor. She enrolled herself in school, bought the groceries, wrote the rent check—when they had the money for rent—and vowed she would live a different life.

Her chance came with the full scholarship to Boston College. Her mother had wanted her to go to school in Tampa, to stay nearby. Eleanor wouldn't consider it.

"You can't wait to get away, can you?" her mother had finally asked. Without her winsome smile, Connie Garrett had looked older than her forty-one years at that moment.

That was exactly what Eleanor did want. To get far, far away. But she couldn't say that, so she said nothing.

"Why? Norman and I love you. Have we ever been cruel to you? We haven't always been able to give you the things we wanted, but now, with this new line of calendars Norman's working on—"

"Stop it, Mother." Eleanor hadn't meant to sound so cold, but she couldn't bear another delusion. They'd given her that in plenty. "Just stop it. I'm going to Boston."

She'd gone to Boston, and she'd stayed, working summers there instead of whatever promised land her mother and Norman had found. She'd seen her mother twice since then—at her college graduation and at her grandmother's funeral. Eleanor had been surprised they drove up from Baltimore for the funeral. Her feelings had been less easy to classify when her mother took her hand at the graveside and said, with tearing eyes, "You're a lot like your grandmother in some ways, Eleanor. Very much a Thalston."

A lot like that hard and cold old woman? A lot like the dragon who had terrified her as a child because of the ease with which she brought tears to her mother's eyes? Just because she had sense didn't mean she was like that.

She rejected the words. But maybe they were there in the back of her head when she and Val inherited the houses from Great-Aunt Susan. Maybe then they'd still rankled some.

Val had immediately come up with the concept for The Fishwife and wanted to plunge in. The memory of her mother's comment stilled Eleanor's first impulse to dismiss the idea out of hand as too risky. That certainly would have been her grandmother's reaction. Deliberately, she delved into feasibility studies. Soon, she was researching pubs, adding night courses in restaurant management to her work load and drawing up financial plans. Val grumbled good-naturedly about the delay but went along with her strict budgets. So far it had kept them in business.

"Is that it, then?"

Cahill's question brought her back from her memories. She'd brought them along the narrow path almost by instinct, right up to the rock as big as a house that hid the opening to the secret spot she and Val had found as children.

She led him around the rock, laughing at how much smaller everything seemed now, and into the clearing. There was just enough room on the thick wild grass for the old bedspread. Beyond that was a curved tumble of rocks. Ocean waves rolled in and shattered against it into sparkling sprays of light.

They left the picnic, working their way down the rocks.

"Was it difficult growing up with a stepfather?"

She considered the question. "Norman? He's a nice enough

man. I guess I'm lucky I don't have any of the wicked-stepfather stories some of my friends have told me." No, it wasn't difficult growing up with Norman as a stepfather. It was difficult growing up with only dreams to live on.

"Actually," she continued, once they'd settled as near to the water's edge as they could without being soaked, "in my case it probably wouldn't have been much different if my father had lived. From what I understand, he was a lot like Norman is."

He gave her an intent look. "And how is that?"

"Well..." She hesitated as she stared into the restless water and thought of the days before her father became ill, before Grandmother Thalston's frequent scoldings left her mother in tears. "He loved a good time. I remember him laughing, and trying to make me laugh. He and my mother always spun these wonderful tales about the future. As a child, I thought he was like Aladdin, and all he had to do was make a wish for the tales to come true. After I grew up, I saw he had no more sense than my mother."

She sent him a quick look. She hadn't meant to say so much, to sound so harsh. But his face held no censure, only an arrested look she had difficulty interpreting.

"Hard Yankee common sense seemed to miss that generation entirely," she said with an attempt at a laugh.

"It makes no matter what flaws a person you love has, or how clearly you see them," he said in such a soft, musing voice that she wondered if he'd meant to speak out loud. "When that person's gone it's like having a layer of skin pulled away—a protection between you and the world...."

Of course. He'd lost his father, too. All the talk about his mother and brother, but never one word about his father. She rested her hand on his forearm where it wrapped around his knees. Her palm absorbed the texture of the fine, dark hair on his arms.

He turned at her touch, and she saw sorrow in the depths of the green eyes. Sorrow that still left room to absorb her pain. His other hand covered hers, pressing his warmth into her skin. This ran deeper than easy charm, didn't it?

A stronger wave attacked the rocks and sprayed them. The sun caught the red highlights in the dark depths of his hair. Was she really seeing things in him she hadn't noticed before, or did she only wish to see them?

She pulled her gaze away, standing quickly. "C'mon, let's eat. I'm starved."

They lunched in companionable silence, and with the remnants of the picnic scattered around them, Cahill stretched out and Eleanor sat by his side. The warm sun felt comfortable with just the faint mist of the waves reaching them.

She thought Cahill had fallen asleep when he pulled himself up and started unbuttoning his shirt.

"It's hot," he complained.

"This is a very mild summer day," she said.

"In Ireland, over seventy is grounds for heat prostration" came the muffled reply as he peeled off the shirt.

Power. It was the only word her mind could form as she took in his broad shoulders. The smooth muscled surface of his back. The narrowing to his waist. The slight, suggestive gap at the back waistband of his jeans when he leaned forward to lay the shirt next to their picnic bag.

"With that fair skin and those freckles, you're sure to burn." She gave the warning around a sudden lump in her throat. Her fingers tingled with the temptation to trace the dusting of freckles that spread across his shoulders.

He turned to her, and the lump in her throat was forgotten in the clattering of her heart against her ribs. Dark, curly hair covered his chest more thickly than his arms, but not so thickly that she couldn't see the hard flesh below it. The curls that peaked through his shirt every day were the beginning of a triangle that narrowed to a line that disappeared into his jeans.

"You need sunblock. Or..." She met his eyes. A mistake. Raw, hungry desire wasn't a thing she saw in men's eyes so often that she could be unaffected by it. To be honest, even if she'd seen it every day of her life, she suspected that this look still would have had her skin humming and her mouth fumbling for words. "Or...or you'll burn."

How had he gotten closer without her seeing him move? How had he gotten right next to her so his green eyes mesmerized her from only inches away, so his fingers wound into her hair, so his lips hovered near hers?

"I already burn," he murmured just before his mouth touched hers.

He did burn. Heat poured from him into her. His mouth was hot, so hot. It seared her, setting flame to every molecule of her skin.

His weight carried her down, and he cushioned her head in one large palm. She felt the solid mass of his chest resting against her, the sensation of the fine curls teasing her nipples through the layers of cloth that covered them. She raked the wavy hair at his nape with fingers that wanted to tremble but wanted more to feel the surprisingly silky texture of those thick strands.

His tongue stroked a line of fire along her upper lip, then the bottom. There was no denying that claim. She parted her lips to him and an electrical fire charged through her veins as his tongue touched hers.

A moan rose in her throat and passed to him, where it echoed deep in his chest. He lifted his head only for a breath, then kissed her again, and again.

Like a man who did this often. The thought sent ice across her heated skin. Pushing against his chest, she ignored the sensation of the hair and solid muscle against her palm. "Cahill—"

He claimed her mouth again, stopping the protest. His hand slid along her rib cage, his thumb stroking the curve of her full breast, gliding across the erect tip.

She gasped, then bit her lip as she twisted away from him, and temptation. This didn't mean anything to him. It was just his way. And she couldn't bear that.

"Stop, Cahill."

She sat straight, not looking at him.

He reached for her again, the desire a green flame in his eyes. It was almost her undoing. Almost.

His lips trailed down her throat. She stood to escape him, but he followed.

"Noreen, why do you turn away from me again and again? I'll not believe I'm feeling this alone."

"You can believe what you want." Why couldn't he really mean it? Why couldn't he feel as much as she did? And why couldn't wishing on stars make things come true? Stop wishing for things that cannot be, Eleanor Thalston.

"Then I'll believe that it's your words that are lying."

She tried to move away, but she was caught between the huge rock and him. He brushed his lips against hers, trailing a line of fire with his tongue.

"And what's telling the truth is the way your mouth feels on mine." One broad hand held her tightly against his hardness. "The way you fit against me." His free hand dipped below the opening of her shirt, fingers skimming the top of her breast, then slipping under the silky fabric. "The way your body—"

"Cahill." She barely got the name out, but she had the strength to spin away from him. "Stop."

"Why?" A glance over her shoulder showed his face matched the harshness in his voice.

She started to climb back onto the rocks, but he followed her. She stopped.

Maybe he did feel something. Eleanor straightened her shoulders and turned. Or maybe he was just so used to charming his way into what he wanted that he couldn't believe it when someone said no. Well, he'd better believe it.

"Not everyone takes these things as lightly as you do, Cahill. Flirting isn't my style. I suggest you find someone who shares your interests." She'd meant to stay calm, but the thoughts pounding in her head wouldn't allow that. "With all the conquests you've made at The Fishwife, I'm certain you could find several who'd be willing. As good as your flirting is for business, I'm certain you could also make it pay off for yourself."

Mortified, she snapped her mouth shut. She sounded like a fishwife herself, a jealous, frustrated, strident fishwife.

She'd made a fool of herself. She looked into Cahill's face, expecting amusement or sneering or disgust. Almost anything except the storm that harshly sculpted his face.

"It's flirting you think I am? It's—"

She could see the taut tendons along his neck, the muscles tightened across his shoulders. His chest rose and fell as he tried to master his breathing. The skin across his jaw tightened. For an instant, she thought he struggled to say something.

He spun away so abruptly she stepped back and nearly lost her balance on the uneven rocks. In the few seconds before she looked up, he crossed the clearing. He didn't stop to pick up his shirt. Two long strides and he'd rounded the huge rock and disappeared from sight.

She felt as drained as if she'd fought a storm. And as dazed. His reaction couldn't have been feigned—he'd been hurt. But did that mean he really cared? Had she hurt him or only his pride? Some men would have that much ego. But Cahill? Was he like that?

She began collecting the remnants of their picnic, stuffing them in the bag and shaking the blanket. Something fell. Cahill's shirt. She held it between her hands and had the crazy idea that the warmth of the fabric came from his body. Ridiculous. Silly. Just the sun.

She watched her own hands begin to draw the shirt closer, as if to hug it against herself the way she wouldn't allow herself to hug the man.

No! She jerked the cloth away from her, stuffing it untidily into the bag. Grabbing the bag and the blanket, she headed for the car.

He joked and laughed with everyone so easily. People were easy for him. Not like her. He didn't feel about her the way she felt about him.

The way she felt about him?

She skidded away from that question, concentrating on starting the engine and maneuvering the car onto the road. The only way to feel about him that made sense was to feel he was a good employee and a pleasant human being.

He wouldn't come back to the cove, she knew that. But she looked for him along the road as she drove. It was a long walk across the cape, especially for a stranger who didn't know the way.

She saw no sign of him. She told herself not to worry. Aidan Padraic Cahill McCrea could take care of himself.

Still, the tightness at the back of her neck didn't ease until she saw a second-story light come on at The Fishwife near midnight. She was walking on the beach, hoping it would make her sleepy. It worked, for abruptly she felt bone tired.

Chapter Five

"Ouch. Looks like you stayed in the sun too long yesterday, Cahill."

Despite her cheerfulness, Valerie sounded sympathetic. Cahill wouldn't refuse sympathy today, even misplaced sympathy. The hurt from his reddened skin could be seen; the other couldn't.

He was caught and he knew it. Everywhere he turned, Eleanor Thalston tormented him. Gray eyes haunted his dreams. Gentle fingers touched him as softly as the drift of a sheet across his legs. A calm voice murmured with the water of his showers. But she thought him the shiftless kind who'd flirt away an afternoon and think no more about it.

He'd tell her he wasn't the wastrel she thought him, if that would help. But it wouldn't.

With her regard for practicality, what would she say if he told her he'd left his share of the Inishowen Hotel in his mother's care while he came to the United States to pursue the elusive goal of citizenship? She'd call him daft, to work so long and so hard for security in one country, then turn his back on it to try his luck in another.

No, telling her those things wouldn't help because Eleanor Thalston was a hardheaded, practical woman. It was part of what appealed to him. It was part of what prevented him from telling her exactly how much she appealed to him.

He knew that after listening to her talk about her family. He didn't think she knew how much she'd revealed about her feelings for her mother—frustration, confusion, and yet, love. But love without understanding, without respect.

He'd thought about that during the hours he walked along the rocky coast as afternoon waned into night. It explained a lot. It explained the way her body responded to him, yet her words pushed him away. She felt attraction, but she didn't want to. Because she didn't understand him, either.

He ached with a longing for her to look beyond his surface. But he couldn't expect it.

And he wouldn't fight the unfairness of it. He'd felt the hot words rising into his throat when she accused him of flirting, and they'd nearly escaped. He couldn't let them. He couldn't risk letting his anger go, not ever again.

Cahill looked up from tuning his guitar and met Eleanor's eyes in the mirror behind the bar. "Yes, I was burned yesterday."

"Phone for you, Eleanor." Manuela handed her the receiver in the middle of the Wednesday predinner bustle.

"Ms. Thalston? This is Rod Church. You asked me to call if I found anything."

The repairman. When he hadn't called after fixing the dishwasher Friday, she'd thought her hunch had been wrong. She'd hoped she'd been wrong. Now...

"And you did?"

"Yeah. I wanted to check it out on a machine set up the same way, and I had the feeling you wouldn't want me doing it there in your kitchen, with everybody looking."

"You were quite right." The words pushed past a lump of

distaste at her distrusting her own employees. "I appreciate that."

"Yeah, well it took me a while to find a similar setup. But I did."

He paused, and Eleanor thought he searched for his words. If so, he found blunt ones.

"Somebody cut one of your hoses, Ms. Thalston. Not quite all the way through, but enough to guarantee it would burst after a load or two."

"But couldn't—" She stopped.

What could she say that wouldn't give away their conversation? She glanced up to where Sandy, Hillary and Jean filled salt-and-pepper shakers. Henry worked at the chopping block next to the counter where Val and Manuela poured batter into muffin tins. Tom Hustine chatted with Rae by the desk, both having come in on their day off to pick up checks. Cahill, just back from a walk, stood alone between the pantry and a small closet where the staff stored belongings during their shifts.

Anything she said could be overheard by these people, or easily repeated to the few staff members not on hand. If Rod Church was right about someone having sabotaged the dishwasher, it had to be one of the employees. As much as she disliked the fact, she acknowledged the logic. She had to watch every word.

"No. I checked it out very carefully, Ms. Thalston. That's why I had to see another washer set up like yours. I wanted to be sure a knife couldn't accidentally have worked down there. No way, Ms. Thalston. Not with that angle."

"Oh. Well, thank you very much for calling to tell me about this, and…um, for your extra service."

"No problem, Ms. Thalston. Give me a call if you need any more help. Or a witness or anything." The repairman's voice held a note of excitement. He could probably already see himself testifying in a packed courtroom. "I kept the hose, in case you need evidence."

Eleanor hung up the phone with a feeling of despair. She should be glad evidence existed. Instead, she felt slightly nauseated at the confirmation that someone inside The Fishwife really meant harm. She'd grown used to considering Franklin Britt the enemy; he was annoying but at least safely on the outside. Now she knew there was an enemy inside. But who?

She wished she could talk to someone.

Not Val. Val would fly off the handle. Even if Eleanor convinced her to hold off confronting the staff, whoever was guilty would need only one look at Val's thunderous expression to know suspicions had been roused. And Eleanor figured the best—maybe the only—way to catch the saboteur was to lure him or her into trying again.

Besides, she really wanted to confide in Cahill.

Automatically, her fingers sorted money for the cash-register drawer, but her eyes went to the tall figure leaning against the wall. Logically, he ranked as high on the suspect list as any of the others. These inside attacks started the same time he began working for them. But she knew Cahill wasn't guilty. She knew it with a certainty that made logic seem puny and pale. But that was why she couldn't confide in him.

He'd said he burned. Well, she agreed. He was fire, and she had too much common sense to put her fingers in the fire. Even when the bright flames drew her.

In the brief lull between Saturday's hectic lunch and frenetic dinner, Val brought up Cahill's behavior.

"Has he seemed quiet to you?" she asked Eleanor as they drank iced tea on the side steps leading to the nearly empty deck.

Eleanor couldn't pretend she didn't know who Val meant, but she did stall. "Quiet? What do you mean?"

"Quiet. You know, like not talking a lot, not joking, not laughing. In general, not being Cahill McCrea."

"Even Cahill McCrea's allowed to have moods, Val," she said in her most reasonable voice.

Val shook her head. "I think it's more than that. And I think I know what it is, El." Eleanor flashed a look at her cousin, but Val stared out across the marsh grass as she added, "At least partly."

She turned back to Eleanor. "Remember Thursday when I brought in the mail? It seemed to me he got awfully quiet right after that. I think it was something he got in the mail that day."

Thursday, not Tuesday. The mail, not her. Relief warred with something else. Disappointment that his concern didn't involve her?

"What kind of something in the mail?" she prompted.

"I don't know exactly, but he got two letters that day. An official-looking envelope that I just caught a glimpse of and one of those blue airmail envelopes from Ireland." Val's worry showed in her brown eyes when she looked at Eleanor. "It looked to me like a woman's writing on the envelope."

A letter from home? Perhaps his mother, asking him to come home. If his brother, Kiernan, needed him, he'd go, she knew that. She'd never see him again.

She looked down at the beach. The sun's reflection on the retreating waves was so bright her eyes burned.

"Maybe there's a problem at home he's worried about," she offered, turning back to catch an expression on Val's face that she didn't understand. If she didn't know any better, she'd describe the look as almost protective.

"Maybe," Val said with no conviction. "El, I know how sensible you think you are, but even the most practical women have hearts and—"

"Val? Val, how do you want those tomatoes done for garnish tonight?" Manuela came up behind them. "Slices or wedges? And we need some help with the herb dressing, and—"

Val gave a deep sigh and patted Eleanor's knee before standing up. "I guess I'd better get ready for the hungry hordes," she said. "We'll continue this talk later."

"Be grateful we *have* hungry hordes this year," retorted Eleanor, resolving that a conversation that linked Cahill McCrea's mood and Eleanor Thalston's heart would never resume if she had her way.

No conversation beyond the absolutely essential took place the rest of that day or that busy Sunday. Falling into bed in the early-morning hours of Monday with the consolation of a tidy weekend income, Eleanor reminded herself to beware of being cornered by Val for the threatened continuation of their talk.

But Val didn't bring up a topic that touched on odd moods and unsettled feelings. Cahill did.

The knock on their front door Monday morning wouldn't count as early by some standards, but the noise startled Eleanor. Not many strangers found this stretch of beach, but anyone knocking at their door some three hours before noon had to be a stranger. Their friends and relations all knew the hours they kept. Val would still be asleep. Ordinarily she would have been, too, but she'd finally abandoned her restless tossing, and showered and dressed in T-shirt and shorts.

Her pulse pounded with an undefined anxiety as she quickly descended the stairs, automatically skipping the one that squeaked. She took a deep breath, then pulled open the door.

"Cahill." He stood there looking as solid as the wooden door. The morning sun behind him obscured his face, but something about his stance pulled the question from her, "Is something wrong?"

"Morning, Eleanor. I've need to talk to you."

She wanted to close the door and shut out whatever he was going to say. She didn't want to hear it. But she swung the door open.

"Come in." She wouldn't run away from this, whatever *this* was. "I was just going to have breakfast."

She started down the short hall without looking to see if he followed. Still, she knew when he came around the corner, and leaned against the edge of the refrigerator with an air of ease. It took her three tries to get the coffee-maker plug into the outlet.

"Why don't you have some breakfast while you talk."

"I don't want—"

"I know," she interrupted. She needed an occupation to steady her oddly skittish nerves, and fixing him breakfast was the most logical. "But if you eat breakfast here or at The Fish-wife, it basically comes out of the same refrigerator."

She gestured to the kitchen table and after a moment's hesitation, he sat. He cleared his throat once, then launched into a humorous story about his mother fixing oatmeal when he was a boy. Eleanor nodded at appropriate intervals and covertly studied him as she prepared juice, coffee, toast, cereal and fruit.

Even before the Saturday discussion with Val, she'd noticed that his manner had bordered on brooding. Everyone had noticed. Everyone had commented. Most of them had asked if she knew what was bothering him. No one seemed to believe her when she said no.

Now, he smiled and gave her a light word of thanks as she sat at the end of the table. But she didn't believe in this new mood. This briskness wasn't the real Cahill; it lacked his underlying warmth. And he didn't look at her at all. She watched his strong neck as he swallowed the orange juice as if he were parched.

She hated this waiting, this not knowing. Why didn't he just tell her? Why did he drag it out this way and make it hurt all the more?

Hurt? Why should it hurt you?

"What do you have to tell me, Cahill?" Her words crackled with impatience. His mouth smiled, but his eyes didn't meet hers. He seemed to look at her hands.

"I'm sorry to be saying, I'll be giving my notice." His smile didn't falter and his tone remained light.

"You're leaving? Why?"

The suspicion and accusation in her voice surprised her more than Cahill's words. The possibility of his leaving had nibbled at her since Saturday. She couldn't even find it in her heart to fault the man. How could she expect him to put the good of their business—because that, of course, was the reason for her sudden desperate desire to beg him to stay—ahead of his family in Ireland? So why had she sounded so...so betrayed?

He turned to her and before she looked down at the cereal spoon clenched in her hand, Eleanor caught a shadow of his surprise, too.

"It's not entirely by choice, Eleanor," he said with that

slightly mocking lilt. "It seems that after the twenty-sixth day of July, I'll not be welcomed in this great country of yours."

"What do you mean?" This didn't sound as if a problem at home required his return. What was going on?

"I mean my visa expires that day and there'll be no extensions, no renewals." He said the words lightly, almost cheerfully.

She should be happy for him, relieved that there was no family crisis. Instead she felt only a vast, yawning emptiness. Disappointment, she supposed. Disappointment for him, at his having to leave the country he longed to join. Disappointment for The Fishwife, which would be losing such an integral part of its summer success. Disappointment for the staff, who would miss his good humor. Disappointment, not loneliness.

"So you're going back to Ireland."

He met her statement with silence.

"Cahill." He didn't look at her. "Don't do it. If you stay illegally—"

The need to touch him, to sway him, sent her hand out just short of the hair-dusted forearm exposed by the rolled sleeves of his plain white shirt.

"It doesn't matter." At last he looked at her, but with his eyes shadowed by the heavy brows, she was certain he could read more in her face than she could in his. "It doesn't matter. Either way, I'd be leaving here."

He smiled with only his mouth, and pushed down on the table as he stood. He hesitated a moment, standing above her, as if he'd left something unsaid.

"So, come the twenty-sixth of July, you'll be needing a new singer at The Fishwife."

Eleanor didn't try to stop him when he walked out. She leaned her elbows on the table, staring at nothing.

"Was that Cahill's voice I heard?" Val came in yawning and tying her bathrobe around her waist. She plopped down in the seat he'd just vacated and eyed the barely touched breakfast with distaste.

"Yes."

"What did he want?"

"He's leaving." That she could respond to Val's questions without thought, without emotion, surprised her.

"Why?" Val's voice had too much tartness and something that sounded almost like concern.

Eleanor looked at her cousin's fierce frown. "It's his visa. It expires in late July and the Immigration and Naturalization Service won't renew it. He has to go back to Ireland, or—"

"His visa? He has visa problems? That's what this is all about?" Disbelief gave way to relief in Val's voice. "I thought it was another woman. I was really worried how you'd take that. But a visa, that's not so bad. Ellie, you can deal with that."

"*I* can deal with that?" repeated Eleanor in amazement.

"That's something you can handle. That won't—"

"Val!" Eleanor stopped her cousin. With the clarity of a lifetime of knowing her, she saw exactly how Val's mind was working.

Val had thought she'd lost her heart to Cahill McCrea, and had worried about her. That explained, too, why Val had kept her dealings with Cahill strictly as a friend. She must have thought she'd seen signs of Eleanor's attraction to him, so she'd stepped back. How could she not love Val for her concern, even such misguided concern?

That other element in Val's voice just now *had* been concern. That look on the steps of The Fishwife Saturday afternoon *had* been protective. When Val talked about a woman's handwriting on the letter from Ireland, she hadn't been thinking of Cahill's mother; she'd been thinking of an entirely different woman in his life. Compared to that, an expiring visa was nothing in Val's mind. An expiring visa wouldn't break Eleanor's heart the way another woman might.

"Well, what are you going to do about this, Ellie?"

"What can I do?"

"If I knew, I'd do it myself," said Val impatiently. "But you can't just let him go like this. Not when you feel the way you do. I can see—"

"Val, I don't know what you think you see," Eleanor interrupted hurriedly, "but you're wrong. I think your romantic imagination has gotten away from you again."

"You mean you don't care that Cahill McCrea's leaving?" came Val's challenge.

"Of course I care. We've had tremendous success at The Fishwife this summer, thanks in large part to him." Val stared at her skeptically, and Eleanor faltered a little as she added. "And...and I hate to see him disappointed this way. He seems to like it here so much and to feel so strongly about becoming an American. And he's—" she faltered again, before finishing lamely "—a nice person."

Her cousin's look grew disgusted. "Yeah, you think he's just a nice person and I'm going to stay at my next job long enough for a twenty-year pin and a retirement watch. Tell me another story, El."

Eleanor smiled her most calm and rational smile. It drew a response that wasn't at all calm and rational.

"Dammit, El, stop trying to look so smug and superior. It doesn't suit you. Are you trying to tell me you're not attracted to Cahill? Are you trying to tell me you don't think he is one hunk of good-looking Irishman?"

"I'm not blind. Of course I think he's attractive," she responded tartly, before schooling her tone. "But that doesn't mean any more than what I said—I think he's attractive."

"Well, at least you admit that."

"I also think certain movie actors are attractive. That doesn't mean I have any special feeling for them as individuals."

"Oh, come on, El. How can you put Cahill in the same category as some distant film images when he's a living, breathing person right here and you're nuts about him."

Unbidden, unwanted and ungovernable, the memory of Cahill's body pressed against hers rose so strongly that fire again surged through her. Nuts about him? She certainly had been for those moments in the cove. But she'd be crazy to let those feelings rule her. Crazy to rely on a dreamer's charm.

"Val, just because you think I feel that way about him doesn't mean I really do."

"Of course you do. Why else would I have been pushing you two together as fast and as hard as I could manage?" Val asked.

"You've been what?"

"Never mind that." She brushed aside Eleanor's open-mouthed amazement with an imperious hand as she grabbed a coffee mug from the cabinet. "I know Cahill and I are very similar. We both like being with people and talking and having a good time—"

Charmers, Eleanor thought.

"—and we see the potential in ideas. We like to spin out the possibilities—"

Dreamers.

"—but where I like to be on the move, Cahill would rather settle down, raise a family, sink his roots into American soil."

Val reached across the table and rested her small hand on top of her cousin's. Eleanor had the oddest impression that this time Val would be the one imparting mature, practical wisdom.

"You know, in his own way, he's very steady and responsible, just like you. You two would be good for each other. A good balance. I'm sorry if you really don't have feelings for him, because I think he has them for you."

Does he? Under the charmer and dreamer is he really the steady and responsible person I'd like to see? Or is that only another illusion—mine and yours? Eleanor's gaze flashed to Val's watchful eyes, then dropped.

Val sighed deeply. "Well, putting all that aside, I still think we should do everything we can to help him stay here. If he leaves, it'll be bad for our business and bad for him. Agreed?"

"Yes," Eleanor got out.

"I've still got some connections in Washington—carryovers from those fourteen months on Capitol Hill. But I'm not sure how much good they'll be able to do. INS tends to be a law unto itself. They've got their own system and their own bureaucracy. That'll be your job," Val said. "You know the ins and outs of that kind of system, you even know how to make it work. You're resourceful."

"I don't know much about the INS, Val." They looked at

each other, and Eleanor saw in her cousin's face the realization of the size of their task. Maybe Val had more common sense than she'd given her credit for. "But I'll see what I can find out."

From the front porch, she watched for him. Nearly an hour passed before she recognized his stride. He continued past the house, on to Boulder Point where he found a seat on a rock looking out to the water.

Crossing the sand didn't take long. But then she hesitated, wondering if he'd consider her an intruder. Their last talk hadn't ended very well. Maybe he wouldn't want to talk to her now. Well, she'd never know by standing four yards behind him procrastinating.

"Hi."

He turned as she clambered onto a nearby boulder and smiled at her; a little tentative, a little tired, but a true smile. "Hello yourself."

"Val and I," she started, gesturing toward the house, "wondered if we could do anything—"

"Thank you to you and Val, but there's not a thing."

She had a clear view of his harsh jaw. At least he seemed to accept her presence, if not her help.

"Val and I thought that maybe with my background…I mean, sometimes when you're not used to a system like the INS, the bureaucracy can be so cumbersome that you don't see all the possibilities. Maybe one person can't see all the possibilities because there are so many rules and regulations. I mean, look at the tax system. You can call up those toll-free numbers for help on your tax form and you end up knowing more than the people who're supposed to be helping you. So maybe if I looked into it I could find something out, because I do know some about how organizations like the INS work—"

He cut her off without turning. "I've made my appeals. There's no more to be done."

The day he went to Boston, she thought. That explained the suit—and the weariness when he returned. He must have already had an indication then. "There may be other people, other ways."

"I've tried the ways, I've talked to the people."

"You could fight it."

He looked at her then for an instant, an instant that chilled her. His perfect stillness reminded her of that first night she'd seen him in O'Herlihy's Saloon, when the old man had said he'd fight him for a song. And she remembered Eamon's odd tension, and her own feeling of watching a drama she didn't understand.

She still didn't understand, but she'd lost her detachment. She cared now.

"I'll not fight," he said. There was no arguing with that tone.

She looked up at the profile he'd turned to her, with the straight line from his high forehead and the bump on his nose and the stubborn jaw. The face of a fighter. No, that wasn't right. Because, despite the scars and strength, she didn't associate him with the boxing ring or fistfights, but with the strength to pursue what he wanted, what he needed. But he wouldn't pursue this. Why?

I'll not fight.

She remembered Cahill's squaring off with Tom Hustine in the kitchen after dispatching Mr. Mullen. He hadn't fought then, either, though she'd sensed his tremendous battle with himself. He'd turned and walked away. Tuesday, when she'd accused him of merely flirting with her, she'd seen a similar battle with himself. Again, he'd walked away. Would he do that now?

Wasn't that what people like him did? When the fantasy didn't materialize, they walked away and tried another. Walking away rather than working, rather than *fighting* for the dream the way she worked and fought. How many times had she seen her mother and Norman do that?

Her teeth caught her bottom lip. But when Connie and Norman Garrett moved on to the next illusion, they went without a backward glance, almost cheerfully. Grim, not cheerful, described Cahill's determination to turn his back on this fight.

"Do you want to go back?"

"No." He seemed to regret the word as soon as he'd said it. He glanced at her. A wave rolled in, tossing its white-topped crest at the shore, then retreating slowly back to the sea. He stood up and held a hand out to her. "But I will."

It's not right! He shouldn't leave. The words rang in her head so loudly, she thought for a moment that he must have heard them. But he just continued guiding her down the treacherous rocks with careful attention.

It wasn't right. He'd wanted to come to America since childhood. He'd said it, Eamon had said it. She remembered his words by the Fisherman's Memorial. Remembered him speaking of his father's desire to come to this country and how he'd caught it. *This country opens wide to hold so many things, so many possibilities.* Surely it could hold Cahill McCrea.

When their feet reached the sand, he dropped her hand.

"Will you go back? Will you really?"

He quirked an eyebrow at her. For once his smile failed to soften his features. "And how would you be wanting me to answer that? Better, by far, if you can tell anyone who might ask that one Cahill McCrea indicated his intention to comply with the notice that his visa would expire." The smile faded and a deeper note sounded in his voice. "Either way I'll be leaving The Fishwife. I'd never involve you and Valerie in anything illegal."

"That's just great. But how about not involving yourself in such a thing?" Her sarcasm didn't move him in any way that she could see. "Cahill, think about what it would mean to be an illegal alien here. If they caught you, it would mean the end of a chance to immigrate. Think about living every day worrying that you might get caught that day. Think about having to watch—"

"What you say, who you know, who you trust." He finished for her. "I know the drawbacks, Eleanor. The papers back in Ireland are full of the stories. Tens of thousands of illegals are here from Ireland alone. I know some of them, I know their lives. No medical insurance, no rights, no peace. That's why

I've filled out so many forms, talked to so many officials, filed so many petitions."

Eleanor found herself remembering how on first meeting him she'd fancied that the strongest gale could make no imprint on his face. She was wrong. He fought some sort of storm inside now, and it showed in the taut line of his jaw, the deep frown of his brow, the compressed thread of his lips. "I've tried their damned system, the officials and their orders and their red tape. I've tried. It doesn't work. The systems never work for the people caught in them."

His bitterness silenced her. A bitterness, instinct told her, that ran too close to the bone to be from this incident alone. Had his frustration over immigration driven so deep into his soul, or was this another hurt speaking?

"Cahill, systems can work."

He stooped to pick up a shell stranded by the retreating tide. With two long strides, he sent the shell spinning out deep into the water. She knew that he had made up his mind.

He turned, and she saw his decision. He wouldn't confide in her. The truth behind his bitterness, the decision to stay or go— he wouldn't tell her. No doubt, he thought of it as burdening her.

"There's no help for it, so there's no sense worrying," he said with a nearly believable imitation of his usual light tone.

He started walking along where the ocean met land. She fell into step with him.

"Have I told you why the Irish never worry?" he asked.

"No, you never have." If he felt the need to talk nonsense, she'd listen to nonsense. For the moment, while she worked on her own decisions.

"The Irish figure there's no sense in worrying because there are really only two basic things to worry about—are you going to succeed in life, or aren't you? If you succeed, there's nothing to worry about," he said with a shrug.

"If you don't," he continued, "there's only two things to worry about—do you have your health or don't you? If you have your health, there's nothing to worry about. If you don't, there's only two things to worry about—will you live or will you die? If you live, there's nothing to worry about. If you don't, there's only two things to worry about—will you go to heaven or will you go—'' he quirked an eyebrow at her and gestured to the sand that oozed around their feet with each step ''—somewhere less desirable? If you go to heaven there's nothing to worry about. And if you don't you'll be so busy greeting all your friends, you won't have time to worry. So what's the sense of starting in the first place?''

She gave him her laugh. But her mind pursued other matters.

Late that morning, she made her first stop at the Sawyer Free Library in Gloucester.

What information she found was confusing and obtuse and wordy. Reading the Immigration and Naturalization Service regulations reminded her of tax-return instructions from the Internal Revenue Service.

Next, she walked down the hill to the office of an immigration lawyer. He provided help, but not much hope. Mostly, she thought an hour later as she emerged into Main Street, he confirmed what she'd read at the library.

Without being the spouse, parent, sibling or child of a U.S. citizen, he'd told her, Aidan Padraic Cahill McCrea's best chance for immigration status came under the provision for ''members of the professions or persons of exceptional ability in the sciences and arts.'' This required another whole level of paperwork from the Labor Department to secure a job certification, plus a job offer from a ''qualified employer.'' With as much tact as possible, the lawyer said The Fishwife didn't meet the standards of a qualified employer because of its insecure financial status. He also pointed out the small percentage of visas granted to people from all over the world in this category.

So Eleanor didn't expect keeping Cahill in the United States to be easy, even when the man at the Boston INS office agreed to see her in two days. But neither did she realize the facts and figures he'd pull from his neat file would be so daunting.

Jeffrey Hanson was pleasant but firm. In his late thirties, he resembled many men she'd encountered at the accounting firm. Like them—and like her—he was a hardheaded businessman, as professional and precise with numbers that represented people as she was with numbers that represented dollars.

"Your restaurant sounds charming," he said with a cordial smile. "I'll have to make a point to get to Gloucester this summer to try your fare."

"I hope you do," she said, the warmth of her smile one degree short of his. "I'm sure you'd enjoy hearing Mr. McCrea perform."

"I'm sure. He enjoys his full share of Irish charm, doesn't he?" He seemed to expect no answer to that, and with his next words, Eleanor knew the pleasantries had ended. He was on to business. "But as much as I may like him as an individual, Mr. McCrea does not qualify at this time for an immigrant visa. As I've told you, the waiting list can stretch into several years."

"While he's waiting, can't his visa be extended so—"

"Mr. McCrea has already had numerous extensions over the years. When we had cause to review his case, that became very apparent. Indeed, looking at his file," said Jeffrey Hanson as he did just that, "it's clear Mr. McCrea has had extensions on his visa every time he's come here."

"Which indicates how eager he is to immigrate to the United States," Eleanor pointed out.

"Many people are, Ms. Thalston. Mr. McCrea has been luckier than most in having so much time here and," he added, "with having such loyal friends. But I'm afraid the only thing he can do now, since he doesn't have a parent, adult child, sibling or wife who's a U.S. citizen, is return to Ireland and hope for a spot to come open."

A wife who's a U.S. citizen. A wife. A U.S. citizen.

She couldn't. She didn't dare. But it would be Cahill's best hope, maybe his only hope. She'd think about it, look at it carefully, maybe talk to him....

His eyes turned stern as he continued. "He can consider himself lucky that we are overlooking his performing at your restaurant. His visa does not include working in this country. That's a deportable offense."

"Deportable!" This new danger temporarily quieted her internal argument. "But we're hardly paying him anything at all. It's mostly tips."

"But you are paying him, plus providing room and board, and that means he's holding a job—a job that could be filled by a citizen of this country."

Someone else fill Cahill's place? No.

"If he weren't leaving anyway, I wouldn't be able to let this slide. In fact, even with just one employee I should issue you an official warning as the employer and put a notation on his permanent file."

A notation that would surely make it more difficult for Cahill to ever achieve citizenship. Unless…

A wife who's a U.S. citizen. A wife. A U.S. citizen.

If she was going to do it, she had to do it now. She couldn't wait to see if Cahill would go along. There wasn't time. If they came back later and made the announcement, Hanson was bound to be suspicious. If she said something now, right this instant, without thinking about it, without imagining Cahill's reaction, without a moment's sane consideration, it just might work. Maybe. She had to try.

She beamed a smile at him, while a voice in a far corner of her mind whispered, *What are you doing? What are you doing?*

"Oh, that's quite all right," she assured Jeffrey Hanson, a part of her rather enjoying the puzzlement that slipped through his polished guard. "We'd planned to wait until after the summer rush if he could get the extension. But we can change our plans."

"I'm not sure I understand."

"The wedding. We'll just have to move up the wedding. Then the visa extensions won't be necessary, because Cahill will have a wife who's a U.S. citizen—me."

Chapter Six

All the planning and plain hard work to open The Fishwife had been a day at the beach compared to this, Eleanor decided. Five days had passed since her bold words to Jeffrey Hanson. In three weeks and three days, the United States government would no longer welcome Aidan Padraic Cahill McCrea on its shores.

And she didn't have the slightest idea how to go about proposing that he marry her so he could stay.

Automatically, she checked supplies behind the bar. Val had stayed at the house to do laundry. In the kitchen, Manuela unpacked replacement dishes. Cahill had gone for one of his long walks. The rest of the staff had scattered to off-hours pursuits. After the weekend frenzy and a busy Monday lunch, she welcomed the restfulness of performing this mundane chore alone in the early-afternoon quiet. A small part of her mind wondered why Tom hadn't mentioned they'd nearly run out of vodka, the rest wrestled with other considerations.

What if Cahill misunderstood? She'd have to make it clear

that her proposal constituted a mutually beneficial, rational arrangement. She would marry him to give him an opportunity for citizenship, and in return he would remain at The Fishwife, and help their business. Then, when he had his citizenship, they would go their separate ways.

The kitchen door swung open and her gaze slammed into Cahill McCrea's smile. Lord, was she crazy thinking she could be married to this man as a business deal?

She mumbled something and ducked her head as if studying the tonic-water dispenser. No, not crazy, just undisciplined. *Get a hold of yourself. Think about what he means to The Fishwife. That's what's important.*

After taking a deep breath, she straightened and met his slightly puzzled, slightly guarded look. The smile had faded. She should talk to him now. Now, when it was quiet, unrushed. They'd sit down at a table, not a booth where he invariably sat much too close to her, and talk this out calmly. One more deep breath, and—

The front door burst open. Breathing hard, a dark-haired girl of about eight, her dark eyes huge in a pale face, ran inside and tugged on Cahill's arm. Words tumbled out of her mouth.

"My sister, please! She's hurt. The rocks. You've got to come. There's blood. Annie's hurt. Please!"

Cahill bent down to the little girl. His gentle hold on her shoulders seemed to quiet her trembling.

"What's your name?"

"Meg."

"Now tell me Meg, slowly, what happened to Annie?"

The girl sucked in a breath. "We were on the rocks. We like to explore, and we're careful. But Annie slipped. She fell all the way down." Eleanor felt a shudder echo through her. The rocks in front of The Fishwife rose nearly as high as a house. At low tide a spit of sand allowed passage from Tide Beach to Rock Beach, but at high tide the water could run shoulder deep. And the tide was coming in. "I called and called, but she didn't answer. I—" A sob wracked her thin shoulders. "I saw her move. There's blood on her shorts. Her new shorts. She's crying. Annie's eleven. She doesn't cry."

"Okay, let's go take care of Annie," Cahill said, his tone calm. Moving quickly to the door, he threw Eleanor a sharp look.

"I'll be right there with the first-aid kit," she said, and mouthed the word "ambulance." He nodded.

Pulling the first-aid kit from the pantry, she ordered, "Manuela, call Emergency and get an ambulance here right away. A little girl fell from the rocks."

She barely paused to see that Manuela understood before she sprinted outside. Although she almost lost her footing on the sand-slickened concrete ramp that sloped to the beach, she didn't slow down.

Water already covered the sand bridge to Rock Beach. Kicking off her shoes, she waded carefully into the calf-high water. The footing could be tricky and she didn't want to risk falling with the first-aid kit.

Around a rock bulwark, she found Cahill and the girls. Annie lay in an area that grew smaller with each wave. Her left forearm protruded at an unnatural angle; Eleanor didn't need any training to guess it was broken. But the six-inch gash just above her right knee alarmed Eleanor more. Annie certainly needed stitches and she'd already lost a good deal of blood.

Eleanor dropped to her knees next to Annie and shared a long look with Cahill.

"The arm, the leg and some ribs, I think," he said.

Eleanor knew they agreed they couldn't wait for the ambulance. The water was coming too fast. If that salt water touched the wound, the pain would certainly throw the child into shock. Not to mention the potential for infection.

"We'd best move her now," he said. He stared at the water with a look that was hard to read.

"As soon as I wrap up that cut." If she lost too much blood, the danger of shock increased.

Cahill bent to the younger girl. "Meg, we need you to go

back to direct the ambulance when it comes. You can do that, can't you, Meg girl?''

Tears spilled down her cheeks but she did as he asked.

Eleanor started to wipe sand from the raw wound, but Annie cried out and tried to kick her away.

"Shh, shh. Annie, girl. I know the pain's fearful, but hold on now, hold on." Eleanor wound the bandage tightly while Cahill wrapped Annie's arm in a rudimentary splint.

"Eleanor! Eleanor!"

She looked up from a final knot in the bandage. On the rocks high above, Manuela leaned over. "There're no ambulances, Eleanor. There was a huge accident out on Route 128 and they're swamped."

Damn! She met Cahill's eyes, and again they seemed to come to an unspoken agreement.

"Get Val's car and back it up to the ramp."

"All right." Manuela disappeared.

"You'll have to carry her, Cahill."

He looked at the ashen-faced child. "C'mon now, Annie, girl. We'll be taking you right out of this little cubbyhole now."

He lifted the girl with infinite care, but still Eleanor heard her whimper of pain.

"That's all right, Annie, girl. You hold on to my neck, and whenever it hurts, you squeeze with all your might."

Eleanor threw the supplies back into the kit and followed him. Meg stood at the edge of the water, clutching Eleanor's canvas pumps. "They haven't come."

"It's all right," Eleanor told her. "We're going to drive Annie to the hospital."

Cahill had stopped a moment at the base of the ramp. She saw the strain in the taut skin of his face, in the tendons standing out on his arms and neck. Not only from the effort of carrying Annie, but from pushing through the deep water and trying with every fiber of his strength to make it as painless as possible for the girl.

Eleanor stayed behind him, a hand resting on the small of

his back. Not so much to aid him—she probably couldn't have stopped it if he started to fall—but to let him know she was there. She didn't think Cahill looked up once from the careful placing of his feet until they reached the top.

"Okay, Annie girl, we're going to put you in the car. Easy as can be," Cahill said soothingly as he lowered her to the blankets spread on the deck. She gave only one short sob of pain, until Cahill started to ease out of the cramped quarters.

"Don't leave me! Don't leave me!" she screamed, clutching the front of his shirt.

Meg burst into tears and begged him not to hurt Annie.

Already in the driver's seat, Eleanor twisted around. Cahill had gone so white she instinctively reached for him.

"Cahill!"

Her voice seemed to pull him back from a long distance filled with pain. He blinked once, then she saw him fo-cus.

"It's all right, Noreen. I'll ride here with Annie. Shh, shh, Annie, girl. I'm not going anywhere."

Eleanor nodded. "Meg, stay with Manuela. She'll call your parents, then she'll bring you to see Annie. Okay, Manuela?" Manuela nodded, and Eleanor put the car in gear.

She heard Cahill's soft crooning to the hurt girl, but otherwise her concentration on driving was complete. At the emergency entrance, hospital personnel met them with a gurney and had Annie on her way in seconds, with Cahill loping alongside. She parked, longing to drop her head to her hands and sleep for a week. Instead she hurried inside.

"Ms. Thalston?" the emergency-room clerk asked. The middle-aged woman was the only other person there.

"Yes?"

"Someone from your restaurant called. They said to tell you the girl's mother should be here anytime."

"Thank you." Thank God. And thank God for Manuela.

"The little girl who just came in, is she—"

"She's in treatment. We won't know her condition for a while." The words came out like a poem learned by rote.

"Do you know where Cahill—the man with her is?"

The clerk's professional demeanor eased a little. "The doctor wanted him to wait in the waiting room. He wanted to stay with the little girl. The doctor lost."

To her amazement, Eleanor found herself sharing a grin with the woman, who pointed to a small couch against the wall. "Why don't you sit down over there?"

"Thanks." She turned, then remembered. "The big accident on Route 128...it doesn't seem very busy here."

The clerk grimaced. "It wasn't much of an accident, after all. All the ambulances got there, and there stood one truck driver with a bump on his head. They're all coming back now."

Eleanor mumbled a thanks before sinking into the couch. Then the automatic doors opened and a dark-haired woman ran in. "My daughter...I had a call. I'm Roberta Cortine. Where's my daughter Annie?"

The clerk said soothing words Eleanor was sure the other woman didn't hear as she led Annie's mother to the examining room.

When the clerk returned alone, she came directly to the couch. "The doctor says Annie's going to be fine." She patted Eleanor's arm before heading down another hall.

"Thank you. Thank you."

She wouldn't cry. She never cried. She kept her head. She stayed calm. That was what she had to offer.

No tears fell. But they pooled so thickly that she didn't see Cahill until he sat next to her. Even then, she felt his presence more than saw him, felt his weight dip the cushion, felt the welcomed warmth of his body. He slid an arm around her shoulders and dropped his head back.

"I had a sister about her age." His words were ragged, as if they came through a long tunnel full of pain's sharp edges. "Patsy."

She turned to him. The thick lashes masked his eyes, sweat darkened his hair and gray tinged his skin.

"What happened, Cahill?"

"She died." The muscles around his eyes contracted. "Three weeks before my father. A long time ago."

"Annie's going to be okay," she reminded him, hoping to lead him away from the past pain. She couldn't watch him bleed.

"Annie's going to be okay," he parroted without inflection. Lord, he looked so tired. She wanted to soothe the tension creasing his forehead and bracketing his mouth.

"Thanks to you," she pursued. "You were so good with her, with both of them. They trusted you. You were so calm. If you hadn't gotten Meg to tell us the situation so quickly, or if you hadn't kept Annie calm..."

He lifted his head, tightening his grip on her shoulder and aiming a grimace of a half smile at her.

"And thanks to you. You're a good woman to have around in an emergency. You marshaled the troops like a general— organized, calm, resourceful." His smile softened. "We make quite a team, Eleanor Thalston."

The first touch of his lips to hers was a sealing of a strain shared. The second was pure man to woman.

Her hand cupped the curve of his strong jaw, her palm absorbed the sensation of the sharp whiskers already shadowing his face. But the lips that slid over hers were soft. And when she touched her tongue to his, heat exploded.

He pulled back, sliding her hand away from him, loosening his arm's circle around her shoulders. Then he pressed a kiss on her mouth as tender and final as goodbye.

Was that what he was thinking about? Leaving, saying goodbye? A clutch of something very near panic struck deep inside her. She couldn't let him leave.

She should tell him her idea. Now. No more delaying.

"Cahill..."

"Shh. There's no harm in a kiss. I won't—"

The automatic doors opened with a sliding sigh, and Manuela and Meg hurried in.

"How is she?" Manuela divided the question between them.

"She's going to be okay," said Eleanor.

Cahill straightened and smiled at Meg. Eleanor wondered if only she saw how much effort that smile took.

"Your mother's here, Meg." Much of the terror eased from the little girl's eyes. "The doctor's caring for Annie, and your mother's with her making sure everything's done just right."

"Where are they? Can I go see them?" The girl pressed against Cahill as she asked her question.

"Not now. We have to wait for the doctor to finish his work. Maybe in a little while."

"Oh." She accepted that after a moment. "Okay. Here are your shoes," she informed Eleanor. Automatically taking them, Eleanor looked at her bare feet in surprise. She'd forgotten. She shook out the sand and slid them on.

Exhaustion creeped in as adrenaline waned, but she couldn't afford to be tired. The busiest part of her workday hadn't even started. "We'd better get back. Dinner's going to start soon."

"I'm staying a while longer," said Cahill, then grinned crookedly at her as he belatedly added, "If it's all right with you. I promised Annie I'd see her again."

Nothing would make him break that promise. Eleanor knew that much about him. "Of course. I'll go with Manuela. Here are the keys."

"You'll trust my driving?" A ghost of a smile showed.

"It's Val's car." She shrugged and was rewarded with a genuine grin.

Cahill arrived for his first set about forty-five minutes later than usual, bringing the news that Annie had been officially declared out of any danger, although she was staying overnight in the hospital for observation.

Roberta Cortine came in as they were cleaning up shortly before midnight, tearfully thanking Cahill, Manuela and Eleanor, then thanking them all over again.

"I don't know how many times I've told the girls to stay off those rocks. If I didn't have to work, I could watch them. Annie keeps saying she's old enough to look out for both of them. They're good girls. When I think of what could have happened…''

They reassured her again, and after she left, they finished closing up.

"Uh…Cahill, could I…talk to you for a minute?" Eleanor stumbled over the words when they were the only two left. It had taken a lot of urging and a bald-faced lie about working on the books to get Val to go without her.

"Sure," he said, with an ease that made her wince at the contrast with her own discomfort. "I was thinking I'd take a walk along Rock Beach. Would you care to join me?"

"That would be nice. Thanks."

Nice? What would be nice is if she had the gumption to get her words out even halfway coherently.

They walked the length of the narrow embankment behind Rock Beach without speaking. The tide, coming in again, sent waves rolling over softball-size stones that gave the beach its name. As the ocean sucked each wave back to its home, it tumbled the rocks against each other, creating the sound of bass-toned hail.

Cahill had told himself he chose this walk because he liked the sound. He did like it. But, standing below the big white house Roberta Cortine had told them was hers, he acknowledged another motive.

That house had caught his eye the first time he'd come here. Too big, too much in need of repair, too idiosyncratic to suit many families, Cahill had taken one look at it and known he'd choose that house to turn into an inn. It was even for sale. It was perfect.

If he weren't being sent back to Ireland in a little over three weeks.

In a way, he'd come to say goodbye, the way he'd said goodbye to Eleanor in that kiss this afternoon. At least the harsh exchange at her cove would not be the final expression of the—he searched for a way to describe what he had, what he wanted, what he hoped for with Eleanor, and failed—the *feelings* he had for her.

Eleanor cleared her throat. She'd done that often on this walk. He turned from the house to face her.

"Cahill, I want to talk to you about...about your immigration status," she plunged in, then stopped abruptly.

He shrugged. "There's no status to be talked of, for I'm no immigrant. Three weeks, and it's back to Ireland with me."

"I talked to that INS agent. Jeffrey Hanson. He was really very nice."

"Oh, was he now?" He would be to her. Jealousy clutched an angry fist in his gut. Jeffrey Hanson was a sensible, gray-flannel sort of man, just the type Eleanor would pick for herself. Pick with her practicality, not her soul. But that wasn't the right sort of man for her, not if he knew anything about her at all. He wouldn't stand by and let her settle for the wrong man. Not if he had anything to say about it.

The anger whooshed out of him. He wouldn't be having anything to say about it. Not in another three weeks and three days. Not with him five time zones away, back in his old world with all its old dreams, and one new hurt.

Gradually, he came back to her voice, and realized she was recounting the options he'd gone over and over in his own mind.

"...and I checked about finding a sponsor, but they said you'd have to go back to Ireland, and we could try to put the paperwork through. But there's so much competition for the spots, and even then it can take so long..."

Didn't he know that? The developer in Rhode Island, despite being set back by a new rash of delays and a tight budget, still wanted him to take the job. But they both knew that with Cahill back in Ireland, the paperwork to be sponsored for a job was stacked against them. And that was if the venture qualified at all.

He watched her straighten her shoulders, and saw the determined cast of her face. Only a thread of a tremor in her voice and an uncharacteristic uncertainty in her words betrayed her matter-of-fact demeanor.

"...we could try that, but it's a half measure, and there are risks, and we don't want to take risks, especially with your future work, because that, of course, is essential. That's really the whole reason. I mean if you weren't singing at The Fishwife, it wouldn't make sense, there wouldn't be a reason. But the numbers show the sense of it. The numbers show just how much difference you've made. I mean—''

He stopped her with a hand on her arm and turned her to face him, calming her spate of words. He couldn't help the hint of a smile in his eyes, but he kept his mouth solemn.

"And just what is it you're meaning, Eleanor Thalston? What is it you're trying to say to me?''

The deep breath she took had some rough edges, but her direct gray eyes met his. "The surest way for you to stay in America, the fastest way to have the opportunity to become naturalized, is to marry an American citizen. You wouldn't have to leave if you were married to me.''

His grip on her shoulders tightened, but she didn't flinch under the bite of his fingers.

"Are you asking me to marry you, Eleanor Thalston?''

He heard the gruff rub of his voice, but her eyes didn't shift from his.

"Yes."

Calm and flat, she dropped the word into his life.

Her voice went on, talking of profits and visas and mutual benefits, but it left him behind. Marry her. Stay in America. Work at The Fishwife. That was what her voice told him. But another conversation went on in his head. Be her husband. Share her house, her bed. Have her as his wife. Children. A baby with wide gray eyes and a solemn chin. See her not just for three weeks more, but...forever?

"...and in two years, you could apply for permanent residency. Then three more years and you can apply for citizenship. You could bring your family over.''

He couldn't stop staring at her. A simple word and she'd offered him two dreams. Just like that.

"I...I, uh, know it's not supposed to be done. But with your time running out...and we could keep working on other ways in the meantime. And of course, you'd be free afterward. Divorces aren't that hard to get...."

"My practical Eleanor," he murmured, not in answer to anything she'd said. Just in bemusement, that someone who prided herself on her level head and foresight, saw only the first step— getting married. But first steps could lead to second steps. Staying in America could lead not just to a job, but to owning his own inn here. A wedding could lead to...a marriage.

"If you're worried I'd be taking a big risk, I wouldn't. I looked into that. If we got caught—but we won't because we won't tell anybody, and we won't put anything on paper. Anyhow, if we *did* get caught somehow, I don't think anything would happen to me. But there is a risk for you. If you were found guilty of fraud, you'd be deported. So, if you think it's worth the risk..."

Risk? Yes, he knew about the risk. Yet the risk he weighed had nothing to do with the INS.

If she was attracted to him without understanding him, could he change that? Could he win her love, all her love?

He faced the waves that finished their journey by tumbling against the rocks. A journey that might have started in Lough Swilly, spilling out of the rocky shores of Donegal and heading west to America. Just as he had.

"I understand you might not consider this a good idea. I mean, if there's someone...if you have someone you're involved—"

"No. I've not been a monk, but now, no. No one."

"Oh. Still, you'll want to know this would be a business situation, Cahill. There wouldn't be any question of...of, uh, other obligations...um, marital obligations."

He heard the tightness in her voice, and even with his back turned, he knew a blush stained her cheeks. Obligations? What of desire, hot and pressing? What of want, deep and sweet? Lord in heaven, she thought she reassured him by telling him it was only business!

He bent to pick up a rock. That was how she viewed it. He had to realize that. That was how her mind worked. Hadn't she made it clear enough she regretted the moments when passion had taken them? If he was realistic, he'd accept that she had no thought of beds and babies. If he was realistic, he'd tell her no and give up the thought of America. Or he'd tell her yes and give up the thought of the kind of marriage with Eleanor Thalston he'd not allowed himself to consider until two minutes ago.

That was what he should do.

But that wasn't what he was going to do.

Uncoiling a gambler's heart, he heaved the rock back into the ocean. If the good Lord had meant him to be cautious and careful, he'd have had him born an Englishman, instead of a County Donegal man about to take his chances on the double dream of country and woman.

"All right then, Eleanor Thalston, I'll marry you."

Chapter Seven

What have I gotten myself into?

Eleanor pressed her fingers against the rough surface of the brick doorway. In exactly three minutes, she was supposed to walk down the aisle of this church.

What have I gotten myself into?

She must have asked herself that question a thousand times in the past three-and-a-half weeks.

From the moment Cahill had said yes to her proposition—proposal, actually—she had somehow lost control of this wedding.

He'd said she had so much to do at The Fishwife and he had more free time, so it made sense for him to arrange the wedding. That seemed reasonable. She told him there shouldn't be much to do. Just arrange for the blood tests, then take the results to the city clerk at the city hall in downtown Gloucester. After they'd filled out the forms to declare their ''intentions'' and a three-day waiting period, they'd have the license and all they'd need would be a judge to perform a brief ceremony.

Then they could start the process of INS applications and interviews. Eleanor as "spouse" would petition for her "alien husband" to be granted permanent status. After an initial interview, Cahill would get two-year conditional permanent residency. Ninety days before their second anniversary, a second interview would determine if the INS lifted the "conditional" status. He could become a citizen after a five-year waiting period, even if he was no longer married to a U.S. citizen.

The night Cahill agreed to Eleanor's idea, they decided no one else would know their marriage was a business arrangement. The INS investigated few such marriages beyond the interviews, but with cause for suspicion, they could investigate. The fewer people who knew, the fewer people who could make a slip, Eleanor said. Cahill agreed.

So Eleanor could discuss her growing uneasiness with no one except Cahill—the cause of her uneasiness.

The urge to call her mother surprised Eleanor. She stifled the impulse, deciding it made more sense to call after the wedding, so her mother wouldn't think she had to come to Gloucester for what would be a very short ceremony.

Not telling Val the truth was excruciating. A dozen times in the first few days Eleanor started to tell her the whole story. She was still working up her nerves to tell Val the lie when Cahill "surprised" her—more accurately, stunned—with a small, simple and perfect diamond ring during the Fourth of July rush in front of nearly the whole staff of The Fishwife. The only three people who didn't squeal with delight were herself, Tom Hustine and Cahill. Even Harry said a couple of words.

Eleanor tried to convey to Cahill the inappropriateness of the gesture that night as he walked her home long after the fireworks had faded and the revelers had gone. Maybe she hadn't been stern enough, maybe she'd been too softened by the way he'd led the festive customers in a round of American folk and patriotic songs.

He merely said he thought it made the marriage more convincing. In fact, that was how he explained away nearly everything that flustered her over the next three weeks.

From spending a few hours filling out forms, having blood tests and standing in front of a magistrate, this wedding had ballooned into a full-blown, well, wedding. Complete with church and reception.

Although, to be fair, Eleanor couldn't entirely blame Cahill for the reception. Val had a hand in that. Still, he didn't have to seem so darned delighted at Val's plans to close The Fishwife for the Monday evening set for the wedding.

Wedding guests. That was another thing. She'd thought along the lines of a witness or two to make the thing legal. Until she found Val addressing invitations one day. She'd let it slide when a steady stream of Cahill's Boston friends started showing up—to check her out, no doubt—including one grayhaired man whose name she never quite caught, who asked some very nosy questions and who, from his appearance, had spent the day fishing. But sending invitations—that was going too far, she told Cahill when she finally cornered him. He said he and Val would take care of everything and she didn't have a thing to worry about.

Hah! Nothing to worry about? How about the dress Val dragged her out to buy? She'd planned to wear her beige silk suit. It was four years old, but still looked nice. Val looked aghast. So there went two whole afternoons, and it would have been more if Manuela hadn't scouted out some dresses first. Eleanor had to admit the one she finally picked was beautiful. It was silk, like the suit, but that was all they had in common. The two-piece dress made her think of a cloud at sunset and was appliquéd with lace and pearls. An inset of delicate lace filled the deeply V'd front neckline, but the back was left bare, and a handkerchief hem decorated the skirt. Eleanor felt regal and romantic at the same time.

Even the dress conspired to make today seem so much more like a wedding. Just the way Val's announcement a week ago that she'd be moving out of the house made it seem so much more like a marriage.

"Moving out! But you can't." Eleanor felt a flourish of panic in her heart. "Why?"

"Why?" echoed her cousin. "So you can have some privacy, you dope. You're not going to get much of a honeymoon as it is. Just one day after the wedding, and that's about it until after the season."

Eleanor gave a fervent internal prayer of thanks for that.

"So the least I can do is give you as much privacy as I can when you two aren't at The Fishwife."

"But where will you go?"

"Actually, I have two house-sitting jobs lined up, so I'll even make money on the deal. You know that fabulous house down at the end of Good Harbor Beach..."

Val detailed the house's charms, but Eleanor didn't listen. She'd realized that if Val had stayed in the house, she and Cahill would have had to share a room, a bed. This way, they could use separate rooms without anyone the wiser.

That seemed to be a day for fervent prayers of thanks.

However, five days before the wedding, she didn't feel particularly thankful when Cahill announced that they would get married in a church. A Catholic church, complete with priest and vows.

"We can't," she said, turning to look him full in the face as they sat on the rocks of Boulder Point. They'd developed the habit of pausing here when he walked her home each night after The Fishwife closed. "I've read they make couples wait at least three months, usually six months, to think about it because of all the divorces these days."

"That's right," he agreed. "Unless you have special permission."

"Special permission?"

"From the cardinal."

"Why would the cardinal give us special permission to get married so fast?"

"He liked you, Eleanor girl."

"He liked me? I've never met a cardinal in my life."

"Near enough. You poured his most trusted adviser lemonade the Saturday before last."

She stared at him with her mouth open. "That gray-haired fisherman?"

"Aye," he confirmed with a glint in his eye. If he laughed at her, if he dared laugh... "It seems Eamon's cousin's wife on his mother's side is nearest thing to a majordomo for the cardinal. You met the wife, too. That's the Kathleen who came out with Eamon two weeks ago. She told the cardinal all about this couple so desperately in love."

She saw no sign of laughter in his face now. "And she asked that he meet us," he continued. "He couldn't, but he sent Terrence, who preferred to see us in an informal way, to see how we got on together, you understand. And after he did, the cardinal gave permission for us to be married Monday afternoon in the church."

"But Cahill..." Swallowing made the words no easier to say. "In a church...and a Catholic church, what about, um, the divorce?"

His tone was light, but the glow of the moon made his eyes seem very intense. "I've told you the Irish never worry. But if there's worrying to be done, I'll do the worrying when the time comes. For now, think of it, isn't it more convincing to be married in a church? Isn't the INS more likely to believe a man's truly married when he's married in his church?"

She had to agree.

But the feeling of uneasiness didn't disappear. It grew. Meeting the priest who would perform the ceremony made her feel like a hypocrite. Father Riley, in late middle age and burly, didn't hide his disapproval of the hurried wedding. He thawed some when Cahill took her hand as they sat in the priest's office, and softened even more when Eleanor agreed that any children of the marriage should be exposed to the father's faith.

Children of the marriage. It didn't seem too terrible a lie to pretend there might be some. Not considering the other lies she'd been telling.

In fact, her overwhelming impulse now, as she stood outside

the church, was to run inside, grab Father Riley and demand
he hear her confession right that instant.

Not that she'd ever gone to confession. And she didn't think
her Puritan ancestors would approve of her starting now.

No. The only alternative left was to go in the other direction—down the flight of eight granite steps and right along the
sidewalk until this whole thing faded out of memory.

"El, are you okay?"

"Oh! Val? You startled me."

"Of course it's me. Don't look like you've never seen me
before in your life. You're a little pale. And you've got all
these indentations in your hand from the brick." Val pried her
cousin's hand from the doorway and rubbed her palm, fussing
at her affectionately. "Looks like your hand has terminal acne.
That's going to look great when Cahill puts the ring on your
finger."

"It's okay, Val. I'm okay." Another lie.

Tears pooled in Val's eyes. "You know I love you, El, and
I'm so happy you've found someone who loves you as much
as you deserve."

Eleanor was pulled into a hug fierce with protectiveness and
pride and loyalty and happiness.

"Oh, God, Val," Eleanor whispered. She'd lied to Val,
who'd never been anything but a true friend to her. For the
first time she considered the impact this marriage—and divorce—might have on people beyond herself and Cahill. Val
would be upset, would hurt for her. So would Manuela and,
on the other side of the aisle, Eamon. What would her family
think? Or Cahill's? His mother, what would she feel when her
elder son divorced? "Please don't cry."

"No, no, I won't cry." Val snuffled as she released Eleanor.
"And don't you, either," she added threateningly, "or we'll
both look a fright when we walk down the aisle. Which we're
about to do right now."

She tugged Eleanor's hand, drawing her inside the church.
Just behind the last pew, Val hesitated.

"There's someone inside I thought you should know about

beforehand, El. It's a surprise, but I thought maybe you should have a little warning." Eleanor read Val's lips on the last word; she couldn't hear it over the swell of organ music.

They'd even gotten an organist. Somehow that seemed the last straw. How could anyone pretend this wasn't a real wedding with organ music playing?

But she soon discovered it was the second-to-the-last straw. Val's voice rose to reach her above the music. "Your mother's here."

Then Val floated off, down the aisle toward where Cahill, looking powerful and proud in his dark suit, and Eamon, grinning from ear to ear, stood waiting.

Eleanor found her feet carrying her down that aisle, past faces—some familiar, some not—that all looked at her with joy. There sat Miss Garner, her fourth-grade teacher. And Roberta Cortine with Annie and Meg, beaming at her. On the other side she saw a young couple Cahill had introduced her to, the Kazinskis—the proof, he'd said, that all his friends weren't Irish. Billie, Jean, Rae, Harry and a woman she didn't recognize shared a pew. Kathleen, the woman from the cardinal's office, sat next to a man she remembered as a bartender from Eamon's bar. And amid a tangle of her other relatives, Manuela had a spot just behind Val's parents. And then she saw her mother in the first pew, clasping Norman's hand for all she was worth, tears running down her face, and smiling.

"And here's to the bride and groom," toasted Eamon, hoisting yet another glass of champagne. "May you always have sunshine. Or, if it must rain, may you always have rainbows when the sun returns. May you always have a coin or two to jingle in your pockets. Or, if you have no coin, may you always have smiles as your treasure. May you always have good friends to share your joys. Or, if troubles plague you, may you always have each other—" he sent a grin to the guests in The Fishwife "—to blame."

"You old romantic," said Val dryly. "You certainly have the gift of gab, haven't you?"

His answer was drowned by calls for the bride and groom to cut the cake—another nail in the this-is-a-real-wedding box Eleanor felt enclosing her.

The ceremony was a blur. But she must have gotten through it all right because no one had laughed or screamed loud enough to disrupt her daze—until Father Riley said "You may kiss the bride," and Cahill did.

Remembering the kiss now, she thought that if Jeffrey Hanson had seen it, he would have waived all the forms and interviews right then. Being kissed by Cahill at the altar of Saint Andrew's Church made her feel even more married than the gold band that circled the fourth finger of her left hand, along with the diamond ring.

The kiss had roused her enough to be coherent when she greeted her mother and Norman. They'd come in from Atlanta as a surprise and told her how ecstatic they'd been when Val called to say Eleanor had found someone terrific. Within five minutes they'd become fast friends with Cahill. They charmed him and he charmed them, which was only appropriate for such charming people, she thought dourly as she twisted the rings on her finger.

"You're not thinking of taking them off already, are you?" Cahill teased, but there was an undercurrent in his voice that she might not have succeeded in interpreting correctly even on a good day. Today, she had no hope.

"I've something for you," he went on before she could begin to formulate an answer. He held out a small package wrapped in tissue paper.

"Oh. I didn't get you a wedding present," she said, feeling badly, which was silly since this wasn't supposed to have been a real wedding in the first place.

"It's not from me—it's from my mother. She sent it over with a neighbor who's visiting a son in New York, and she passed it on to a cousin coming to Boston. Sort of an Irish Pony Express."

Eleanor supposed his stab at humor was an attempt to cheer

her up; it failed. His mother had gone to all that trouble to send
her a gift....

"Open it, then read this letter."

She fumbled with the tissue paper and drew out a small,
worn jewelry box. Carefully opening the top, she saw a pe-
culiarly shaped cross. A circle linked its thickened arms. It
appeared to be made from the deepest black stone, but when
the light glanced off it, it gave off a shimmer of green. Delicate
gold filigree outlined every line and curve.

She looked up at Cahill, but he only tapped the envelope in
her hand. Reading the flowing script, she remembered her
thoughts in front of the church about how this false marriage
would hurt the people who loved her and Cahill. His mother
sent her love to the woman her son loved, and welcomed
Eleanor to the family.

"I can't," she whispered. "I can't take this."

"You can, indeed," Cahill said, already fastening it around
her neck. "She meant it for you."

"But it's a family piece. Cahill, I can't take this from your
family."

"You're part of the family now." He squeezed her elbow
in reminder of listeners around them.

"But—"

"Did she tell you it's called a Celtic cross?" he asked, pro-
nouncing Celtic with a hard *c*. "And it's made of a very old,
very rare kind of marble once found in the west of Ireland."

"But—"

"It's lovely, Cahill," said Connie Garrett, coming close to
examine the dark cross. "And I'm sure it will be very safe
with Eleanor. She always takes very good care of her things."

Distress over accepting a family heirloom under false pre-
tenses took a back seat to familiar annoyance at her mother's
ability to make her sound like a combination of stuffy banker
and conscientious child. Taking good care of things was not a
trait Connie Thalston Garrett had ever mastered. That smacked
too strongly of responsibility, reality and practicality.

"I will cherish it, Cahill," Eleanor said with dignity.

Strong emotion flickered across his eyes, and she found herself holding her breath for his response. But then Eamon's voice rose, demanding the cake be cut "before the two of you go find somewhere else to give those love looks to each other, and let the rest of us toast your good fortune in peace."

The photographer Val had hired snapped several shots while they made the ceremonial first cut. Eleanor thought Cahill might balk when the photographer asked them to feed each other. But he not only didn't protest, he managed to pull the tip of her index finger into his mouth along with the cake, to the hoots and hollers of the guests.

"Now, if you'll kiss the bride…"

Cahill needed no other encouragement. He held her snugly against him, leading her arms around his waist. His lips were firm and slightly sugary from the cake frosting. When his tongue slid into her mouth without hesitation, she tasted the sweetness of the cake, and a darker hunger.

When he lifted his head, she dimly wondered why he had stopped. She certainly hadn't stopped him. Then she became aware again of the crowd around them.

"And the throwing of the garter and bouquet…"

"No!" Eleanor couldn't take any more of this. It had to stop. Now.

"I think we'll be leaving now," said Cahill and, to Eleanor's surprise, not only did the photographer back off but no one made any suggestive comments.

She got hugs all around, and a kiss from her mother, along with some tears. As he led her to the door, Cahill curled an arm around her shoulders in a gesture certainly protective and possibly possessive. She'd have to think about that when she could think.

"One last toast," called out Eamon. They turned back to see his cheerful face truly solemn.

"May the road rise to meet you. May the wind be always at your back. May the sun shine warm upon your face, the rains fall soft upon your fields and, until we meet again, may God hold you in the hollow of His hand."

Eleanor felt tears rise in her throat. She walked back to kiss him on the cheeks. A second impulse made her push her bouquet into Val's arms.

Then she went to where Cahill waited for her, and they stepped out into the night.

If he'd had his way, they'd have walked along the beach.

Maybe then, the face he glimpsed as they drove around to Harmony Beach by way of the main road, would have looked liked Eleanor instead of this tense, formidable woman. Maybe then, the familiarity of their customary walk would have allowed her to look at him with the trust he'd seen growing over the weeks, instead of the wariness reserved for a stranger, and a suspicious stranger at that. Maybe then, his bride would talk to him.

His bride. His wife.

The words electrified him. His body tightened in an instinctive desire to act out the emotion that surged through him. To claim what was his. To claim her.

He suspected she wouldn't understand that instinct. And she certainly wouldn't approve of it. One eyebrow would arch quellingly over those intelligent gray eyes, informing him in no uncertain terms that he had married a lady who belonged to no one but herself.

He'd seen that warning in her eyes as she came down the aisle toward him. Still, she had come to him. She placed her hand in his. She stood next to him in front of God and their friends and pledged herself to him. She accepted his ring on her finger and placed one on his hand. And all the while his heart thundered against his ribs—not with nerves or fear but with the joy and rightness of it all.

He'd followed a gambler's instinct when he accepted her proposal. And he'd followed the same instinct as he made the wedding as real as she'd allow. Not quite ready yet to put a name to his feelings for her, he still wasn't fool enough to ignore a wondrous gift just because it came in an odd package.

The flaw was that the woman he'd married considered their joining a matter of business, not love.

Even if he tried to explain to her that his claim on her had nothing to do with legalities or ceremonies, and everything to do with the way her mouth molded to his, the taste of her skin under his lips, the feel of her hair against his fingers, she would remind him that leaving the Old World for the New meant leaving behind some old ideas.

But not this one, he thought. Because this idea was as old as man himself. The idea that one woman was right for him, and he would fight off anyone and anything that tried to come between them.

No, Eleanor wouldn't understand.

Not that he'd be daft enough to tell her in the first place, he thought with a wry twist of the lips.

He pulled the car up behind the Harmony Beach house and turned off the engine. He'd done the driving today with the tacit understanding that it was for a special occasion and that he would modify his driving habits to American standards. Now he returned the keys as he opened the passenger door for her.

She bent her head as if fascinated by the keys in her palm. But he wondered if it wasn't more an excuse not to look at him as she got out of the car. "I'll get a set of keys made for you, for the house and everything."

"Thanks."

He took his suitcase from the back seat and followed her to the door. He set the suitcase inside the door that opened between the kitchen on the right and dining area on the left. He loosened his tie and undid the collar and top button of his shirt. Her eyes flicked from the suitcase to him, then away.

His bride was definitely skittish.

If only her nerves came from anticipation of how they would be spending the night if this were truly a wedding night, instead of awkwardness.

"Uh…would you like something? I mean something to drink."

Damn right he wanted something. He wanted her. And she knew it. No wonder she was skittish.

"I do have a bit of a thirst," he said. "But lemonade will do just fine for this thirst."

His reference to her first meeting with Eamon drew a tentative smile. He sat at the table and watched her slip off her high-heeled shoes. She'd never worn high heels around him before. He'd been fascinated when he'd realized they raised her cheekbones to the level of his lips. Maybe he would persuade her to wear them again. Not at work, but sometime when he could hold her, explore this new territory. Maybe if he took her dancing...

"Would you like cookies or something to go with your lemonade?" She hesitated after placing a glass in front of him.

"No, thanks, I ate my fill of the cake," he said. Her eyes met his for only a moment, but it was long enough for him to read her memory of his lips lightly sucking on her finger, his tongue teasing the tip. Long enough for his body to tighten further.

Just as well she looked away.

"You made a big hit with my mother and Norman." She said it for something to fill the silence, he thought.

"They're charming people."

"Yes. Charming," she replied, her finger making patterns in the condensation on her glass.

His eyes narrowed at the emphasis on the last word. Was there a clue there to her relationship with her mother? To a loving that included no respect. Was there a clue there to her feelings for him?

"I said we'd have lunch with your mother and Norman before we take them to the airport tomorrow afternoon. I hope that's all right with you." His voice stiffened with the realization that he really didn't know if she'd refuse to go.

Her hand stilled, then resumed making patterns. "That's fine. I guess I should have thought of that," she said with the air of someone reminded of a duty unfulfilled.

He longed to pull her into his lap and stroke her shining

hair, to soothe a lifetime's disappointment in her mother. He longed for some magic potion that would make her see the good in her mother. He'd watched them together today; Connie hesitant and anxious, Eleanor stiff and reserved. So different from the respect, love, understanding and humor that flowed between him and his own mother.

He'd missed his mother today. And Kiernan. He wanted them to be part of the celebration of his marriage. He wanted them to know Eleanor. He wished his father and Patsy could have known her.

She poured her nearly untouched lemonade down the drain and put the empty glass in the dishwasher. "I, uh, I think I'll go up now. I'm awfully tired. It's been a long day."

"That it has."

She picked up her shoes. "Well, good night, Cahill."

"Good night."

She took two steps and stopped. "Oh."

He raised one eyebrow invitingly. "Yes?" he prompted.

He saw her struggling to find a way to say what was flitted across her eyes. "The, uh, bed in the second room to the left of the stairs has clean sheets. I'm sorry, it doesn't have an ocean view."

He smiled without humor. "It's all right, Eleanor. I'm not here on holiday."

Her mouth formed a small "oh," then firmed immediately. His harshness hurt her. Damn, he hadn't meant to. He'd known what he was getting into from the moment she'd proposed this marriage. It wasn't her fault that now that he had a way to stay in America, he wanted more. He wanted everything. He wanted her.

"It's all right, Eleanor," he repeated, meaning the words this time. "I'm going to stay downstairs a bit longer. I'll see you in the morning."

He watched her going up the stairs, back straight, shoulders slightly dipped with fatigue, hair gleaming with a golden halo from the hall light above her.

"Sleep well," he murmured as she turned into the first door on the right of the landing, but he didn't think she heard.

Sleep well? Nearly an hour after he'd said those words to her, the concept of sleep seemed as alien as quantum physics.

She sat tailor-style in the middle of her bed. Alone.

Moonlit shadows thrown by the old iron bedstead formed a pattern on the rumpled surface of the cream-colored comforter. She'd been lying under it, until she gave up pretending she could sleep.

A board creaked in the living room. What was he still doing down there? He couldn't be pacing; that would have made more noise. But if he sat still, say in the corner of the sofa by the window, looking out to the ocean, there wouldn't be these occasional creaks. Maybe he sat in the easy chair by the floor lamp reading a book and shifting position now and again.

He'd better not be reading a book. The thought came, unexpected and vehement. *He better be as miserable and keyed up as I am.*

Eleanor propped an elbow on each knee and dropped her forehead into her palms. *What have I gotten myself into?*

It was her wedding night. And she was married to a man she'd kissed exactly three times. No, five, counting once at the altar and once cutting the cake. Those kisses definitely counted.

Five kisses. Her breath eased past her lips at the memory. Sensation, like a feather of need tickling down her backbone, made her sit up. Beneath her thin cotton nightgown, his mother's cross felt cool against her skin, just above her breasts. Breasts that were growing tighter and heavier.

Another creak sounded below her, then a click like a light switch being turned off, and a second creak of wood, louder and easily identified as the bottom step. He was coming upstairs. To bed. If he came to her now...

She imagined the door swinging open. His broad shoulders filling the doorway. The light behind him outlining his form. His breath coming faster and harsher. Her body heating and softening at the memory of how his length pressed against her

that day at the cove. Anticipating the way his lips tempted her
each time they kissed. Unbuttoning his shirt. One button.
Shadow obscuring his green eyes, so she could only wonder
what he thought. A second button. The triangle of dark curly
hair on his chest. Unhooking his belt and sliding it away. Un-
fastening the clasp at the waistband of his pants, lowering the
zipper and...

Oh, Lord, what have I gotten myself into?

She dropped her head into her hands once more and stayed
that way until she heard the footsteps pass her door, continue
down the hall to the second door on the left, cross the open
threshold, then be cut off from her ears by the faint click of
the door shutting.

What she'd gotten herself into was being a woman alone on
the night of her business-arrangement wedding, fantasizing
about her husband.

Chapter Eight

Eleanor sat on the end of Dog Bar Breakwater and watched Cahill McCrea walk toward her over granite blocks each as big as a compact car. The Eastern Point lighthouse, rotund and freshly painted white, contrasted with his dark-haired, lithe form. She smiled to herself at the notion of comparing Cahill to a lighthouse.

She felt remarkably cheerful today, considering her lack of sleep the night before and the strain of lunch and farewells with her mother today. Actually, that had gone surprisingly well, thanks to Cahill.

If his presence in her house had cost her sleep, he'd unconsciously compensated by smoothing over the final hours of her mother and stepfather's visit. Eleanor couldn't remember the last time she'd spent four consecutive hours with her mother with less tension. Maybe as a child, before she'd realized wishing for stars was not a suitable full-time occupation for adults.

Cahill steered the conversation largely away from topics that would expose her mother and Norman's flaws, and she dug deep for more tolerance of their Pollyanna-ish views. The worst moment came when Connie thanked them profusely for giving them some of their precious honeymoon time, prompting Norman to nudge Cahill in the ribs and say with a wink that the morning after the wedding night was just the time a man did need a break.

With their flight boarding, Norman gave her his usual crushing hug and she even returned it a little. Voluntarily, she leaned forward to kiss her mother's soft cheek. Connie's voice choked with tears as she said goodbye, but Eleanor knew she'd made her mother happy. The satisfaction she got from knowing that surprised her.

All in all, "mellow" might describe her mood. She must be feeling mellow to let Cahill coerce her into that delayed tour of Gloucester and then out on the breakwater.

"People aren't supposed to go on the breakwater," she said. "It's dangerous. People have drowned."

"I promise I won't let you drown, Eleanor."

"I'm not worried about that, but it's not a good example if any kids saw us."

Cahill looked at her steadily. "It's a good example you're wanting to be? One of those role models they're forever yammering about? How about being a kid yourself every now and again?"

"Are you saying I'm stuffy?" She tried to sound indignant, but it was obvious she truly cared about his answer.

"I'm saying I want to sit with you on the breakwater."

Once he'd gotten his wish, however, he discovered that a granite block sits no softer than it looks. He went back to the car for the old bedspread to serve as padding.

She turned away to watch a small fishing boat come into the harbor. Watching the way Cahill moved started a sequence of thoughts she'd resolved to avoid. She'd had plenty of time last night to make, break and remake the resolution as the hours crept by.

"Now, that looks like a true fishing boat." Cahill nodded at its battered appearance. Salt water was winning its duel with the paint. Lines and pulleys sprouted from the mast like a Spartan Maypole, and nets, buckets, coolers and boxes littered the deck. "Not like those little toys we saw up at Rockport. Here, sit on this."

She accepted the invitation. The folds of material helped make the granite more compatible with her anatomy. "Those were very expensive 'little toys' at Rockport, some of them. But this *is* a true fishing boat. Once some of the finest commercial boats came out of this harbor, and Gloucester still has its fishing fleet."

"I like this," he said with a wave of his hand toward the inner harbor and Gloucester beyond.

"Are there places like this in Ireland?" She felt oddly shy asking him about Ireland, now that he'd decided to make this country his home.

"Mmm-hmm," he confirmed absently, while his eyes tracked the boat's progress.

Perhaps he sensed a change in the quality of her silence, because after a moment, he turned to look at her. A breeze picked up a heavy lock of hair from where it had fallen across his forehead, and revealed parallel lines of a frown. But his voice was light.

"There's a good bit about Cape Ann that reminds me of parts of Ireland. The Irish are no strangers to rocky land and the sea, so the early immigrants here must have felt at home." He paused. "Until that first winter, and then they must've had a hell of a surprise."

He shivered convincingly. "I know I had a surprise the first time I visited in winter. Snow piled so deep I could barely see over it—and the tourists complain about the rain in Ireland!"

"Do you miss your country?" For all his desire to be an American citizen, he spoke so lovingly of Ireland. Could he regret his decision already?

"This is my country, too."

"All right, your homeland."

He gave her a long, steady look, as if trying to communicate something beneath the words he was about to say: "A man loves his mother, but still goes on to the love of a wife. The mother gives him life, the wife is his life. That's how this is for me. Ireland gave me life and I'll love her till I die. But this country is my life now.''

He sounded so very sure. That relieved her.

Other feelings roused by his analogy defied easy classification. Which might be just as well, since her common sense told her they were better left in the dark.

"If you and Cahill had a baby fast, I'd still be little enough to play with it,'' Meg announced.

Driving back from making The Fishwife's daily bank deposit, Eleanor had spotted Meg walking along the side of the road. She'd been in the ice-cream shop down the road for a treat from the man visiting her house to talk business with her mother, the girl explained. Eleanor barely had time to hope the man was a prospective house buyer before Meg started detailing the future prospects for the baby she clearly expected Eleanor and Cahill to get busy producing.

"I'm real good at math, and I figured this out all this morning,'' Meg said. "If you wait a while, I'd be old enough to baby-sit. Of course, I guess Annie's nearly old enough to start baby-sitting now. She kind of baby-sits me when Mom's not home, though it's not real baby-sitting because she doesn't get any money. But she couldn't baby-sit for your baby anyhow, because she's still got the crutches for a week and the cast on her arm for lots longer.''

Apparently either Meg's math or her experience didn't extend to realizing the nine-month lead time required for a baby, Eleanor thought with a grin. But the grin quickly faded.

What was she thinking about babies for? There would be no baby.

Even if…something happened between her and Cahill, she would be sure of that. One thing about living on Cape Ann: news traveled fast. Or maybe it was living with Val. Either way, when Eleanor had gone in for her regular checkup two weeks before the wedding, her doctor had already heard about the plans and asked if they hoped for children right away. Her strangled "no" brought a blunt question about what she planned to do about birth control. She considered telling the truth—abstinence—but decided that would just raise more questions. The doctor asked a few more questions, and in the end prescribed birth-control pills.

Eleanor considered throwing out the packages, but that would mean more explanations to the doctor when she went back for a follow-up appointment. And the only way to get out of the follow-up would be to move out of state. In the end, the easiest solution seemed to be to take the pills.

"I'd like it best if you had a baby right away so I could play with it, but Mom says sometimes grown-ups don't like to rush into these things," Meg said, her careful handling of the last phrase indicating it was a quote.

Eleanor pulled into the Cortines' driveway. A thinning hedge obscured the house, but the car in the drive was visible and easily identifiable.

"So, then I figured if you wanted to wait a while," Meg said, her tone clearly saying that wasn't her first choice, "the baby could be the flower girl at my wedding. Unless you have a boy. Then he'd have to be a ring brewer."

"Bearer," Eleanor corrected absently.

"Bearer? I guess he could be that, too. Well, bye!" She scrambled out of the car, cheerfully waving as Eleanor started to back up. She ran up to Eleanor's window to add, "Thank you for the ride."

"You're welcome, Meg. Come and see us soon," she invited with a smile. "I know Cahill would like to see you."

But a frown replaced the smile as she drove away. What was Franklin Britt's car doing in Roberta Cortine's driveway?

Above the sound of the rain that had kept their Sunday-night business well below average for late July, Eleanor heard the kitchen door open and close. She didn't raise her gaze from the receipts neatly piled on the table of the corner booth and she didn't stop her fingers' march across the calculator.

"I thought as much."

Even the amused exasperation in Cahill's voice didn't pull her head up.

"Shh."

"You said you'd be ready to go home an hour ago and more."

"But I haven't finished. Go ahead without me."

"You can take care of it tomorrow." Less amusement and more exasperation came through.

A part of her noted that he'd ignored her comment about going without her. He still waited to walk with her every night. Though now, the wait wasn't usually as long. Even before the wedding, he'd helped more and more with the running of The Fishwife. Since the wedding six days ago, he'd officially taken over stocking the liquor as well as running many of the maddening, mundane errands. He'd proved surprisingly adept at knowing where they needed help, catching on amazingly fast to the needs of running a restaurant.

But the books she did alone. Still, the workload seemed more reasonable with another pair of shoulders to bear it. Both she and Val put in shorter hours. Maybe they'd needed a third person all along. A sort of manager. She pushed aside the thought that they hadn't needed a manager; they'd needed Cahill, with all his easy ways.

Though right now he sounded annoyed. "If you don't take care of those dark shadows growing under your fine gray eyes, you'll be looking like one of those American football players with the black smears on their cheeks."

At that, she did look up, using her left index finger to mark her spot on the receipts. He stood by the table with his arms crossed in front of his broad chest, the image of determination. No way should she feel anything but annoyed that the first personal comment he'd made to her in nearly a week concerned how exhausted she looked. Especially when it was his fault she wasn't sleeping well.

The skip in her heart didn't indicate annoyance, though.

"How kind of you to point that out, Mr. McCrea. That, I take it, was an example of the vaunted Irish gift of gab."

Inexplicably, her sarcasm swept away his frown, and a smile eased in. "That it is. The blarney, as pure as the moment I kissed the stone. And if you don't want to bear the responsibility of wiping out an entire tourism industry by refuting the power of that stone, you'll come away from your work now."

"I hate to cast any doubt on the efficacy of the Blarney stone," she answered, keeping her voice level but unable to stop the quirk at the corner of her mouth, "but I have to finish this."

"It'll keep another day. Those circles won't."

"But these are the weekend's totals, and before I do next week's projections, I have to know this week's results." Her moment of amusement faded as she considered the totals she'd arrived at once. She didn't really expect the number to improve with refiguring, but she had to try.

Losing Monday night's business because of the wedding, and having the bad weather had produced their worst week of the season. At least her phone calls to all their suppliers to double-check any changed orders had paid off. The woman who sold them homegrown vegetables had asked if she really did want to halve their tomato order. That prevented the disaster of having to scratch Val's special lasagna from Thursday's menu. The vegetable woman hadn't been sure if the caller had been a woman speaking gruffly or a man trying to disguise his voice. Eleanor hadn't had much opportunity to consider the sabotage lately, not since the issue of Cahill's visa came up. And then with the wedding... Maybe she could talk to him about it now. Their relationship was clarified, after all. It was a straightforward arrangement. The fire had a screen around it, didn't it?

"Is that what you're frowning so fiercely at?" His arms dropped to his sides and she saw a gentleness come into his face that did nothing to diminish the determination. "Bad?"

"Not good."

"The rain all weekend's kept people away, I suppose."

Eleanor's attention was divided between noticing that he didn't just wave away her concern the way Val too often did and noticing the way his accent made him emphasize the second syllable of "weekend."

"Maybe. But rain or no rain, the bills have to be paid."

He lifted an eyebrow at her. "Do you know you've a way of starting every sentence with 'but'? It's a mite negative, now isn't it?" Before she could answer, he'd moved on to another question. "And didn't we do better than you expected last week?"

"Projected," she corrected him. Expectations, like hearts, could be disappointed. Projections belonged to the realm of reason. "But, yes, we did."

"Then what's the worry? Add the two weeks together." He moved next to her, leaning over her shoulder and casting a shadow consisting more of heat than darkness over her body. "Go on," he instructed, pointing an imperious finger at the scratch pad. He sat on the bench, and she felt the pressure and warmth of his thigh all along hers before she eased away. The pen felt slippery in her hand. "Good. Now divide that by the two weeks and see what you have. And how's that to your projections?"

"But—"

Too quickly for her to prevent it, even if she'd had the presence of mind to do so, his hand covered her mouth.

His gentle touch didn't cut off her air, but still she didn't breathe. The solid warmth of his palm pressed against her lips, his fingers curled along the line of her jaw, seemed more intimate than a kiss.

The contrast to the few touches they'd shared during their six days of marriage was startling...and, Lord help her, exhilarating.

For six days he'd adopted an attitude of easy camaraderie. But if he'd meant this gesture as a friendly tease, he'd missed the mark entirely, Eleanor decided. A tease, maybe, but not friendly. Her only compensation, as she met his look and watched his green eyes darken and narrow, was knowing she was not the only one affected.

"No buts," he said, and she heard a roughness in his voice. He lowered his hand so the fingers curved around her neck and his thumb stroked her mouth. Her long-held breath came out in a quick sigh. She knew he must have felt it across his thumb. He stilled, then his gaze dropped to her lips as he softly traced them with the side of his thumb. "The only thing I want to hear from between these lips is a simple answer. Taking the two weeks together, are we over or under your projections?"

She swallowed, and he looked up to her eyes again.

"A little over." The voice was definitely hers, but it had an unfamiliar huskiness. If the man didn't stop that…that stroking on her lips, she'd…she'd…

Cahill dropped his hand but kept his eyes on her face. She swallowed again and turned back to the pile of papers on the table.

"Well, then," he said.

"Well, what?" He'd stopped stroking her lips. Now if only he'd stop looking at her that way. Even turned away, she felt his stare.

"Aren't you satisfied?"

"Oh, 'satisfied.' Yes I guess so."

He stood abruptly, his voice and movements a brisk contradiction to the languorous touch of a moment ago. "C'mon," he ordered.

"C'mon where?"

"You need a walk to clear that head of yours and see just how good being a little over really is."

"But it's raining."

"There it is—another of your buts! No more, do you hear me, Eleanor Lynn?" Ever since he'd learned her middle name from the forms they'd filled out before getting married, he'd taken to using it to emphasize points. She couldn't help but smile at his affectionate scolding, even as his hand enveloped hers and tugged her to her feet. "I know I won't melt with a bit of rain and it's as certain as a rock that that hard business head of yours isn't made of sugar.''

Her resistance as he drew her toward the front door was only token. "I've got an umbrella in back." Maybe it would help clear her head to get out for a while. Then she could come back and start fresh.

"No need."

"Oh?" She followed him into the small entryway. "Do you have one here?" The pegs and bench were empty.

"No. I've never owned one in my life."

"But I thought it rained all the time in Ireland."

"It does," he agreed as he opened the door. "And if you bothered every minute with umbrellas, you'd never do anything else." With that, he pulled her out into the soft rain and the dark, shutting the door behind them.

"Oooohhh," she protested. She put her hands over her head until he pulled them away, capturing both her wrists in one strong hand. With the other, he tipped her chin back until her eyes met his, and the gentle moisture touched her face.

"We call it liquid sunshine in Ireland," he said. She didn't know if he meant the rain alone, or if he also knew of the liquid rays of heat streaming through her veins at his voice and touch.

"It happens to be dark and we happen to be in Massachusetts at the moment," she protested.

He could imagine a century or two of Puritan ancestors standing in a long, straight line behind Eleanor, nodding approval at her calm, even tone. But they couldn't feel the way her hand meshed with his as he guided her down the slickened ramp. They couldn't smell the summer-scented rain. They couldn't hear her soft sound of accomplishment when they negotiated the final obstacle.

"Take your shoes off." He removed his own as he gave the order.

"What?"

"Take your shoes off, woman. It's part of the therapy."

"I didn't know I was in therapy," she objected.

"And there's few in greater need, to my way of thinking," he said with a grin as he tied the laces of his running shoes together and stuffed his socks in the toes. *Sometimes you're too serious by half, my Noreen.*

"That's another fulsome Irish compliment, I take it," she said. His grin deepened as he watched her bend to untie her shoes. "I'd like to know what bare feet have to do with clearing my head."

"They're directly connected. It's a well-known fact." He'd thought perhaps she'd lean on his shoulder for balance while she took off her shoes, but she did it on her own. The faint glow from The Fishwife's lights turned the sheen of moisture on her hair into a fall of golden crystal.

"Another well-known fact? Like the Irish beat Columbus to America by a century?" she asked as she straightened with shoes and socks in hand. "Oh...that's wet."

He took her shoes and socks, repeated the actions he'd taken with his own, and hung both pairs over his shoulders by their knotted laces. "A well-known fact exactly like that. And another one's that sand that's rained on often is wet."

She made a face at him, but it didn't deter him from grasping her left hand firmly in his right and starting off along the sand. His fingers stroked the double band of rings on her finger.

He knew he'd caught her off guard. It took her several strides to fall into step, and some thirty yards before her hand relaxed in his, but he didn't slacken his pace or his hold.

The small voice of caution in his head told him to be satisfied that he had her out in the fresh air, free of the responsibilities she carried out so conscientiously. And he had the pleasure of having her hand in his. He liked the feel of it, the fine, soft skin covering the long, clever fingers. He'd liked watching them move over the calculator, sure and competent, just like her.

His imagination conjured up the possibility of those fingers moving over him. He recognized the clenching in his gut, but didn't realize he'd tightened his hold on her hand until she turned a questioning look up at him.

He grinned at her until the faint frown gathering between her brows lifted. Then, instead of releasing her hand, he pulled it around his waist and caught it with his left hand. He circled her waist and tugged her closer so they walked hip to hip along the sand.

"Also part of the therapy?" she asked. That was supposed to sound peeved, he thought. But she didn't try to pull back, and the way her body moved in rhythm with his told another story—that she enjoyed the feel of it, and him.

"Indeed."

They walked in silence, bound together by the quiet they created in the midst of the ocean's roar.

Rain still fell, but the clouds broke up under the freshening wind. He leaned close so the breeze feathered his cheeks with the ends of her hair. The moon peaked out from behind a silver-gray gauze. But neither its glow nor its mystery could match his Noreen's eyes.

"About the INS appointment on Tuesday..." Eleanor started.

He smiled ruefully to himself. While he thought of the feel of her hair and the mysteries of her eyes, his practical Noreen considered the next hurdle to jump.

"The interview, yes?" He prompted her after a long pause.

"I...I was wondering what sort of questions they're likely to ask. I'm not always very good at...situations like that where you have to, um, pick out what to say."

"You're saying you're not a good liar?" he asked. "That's a very grave failing indeed, Eleanor. If I'd known that before the wedding, well..." he finished on a rising note of doubt.

She grimaced. "I wouldn't worry about it. I've been getting so much practice the past few weeks I should qualify as a professional pretty soon."

"Does it bother you, the lying?"

His abrupt change to seriousness seemed to surprise her. She stopped, and he faced her. Her eyes opened wide as she met his searching look.

"I can't say it doesn't, Cahill," she said. She must have

seen something in his eyes then, because she touched his cheek in a fleeting gesture of consolation. "I made the choice, Cahill. I would make the same choice now. I couldn't stand to see you sent back when you so wanted to stay here."

She drew him along, their arms around each other again. "Tell me what sort of questions they're likely to ask Tuesday."

"Having never been married before, I'm not sure myself," he told her dryly. "But if it's anything like the other interviews and forms I've filled out, they'll ask you everything you can think of and much you'd never dream of."

"Give me some examples," she pursued.

He tried to remember some of the multipage forms he'd filled out for the United States government over the years. His file must be rivaling *War and Peace* by this time.

"They'll want to know where you were born and when. Your parents' names, birthplaces and dates. Education. Employment history. Immediate family. Health, current and past. If you've ever been arrested—have you?"

"No. You can relax on that one. You haven't married a felon."

"That is a relief."

She squeezed his waist in retribution for that bit of sarcasm, but he only took it as an invitation to hold her tighter.

"What else?"

"They're sure to be asking about our romance, I'd think. About how we met and came to be married. Our plans, thoughts on children. Wouldn't you think?"

She let out a breath before she answered. "Yes. I'd imagine you're right."

"And of course the other things," he added, determined to take that pinched look from her face. "Like which tooth you lost first when you were six years old, and your mother's shoe size."

She laughed.

"What size shoe *does* your mother wear, in case I decide to buy her a pair as a gift?"

"I don't know."

"You don't know very much about your mother, do you, Eleanor? You don't know her well at all."

He felt her arm stiffen across his back and marveled at how quickly they skidded from comfortable companions to awkward near-strangers.

"We've lived very different lives since I left for school. We're very different people. But you needn't worry about having to be some sort of family peacekeeper. We're not at the point of pulling each other's hair out. We just stay away from each other."

He could soothe her ruffled feathers or he could plunge ahead. Or he could try first one, then the other. Besides, he had the feeling that her thoughts about her mother had some connection with her view of him as feckless and unreliable. "It makes me sad, is all. But to tell the truth, it's you who stays away from her, isn't it? To not even invite her to the wedding—"

"I didn't invite *anyone* to the wedding!" she interjected.

"A woman cut off from her only child. It must be hard on her. Why do you stay away, Eleanor?"

"It's a long story."

"We've plenty of beach left to walk before we run out of sand." He'd willingly walk all the beaches to Miami to take those tense lines from around her eyes and mouth. "Tell me, Eleanor." He kept his voice low, lulling.

"All she ever does is dream." For all the weariness in her voice, he heard the pent-up frustration.

"And what's so wrong with dreaming, then?"

The frustration spilled out, overriding the weariness, flooding her reserve. "All these elaborate, grandiose mirages she and Norman create. But they don't do any of the things necessary to get beyond that—the thinking, the planning, the organizing. And then they turn to me with those eager-child looks, and I'm supposed to be all excited, too. If I'm not, then I'm an ogre, like Grandmother Thalston, deflating their excitement. All I can see is all the steps they should be taking to at least try to make the fantasies come true, but they won't take any of those steps.

They never do. And in the end they're always disappointed. Crushed. Like children Santa Claus forgot.''

Puzzlement slid in. He'd thought her problems with her mother had spilled over to whatever her feelings were—or were not—for him. But it couldn't be. Yes, he dreamed. Certainly more than she. And maybe at times he needed her extra dose of practicality to balance him, as she needed him to balance her. But he'd also turned the Inishowen into a well-run, profitable enterprise through long hours, careful management and single-minded determination.

Maybe it was just her caution. Maybe if he went slowly, if he built on the attraction and affection, she'd look for love in this marriage. Yes, he knew now that was what he wanted from her. That was what he felt for her.

He wanted to stop and fold her in his arms right there. His practical Noreen, who took others' disappointment more to heart than they did. She stayed away so she wouldn't have to see their hurt when they faced an empty stocking Christmas morning. She'd forgotten the hopeful joy of simply hanging the stocking.

"Some people never get as far as fantasies at all, you know," he told her gently. "Some people don't have the capacity to hope, to look forward."

"But her hopes never amount to anything." Weariness weighted her voice again.

"Oh, your mother had at least one hope that amounted to a great deal."

She looked up at him, her huge eyes like the moon, with wisps of clouds streaming past its shining surface. Clouds called suspicion, skepticism, confusion, uncertainty.

"You. She dreamed of raising a wonderful daughter. You're her dream that came true, Eleanor. Don't you know that?"

Surprise, then a sort of wondering belief showed in her eyes. At least the start of belief. And finally, a small smile just for him.

"I... I..." She gave up, turning away as tears pooled into her eyes.

Just as well. That smile had nearly undone him.

After weeks of wanting her, nights of lying staring at the ceiling knowing she slept two doors away, hell, a smile was more than enough spark to set off his fire for her.

They reached the end of Harmony Beach and silently turned and headed back. The rain had stopped.

When he knew she'd mastered the tears she hadn't wanted to shed, he rubbed his open palm against her side. "Okay?"

He'd meant his gesture to be comforting. It didn't comfort him at all. He felt her softness under the cotton shirt, knew that just a stretch of his fingers would bring his flesh in contact with the bottom swell of her full breast.

"Fine," she said, but her voice sounded breathier than usual. Her laugh was a little forced, too, as she added, "Perfectly fine. But then, I like being lectured."

"Lectured?" He packed a lot of wounded innocence into the word.

"Lectured," she confirmed, sounding as if she felt on firmer ground. "How would you like it if I started lecturing you?"

"You mean having a heart-to-heart talk with me about some things that could be cleared up, that could maybe make some-one else happy, possibly be the answer to pollution and most certainly erase the national debt?"

"Not exactly," she started to say around a laugh. But he was on a roll.

"I can say with all honesty and humility that I would listen very carefully and take your words most thoroughly to heart. Because I know you'd be doing it for my own good, and you'd have my best interest at heart, not to mention concern for pol-lution and the national debt. So when you stop me in my tracks—"

He halted and tightened his hold on her waist so she had to stop, too. The hell with caution. The hell with business arrange-ments. The hell with everything but the need to hold her in his arms.

"—turn me around to face you," he said, suiting action to words, "and put your hands on my shoulders—"

He slid his hands down her arms to grasp her wrists and lift them to his shoulders. She resisted only slightly, but her hands stayed tense, clenched on his shoulders. He knew she was a heartbeat from calling an end to this. He could hear her firm voice, calling it silliness. But it wasn't. From somewhere inside him, he felt the certainty that it was not silly at all. And it became vitally important that he not let her call it silly.

"—probably wanting to take hold of me and give me a good shake," he added, feeling her arms relax and seeing a smile flit to the corners of her mouth, "I'd know you were doing it for my own good. So I'd listen to every word you said." He lowered his head to hers.

"Cahill..."

He understood the hesitation in her voice, and he responded to it with the answer he wanted to hear. Needed to hear. "Yes."

He leaned toward her, closing the distance to desire.

He'd just touch his mouth to hers. Get the taste of her lips the way his thumb had gotten the feel of them before. Just a touch. Just a taste.

Her taste was intoxicating. He slid his mouth over hers and marveled at the complexities of her. He'd seen her lips thin with determination, tilt with bemusement, droop with tiredness, curve with amusement. But each time he touched them with his own, he felt them molding to his, softening. Felt the line and texture of them as he explored with his tongue.

Noreen... Noreen... He wanted to call the name out, to reach that part of her. Hope allowed him to think of that now. But he cautioned himself not to be too fast, too greedy.

He wouldn't call out. He would take only a taste.

He forced himself to end the kiss. In stages, to make the leaving easier. He kissed the corner of her mouth. Her cheek. Her eyelid. Her brow.

Her lips parted on a small sigh. He felt her breath along his jaw and neck, igniting the skin it touched.

A taste wasn't enough.

He closed his arms around her, pulling her softness against

him. His mouth found hers again. Her lips, still parted, gave entrance to his tongue. Seeking the deeper taste of her, he tightened his arms for the fuller touch of her.

Her arms curled around his neck. He felt her fingers—those quick, competent fingers—tremble just a little as they slid into his hair.

A groan came from the ache deep inside him as he shifted to deepen the kiss, to explore all there was of her. His tongue found hers, drawing it hungrily into his mouth. One arm still circled her back, hand spread wide to claim as much of her as she'd let him. He dropped his free hand lower, curving around her and pressing her against him.

For an instant, she seemed to melt into him and the taste of her was suddenly sweeter and darker. Her body fit against his, her breasts against his chest, her hips tempting his hunger. Then she stiffened.

He could ride out the moment. She wanted him, he could feel it in her. No one could be as desired as she was and not return the feeling.

Abruptly, he dropped his arms, turned away and took two quick strides into the shallow water. It lapped against his calves, soaking his jeans. The cold and wet helped restore his sanity.

What was he thinking? How could he even think that way? No matter how he wanted her, no matter how many weeks, months, years he wanted her, she had to know she could trust him. *He* had to know she could trust him.

He looked over his shoulder at her. The moon showed her eyes open and stunned, her mouth darkened from the pressure of his lips. He swore under his breath.

"Go home. Now. I'll go back and make sure The Fishwife's closed tight."

They'd stopped nearly in front of the house. He could watch that she got inside. From a distance. A safe distance. If any distance was safe.

"But—"

"No more buts tonight, Eleanor." He growled the words.

She was probably thinking of the papers waiting for her at The Fishwife. Thinking of her work and her responsibilities. Thinking of everything except wanting him. He cursed to himself in Gaelic. Well, all right. That was the way of it, then. But he'd be damned if he'd have her walking back beside him and sitting calmly down to do her calculations while he throbbed with wanting her.

"Go home. Go to bed. And lock your damn door."

Chapter Nine

Eleanor knew exactly what she was doing. She was waiting for her husband to come home so she could try to seduce him.

She even knew why she was doing it. The past six days had been frustrating enough. After that kiss on the beach, the concept of living two years with Cahill—but without his touch—ranked as impossible. And practical people knew better than to try the impossible.

What she didn't know was if she'd succeed.

She paced from her neatly turned-down bed to the open door and back. What could be taking him so long? She looked at the bed and wondered for the first time if it was where Great-Aunt Susan and Great-Uncle John conceived all those children.

Lord, what a thought! She paced back to the open door. There wouldn't be any children conceived there tonight, even if she succeeded. A big if.

She'd never tried to seduce someone before. She hadn't dated much until college, then she'd had steady boyfriends. Adam had been the most serious, and they had talked about

marrying the year after they both graduated. But they had
drifted apart, in a gentle and natural parting. She still thought
fondly of Adam—and thanked her lucky stars they hadn't married. Her most serious relationship since then hadn't ended as
amicably, but there had been enough dates mixed in with work
and graduate school that Eleanor figured she wasn't completely
undesirable. Still, her body didn't fit the popular image of perfect: too many curves, too rounded. She'd always been very
aware of that with men.

Until Cahill.

Somehow, he made her feel entirely desirable. She intended
to find out if she really was. She just hoped this floating wisp
of white gauze that Manuela and Val had presented to her before her wedding would do the trick.

Seducing her husband—trying, anyhow—really was a sensible decision. Yes, it would be harder to let him go when the
reason for their marriage no longer existed. Yes, she remembered all her self-directed warnings about playing with fire. But
the question arose of which posed the graver danger—fire or
drowning. Two more days like this, much less two years, and
she'd be ready to walk straight into the ocean.

As he'd nearly done forty-five minutes ago.

In fact, his reaction had finally given her the courage to
consider this step. The desire she'd seen in his eyes that afternoon at the cove had existed tonight in every line of his body
pressed against hers, in every touch of his lips.

The bottom stair creaked under a foot. She'd been so absorbed in her thoughts, she hadn't heard him come in. Quickly,
she moved to the doorway, pressing her hands behind her
against the door frame to keep them from shaking.

A deeper shadow in the darkness, he slowly climbed the
stairs. Dim light from outside bathed her room and spilled onto
the landing. Eleanor sensed the moment he recognized the open
door. He hesitated on the stairs before another, slower step
brought him into the light.

He'd left his shoes off. She concentrated on that, trying to
decide if he'd never bothered to put them back on or if he'd

taken them off to walk up the stairs. Had he left them at the front door? At the bottom of the stairs?

Oh, Lord, why didn't he say something? He stood there and stared at her while her heart thudded so fast the beats seemed to blur together.

"I...I wanted to talk to you, Cahill." She freed one hand for a halting gesture of invitation into her room, then hid it behind her again.

He came as far as the doorway, but no farther, and leaned against the opposite door frame. What if she'd been wrong? What if he didn't want her? Not in any way? Not now, not ever?

Cahill tried to remember how to breathe. From a curved neckline held up by delicate straps, the white gown floated around her body, alternately concealing and revealing. One look, and nearly an hour of walking and self-lecturing vanished. And he couldn't stop looking.

Why was she doing this to him? He'd withstood temptation so far, but this was torment.

"It's late, Eleanor. You should be in be— You should be asleep." He bit off the word, but too late to halt the image of her in bed, under him, that white gown gone.

He could have sworn the breath she let out held relief, maybe even a little amusement. She pushed herself away from the door, standing so close to him without touching. Except where her scent—hers, not a perfume's—sifted into his head, making him dizzy. Except where the gown caught a flutter of breeze from the window and skimmed across the back of his hand clenched at his side.

"Eleanor—"

"It's all right, Cahill."

It wasn't all right. Not as long as his body reacted as if this were a real marriage.

She let out a long, uneven breath and touched her fingertips to his jaw. "I want you, Cahill. I—"

I want you. I want you. The phrase pounded through his

body with the blood that heated his veins. He'd gambled and won—the woman he wanted, the land he wanted.

He gathered her against him with exultant possessiveness. Surprise and the squeezing hold of his arms pushed the air out of her lungs. He barely gave her a chance to gulp it back before he claimed her mouth, his tongue plunging into the warm moistness. Her arms clung to his neck as she answered his demand.

He wanted to show her gentleness, and he would—but not this first time. The joy and the hunger inside him were too powerful to ignore.

"Noreen… Noreen… *A mhuirnín*." Claiming her, he trailed endearments across her skin along with kisses. Her forehead, her nose, her lips, her chin, her cheek, her ear, her throat. All of her.

His big hands looked rough and dark as they pushed aside the fragile white straps and slid the fabric away from her silken white skin. He rubbed his mouth across the line of her collarbone, flicking his tongue into the hollow at its center. Then lower. Across the swell of her full breast, to the tip already pointed and stiff. He covered her with his mouth, circling with his tongue, then gently pulling on her.

A gasp escaped her as she arched toward him. One hand twined in his hair to hold him tighter. The other clasped his shoulder. The gasp held a thread of nervous laughter and pleasure.

What a sound. It burned through him, hardening muscles, melting reason.

He moved to her other breast as he pushed the gown past her waist and the curved swell of her hips to float unheeded to the floor.

"You… Cahill— Oh."

He understood her fingers struggling with the buttons of his shirt more than her words. Impatiently, he pulled it off, tearing loose the final two recalcitrant buttons. He came back to her mouth for a raw, hungry kiss, the stripped off his jeans and briefs.

And he came back to her again. Naked skin to naked skin. Soft smoothness of woman to hard smoothness of man.

He lowered her to the mattress without ever remembering how they'd gotten across the room. The words he heard were his. English. Gaelic. Her name. Endearments. Praise. Longing. Passion.

Her only word was his name. And the small sounds that drove him wilder and wilder.

He skimmed his lips from her shoulder to her breast and down her side until he placed a soft, openmouthed bite on the arch of her foot. Then he served the other foot the same way and came up that side.

She reached for him, and he was there. Her fingers were strong and purposeful, then light and testing, stroking across his shoulders, smoothing down his arms. He slid up her body, glorying in the friction of their skins, to take her mouth again. But she stopped him with one soft palm on his cheek. With only the pads of her fingers, she traced the harsh bones in his face until she reached the odd alignment of his nose.

With a private smile, she pushed back the lock of hair that had fallen across his forehead, then trailed her hands lower. Nails gently combed through the hair of his chest to tickle the hard flesh, and followed its path to the base of the dark triangle, then lower.

He gritted his teeth against the pain of such pleasure.

"Cahill... Now, Cahill." He felt her sigh of frustration against his shoulder when he shifted away from her. He had to. "I want—"

"I know, Noreen. But wait. Shh, my Noreen."

He stroked the softness of her inner thigh, seeking. "Cahill—"

"*A mhuirnín.* Yes. Noreen. Now, my Noreen, now."

He shifted her more firmly beneath him and found her with a sure thrust.

"Cahill." Just his name, on a shallow half breath, but she said it as if he were all there was in her world, and she arched her back, drawing him deeper, fuller into her. He looked into her clear, fathomless eyes and began to move.

He made his claim. She *was* his. As surely as he was hers.

Keeping her touch light enough to not disturb his even breathing, Eleanor skimmed her fingers over the freckled expanse of Cahill's broad shoulders. With his fair skin tanner now, the dots didn't stand out as they had that day at the cove, but she found each of them even in the tentative light of dawn seeping into the room.

Sprawled on his stomach, with one hand tucked under a pillow and the other resting on her far hip, he slept on. Reaching his back required some twisting, since his legs anchored hers. It was worth the contortions. She remembered wanting to do this that day at the cove. Now she could. Just as her fingers had slipped through the dark waves of his hair and outlined the heavy brows and felt the brush of his thick lashes the night before.

Her husband.

This was right. No matter how much greater the pain when he was gone, she'd have this. And she would never regret it. He'd welcomed her to his body with generosity, with warmth and with heat. He'd encouraged her to explore. In turn, he had uncovered her secrets and shown her her own desirability.

"A little lower, please."

His sleepy rumble drew a small, wicked smile.

Her fingers shivered down his spine, trailing the tangled sheet with them as she sat up.

He'd married her as a passage to his American dream, but he did want her. She'd take him on those terms. Want would be enough. She'd make it enough. For the time she had him. She wouldn't look beyond that. She wouldn't consider the bleakness beyond that or ask for promises he couldn't keep.

Her realistic nature would take what was and not long for what wasn't.

Straddling him, she trailed her tongue on the path her fingers had blazed. The Celtic cross, which dangled from her neck and flirted against his skin, was another link between them. His breathing was no longer even or deep. He tried to shift, but she squeezed her knees against his hips to keep him still.

"Noreen…"

"I'm here, Cahill."

"Lord, don't I know you're there, woman!" The rumble was rougher, no longer sleepy.

This was a knowledge he'd given her during the long, heated hours: the compounded joy of giving each other joy. She'd seen him watching her face as she received his caresses, and she'd seen her pleasure reflected in his face, and had felt his pleasure return to her. It was a circle she'd never known before.

"Noreen…you're tormenting me."

"Should I stop?"

A harsh sound came from the pillow. "No."

She bent lower, brushing her breasts against his back. Before she moved away, he twisted beneath her, positioning her hips with large, strong hands, and began his own delightful torment.

He'd move on to another fantasy. All dreamers did. She was lucky; she knew exactly how long this mirage would last—two years. Two years she had him.

Her husband.

"Cahill!"

Her head dropped back as the circle wound tighter and tighter inside her.

"Oh, Lord, I forgot."

She jammed on the brakes a hundred yards away from the Harmony Beach house.

"Forgot what, Eleanor?" Cahill asked from the passenger seat where he sat calmly and handsomely in his dark suit.

"My birth certificate. Val took it out of the safety deposit box yesterday when she made the bank deposit, but I forgot to get it from her."

"So, we'll go to The Fishwife and get it from Val. We've got more than enough time."

His dry tone reminded her he'd been teasing her for leaving

so early for their midafternoon appointment in Boston. She didn't want to be rushed at the last minute, she'd told him. She didn't want anything to have a chance to go wrong, she'd told herself.

She headed the car for The Fishwife. "You're getting a kick out of this, aren't you, Cahill McCrea?"

"If you mean the sight of you putting on and taking off four dresses this morning, yes. Especially the taking off."

He'd made that abundantly clear, succeeding in sidetracking her so thoroughly that the three-hour time cushion she'd built into the day's schedule for contingencies like flat tires, overheated engines, traffic tie-ups beyond even Boston's usual standards, and birth certificates left in the wrong place, had lost an hour. She blushed now at the memory but didn't mind the sensation.

Besides, she knew trying on the other dresses made her more secure in her final selection. The beige silk suit, superseded as her wedding dress, gave her an added air of distinction, reliability and maturity. She needed that bonus of confidence.

"I meant a kick out of the whole thing. Some of us aren't blessed with the gift of gab, you know. Some of us get nervous at interviews like this and stumble over words or say the totally wrong thing."

"*A mhuirnín,*" he addressed her, placing one large, warm hand on her thigh in a gesture intimately comforting. She'd meant to ask him what that word meant, but the moment never seemed right. The other times he'd used it, she couldn't possibly have marshaled her thoughts for a coherent question. Now, she didn't want to distract herself in any way from the coming interview.

"You won't be saying anything wrong. All you'll be needing to do is treat Hanson like one of the suppliers whose delivery's not satisfying you and you'll have the man eating out of your hand. Don't fret yourself. If I worried so before every one of the immigration interviews I've had over the years, I'd be screaming like the banshee by now."

She darted a mischievous look at him as she braked the car to a stop. "I thought that's what you *were* doing last night."

Before she could close the door behind her, he leaned over and swatted her fanny. "And the night before, you vixen. And this morning. In fact—"

"Oh, no. We've got other things to think about now, Cahill." She eluded his hand and closed the door. But through the open window, she heard him mumble something about taking practicality too far. She grinned back at him through the windshield, then hurried up to The Fishwife.

The door closed softly behind her, and she gave her eyes a minute to adjust to the gloom of the front hallway. Before she could move, she heard a voice. Manuela's. Talking on the telephone at the bar from the sound of it. Which was unusual. Unless she wanted privacy, an impossible thing to have in the kitchen at this hour of the morning, with Val preparing for lunch and the early waitress beginning her duties.

Eleanor would just make her presence known, cross to the kitchen and then Manuela would have her privacy.

"...and Franklin Britt knows that," Manuela snapped into the phone. "You can tell him that for me."

The name froze Eleanor. What would Manuela have to tell Franklin Britt? And to sound so angry?

"No. That's not the way it's going to be. No. Don't you threaten me. I'm not afraid of that. I told you what I would do, and that's all. No more. *No más.*"

Phone receiver met cradle with a crack and a stream of agitated Spanish. Eleanor could hear Manuela take several deep breaths. Then the faucet behind the bar ran a moment; probably for a calming drink of water. At last the sound came of the kitchen door opening and closing behind Manuela.

Eleanor consciously relaxed the muscles in her shoulders and neck.

What could Manuela, their trusted employee, have to do with Franklin Britt? *I told you what I would do.* What did that mean?

She knew what it could mean, but she prayed for another interpretation. Not Manuela, was the plea in her heart. *Don't you threaten me.* If someone had a hold on her, if someone forced her...

No, she wouldn't jump to conclusions. She'd wait and see and watch. Watch everybody—Billie, Jean and the other waitresses, Tom Hustine, Harry, Roberta Cortine. And now Manuela. Her circle of trust narrowed to herself, Val and Cahill.

If she had it in her power to make Franklin Britt pay for one thing, it was that.

She breathed in, then out, steadying herself and delaying her entrance so Manuela wouldn't suspect she'd been overheard.

"And I hear Britt's paying his employees below minimum wage at all his restaurants," Billie said as Eleanor pushed open the kitchen door. "How he gets away with it I don't know. Good morning, Eleanor. I didn't think you were in today."

"Such an unpleasant topic for such a lovely morning," Eleanor said with a wide smile.

"What are you doing here, Eleanor?" Did she only imagine the sharpness in Manuela's question and look?

"El!" Val turned from the sink with a dripping colander of fresh raspberries. "I thought for sure you'd be on your way to Boston by now. In fact, I wouldn't have been surprised if you'd camped out in front of the INS office last night just to make sure you were on time."

Eleanor started to retort that she'd found far better things to do the night before, but decided not to open that door to teasing. "I need my birth certificate. I forgot to take it home last night."

"In the drawer." Val indicated the desk drawer that the cousins shared a key to. There they kept important papers they needed more access to than the safety deposit box offered, along with the employees' paychecks. "You all ready for this interview?"

"No," she answered honestly, despite the hours spent gathering the material the INS had asked them to bring to this interview. Not just documents like birth certificates, but pictures of the two of them together, letters addressed to them together at the Harmony Beach address and letters from three friends. After much thought, they'd chosen Val, Eamon and Terrence, the cardinal's trusted adviser.

"You'll do fine," said Billie. "Everything will go great."

"This INS man will see how much a wonderful woman loves Cahill, and he will have no doubt that this is the sort of man to become an American citizen," said Manuela with a fierceness that touched Eleanor, and made her feel guilty for doubting the older woman just moments before.

Surely Manuela would never sabotage them.

She smiled at Manuela. "Thank you. Thank you all."

"You're welcome, you're welcome," said Val with a shooing motion that sprayed water from her hands. "Now get out of here, or you'll only have an hour to sit in the waiting room holding hands with Cahill."

Eleanor made a face at her cousin but followed her orders, waving her goodbyes with the birth certificate in hand.

"Break a leg," Val called after her. Eleanor laughed to herself at Manuela's horrified exclamation and the beginning of Val's laughing explanation of the phrase.

Knowing his feelings weren't entirely reasonable didn't particularly bother Cahill. Maybe they weren't reasonable, but they were real.

And to make them all the worse, Eleanor chatted happily, unaware as she walked by his side through the teeming rush-hour streets of Boston.

"I think it went really well, don't you, Cahill?"

She didn't seem to require an answer because she went right on. "You weren't kidding about the silly questions they asked. What brand of toothpaste we use and what color the digital readout on the alarm is! Can you believe it?"

She chuckled. He didn't find it amusing. Those questions, along with the one about who turned off the alarm clock in the morning, asked of them separately, tested if they really lived together, in addition to having gone through a marriage ceremony.

Still, those questions didn't bother him. Nor did the showing of the pictures from the wedding, nor letting Hanson read the letters her mother had addressed to them together, nor even having their friends write affidavits to their love for each other.

"And Jeffrey seemed very agreeable. I'm sure he'll approve you for the conditional permanent residency as soon as the paperwork goes through. Don't you think?"

What he thought was that Jeffrey Hanson would have been pleased to have sent Cahill McCrea back to Ireland on a raft, preferably leaking, so he could have an open door to Mrs. Cahill McCrea. What he said was a noncommittal grunt that she could take as she chose.

"He really was very nice."

"Of course he was nice. Who wouldn't be nice with you flirting your great gray eyes at him like that?"

His response brought those very eyes around to him as they waited out a red light. "Flirting? Me?" She sounded more astonished than insulted. And there was absolutely no mistaking the pleasure in her next question. "Cahill, are you jealous?"

"Yes." He snapped the answer out as he grasped her arm and started across the street. But truth to tell, he felt mostly amused affection over her almost naive pleasure in such womanly achievements as flirting and rousing a man's jealousy. His anger's seed grew elsewhere.

"Is that why you got so strange when I told Jeffrey I asked you to marry me?"

Ah, now they were getting to it. "It was none of *Jeffrey*'s damned business."

"I thought asking about how we decided to marry made sense, considering his position," she answered with a reasonableness that jacked up the temperature of his anger a notch. "And he only continued on about that because I said one thing and you said another, all at the same time."

"You shouldn't have told him you asked me to marry you."

"Why? It's the truth."

"Because it's proper for the man to do the proposing," he ground out.

The traffic noise abated as they cut across a park to the garage where they'd left her car. He saw the amused quirk of her mouth, though she suppressed it quickly. "That's so old-world."

Maybe so. Maybe he'd never leave the Old World behind entirely. He didn't give a damn right now. "Because the man'll think I don't love you."

"Oh, I don't think that'll be a problem, do you? I think we convinced him. All those questions about the toothpaste and alarm clock and everything—"

"I think it's pretty damn obvious we're living together. That's not what I'm talking about." He stopped her in the middle of the sidewalk, ignoring the grumbles and interested looks from people forced to detour around them. He wanted this very clear between them.

"Then what *are* you talking about?"

"He'll be thinking I didn't propose to you because I don't love you. And that's not the reason at all. But he won't know that. He won't understand that I love you." He looked into the confusion in her eyes. "I do, you know. Love you."

Something trembled a moment in her eyes, then retreated.

"Cahill…Cahill, we agreed…"

Chill crossed his skin. This hadn't been the time to tell her of his love, but he thought she already knew. And felt the same. He thought they'd passed this Sunday night. He'd never given her a chance to say more than that she wanted him, but he'd thought… He'd been wrong. So damn wrong.

"We agreed? To what? A business arrangement? It's gone past that, don't you think?" Pain pressed against his chest. He swung out against it with words. "Or is that how you do business?"

He was saying he was sorry before he'd finished the question. He tightened his hold on her when she recoiled. "Noreen—"

He wanted to say he was sorry for his harsh question, but she looked away from him, to the people streaming past them. "This isn't the place to talk about this, Cahill."

She disengaged herself from his hands and continued down the sidewalk, taking the path they'd agreed on. Just the way she seemed determined to follow the path they'd agreed to before the wedding—straying far enough to make love with him, but not enough to love him.

He'd done it all wrong. He'd thought their lovemaking the past two days meant she understood his feelings for her. And shared them.

She didn't. She didn't understand them. She didn't believe them. She didn't want them.

"Cahill McCrea, as I live and breathe."

Under any circumstances Cahill might have wished that the round figure coming toward him along Gloucester's tree-lined Main Street neither lived nor breathed. Today, with twenty-four hours of silence between him and Eleanor—silence of hearts, not words—he made no pretense.

"Go to hell, Britt."

"Now, McCrea, is that any way to greet someone coming to congratulate you on your wedding?"

Cahill stood silently in the dappled shade. Deliberately, he turned so Britt had to move into the glare of the sun in order to keep eye contact, then watched with pleasure as the other man sweated into his expensive shirt.

"Of course, now that you're a married man, you have more responsibilities. Like that lovely wife of yours. If something should happen to her business..."

Easing the tightening muscles of his shoulders took a conscious effort, but Cahill didn't bother trying to ease the muscles that narrowed his eyes and tautened his jaw.

"Nothing is going to happen to her business, you understand, Britt. Not to her business, not to her, not to any of them at The Fishwife."

"No, of course not, my boy." Britt halted his hand before it touched Cahill's shoulder, apparently thinking better of the gesture at the last moment. "I'm sure you believe that. But if something unfortunate—and totally unforeseen—should happen, just remember that I still want you to sing at The Old Salt.''

Out of the corner of his eye, Cahill saw Eleanor emerge from under the striped awning of a shop across the street and down the block.

''A purely friendly offer, I assure you. I just want you newlyweds to not worry about the future, because you'll always be able to earn a living at my restaurant. Maybe I could even give Eleanor a job.''

Britt said more, but Cahill didn't hear the words as he walked away. He knew she'd seen him and who he'd been talking to. He wondered how long it would take her to ask.

''What did he want?''

She couldn't take the inconsequential talk or the heavy silences anymore. When they returned from town, Cahill suggested this walk along Rock Beach. The retreating water hadn't exposed much of the sand yet, so the beach was nearly deserted. They'd turned and headed back to The Fishwife. This was her opportunity.

''The same.'' Cahill didn't bother asking who she meant. ''More palaver about offering me a job.''

''And you said?''

They walked without touching, without looking at each other.

''I told him to go to hell.'' That was the most cheerful she'd heard him sound since their exchange of harsh words in Boston the day before.

He'd never been more unfathomable to her than this past day. She couldn't tell what he thought, what he felt, though she believed she'd caught an undercurrent of sadness, even in their lovemaking. His wanting her was the only emotion she was sure of. She welcomed his desire because of that certainty, as well as for its own sake.

''That's not wise, Cahill. I know, ideally, we could thumb our noses at him for good, but you have to face facts. He is a prominent businessman and you can't afford to pretend you're some knight in shining armor sure to slay the dragon. That's not—''

"Realistic." His half-angry completion of her sentence stopped her. They faced each other across the sand. "It's not an either-or sort of proposition, you know, Eleanor."

"What isn't?" A little confused, she felt the shift in the conversation without really understanding it.

"Dealing with Britt, facing the world. Life. It's not either the irresponsible illusions of your mother or the never-budging caution of your grandmother. The best of the world's a mix of the two. Creating the mirage, then going after it with all your heart. It can be done, you know." He tilted a wry smile at her, but she detected wistfulness, too. "We stand here, the pair of us, as proof."

"What do you mean?"

"Well, take me, for example. I wanted to come to America and become a citizen, and here I am."

"Yes," she said, not trying to soften the bite. "Abandoning a safe, steady job in Ireland for who-knew-what here."

"Actually, I didn't abandon anything. It's true, I'm not drawing salary from the Inishowen Hotel, but I still own a good part of it, and that investment's safe. Along with others. And it's enough to care for my mother and brother. I could go back if I wanted. It's hard to turn down the owner for a position. But I wanted to come to America, so I set out looking for a job over here. The kind of job I wanted—"

"You...you what? You *own* the hotel!"

"I—"

"I heard you," she snapped. "I just couldn't believe it. Why didn't you tell me this before?"

"I probably wouldn't have told you now, if I'd given it more thought," he said a little grimly. "What's so wrong with finding out I'm not destitute, Eleanor?"

"You threw it all away, you risked it all—"

"I *didn't* throw it all away. I put my share of the Inishowen in safe hands for the care of my family, and I set out searching for what I want in this life. What's so wrong with that?"

"Searching for a dream."

"You say that like you've never had a dream in your life."

"I haven't, at least not the kind to gamble everything I have for."

"Of course you have, Noreen. And there it sits." His gesture took in The Fishwife ahead of them. "You left a safe, steady job. You put your savings into it. You put your heart into it. You gambled, you risked."

It wasn't like that. He made opening the restaurant sound like one of her mother's dreams, and it wasn't like that at all. "I also worked like a slave and plotted where every penny was going! I didn't just leap into this, I planned and prepared for months."

"And you don't think I'd put that same sort of effort into something I believed in? You think I'd just conjure up a pretty illusion and sit back and wait for it to materialize?"

I don't know. I just don't know, dammit. The words echoed with frustration, but only inside her head.

He stared down at her, but she couldn't see his shadowed eyes. She wished she could put her hands up to his cheek and tilt his head until the sun illuminated the pale green of his eyes. Until she could read his soul.

At night, in their bed, there were no restraints in the sharing of their bodies. But here, in the daylight, she didn't feel the freedom to touch him even so innocently.

"I have to get back." She pivoted away from him. "Val will need help."

Striding across the tide-packed sand, she felt his look.

He was a dreamer; she knew that. And the dreamers she knew did just what he'd said: they conjured up pretty illusions and sat back and waited for them to materialize. Could he really be so different?

The question drilled a sharp ache into her head. And in her heart, a small clutch of fear. He had a life, security back in Ireland. He didn't need this life they'd formed on Cape Ann the way she'd thought he did. If he was this different kind of dreamer, he wouldn't need her good sense, her practicality, either. He wouldn't need her.

"Cahill, can I talk to you a minute?"

"Sure," he told Manuela. As she led him to the deserted deck, Cahill smiled a little ruefully, remembering how Eleanor used nearly the same words to start the conversation that ended in her proposal, their wedding and this mess.

At least a mess for him. Eleanor seemed content...as long as he didn't talk of love. When she eluded the topic of their future together a second time, he didn't press. He could almost taste her relief. Their lives sailed along smoothly day by day, and passionately night by night.

As for him, well, he had everything he wanted. Except for his wife loving him and wanting a real, lasting marriage.

"Cahill, you know how much respect and love I have for Eleanor and Valerie."

He nodded, wondering what would follow. "And they feel the same for you, Manuela."

Her brown eyes misted. "But there are some things they don't know. So smart, but in some ways such innocents. Many Americans are that way. I have thought this over and I've decided I should talk to you. I know Ireland is not like where I come from. But you understand about being in this country better than Valerie and Eleanor. What it means to be here. That's why I thought you might help."

Cahill looked for signs of panic in the woman's eyes, the kind of panic he'd seen in the eyes of illegal aliens facing exposure. He saw worry and deep concern but no panic. Tension eased from him. What would having Manuela turn out to be an illegal immigrant have done to Eleanor?

"What is it you're needing help with, Manuela?"

"Franklin Britt."

His dark brows clashed together in a frown. "Britt? Has he been causing trouble here again?"

"No. Not here. At his own restaurants. That's where the trouble is I wanted to tell you about."

With a deep breath, she plunged in. "My nephew works at
The Old Salt. He has told me what is happening there. He has
asked me for help. Begged me. He is so desperate he even tried
to threaten me." She smiled sadly at Cahill. "I was very angry
at him for that, but to be truthful, he wasn't very good at it."

"What is it your nephew's desperate about?"

"Not him alone, Cahill. All of them who work for Britt. He
takes advantage of the immigrants, the people new to this country like you and me. But he finds the people not so strong as
us. He finds the people who have looked and looked and looked
for work and cannot find it. I have been in this country thirteen
years. I have seen a change. Now the law punishes employers
who hire illegals, and many employers won't bother with immigrants. Sometimes not even with people who look foreign.
They don't want to take the risk, they don't want to bother
checking if an applicant is legal, they don't want to do the
paperwork. So they say 'No jobs.' And when the immigrants
have been told 'No jobs' often enough, they go to Franklin
Britt."

Cahill knew the frustration of being told "No job" time after
time, not because he couldn't do the job but because of where
he was from. But he didn't know the desperation. Even if he
had to leave this country, he had a life to go back to, a job,
security in Ireland. He had family and friends, here and in
Ireland. What would it be like to have none of that? An anger
deeper and colder than any he'd known for a long time seeped
into Cahill's blood. "What's he doing, Manuela?"

"He makes promises, lovely promises. But he does not keep
them. He makes them sign contracts that they will work for
him for seven years. He says since he is taking a chance on
them when no one else would, he should have that. He pays
below the wage they're supposed to pay."

"Minimum wage?"

"Yes. Minimum wage. But if they find another job, a better
job, he still has this contract. He says he will sue them. These
people have no money for lawyers. And often Franklin Britt
has loaned them money—to buy cars, to pay rent, to pay doc-

tors. So they owe him money every month, too. They have to stay. They cannot escape.''

Cahill hissed out a word that described his opinion of Franklin Britt. ''My God, he's made them indentured servants!''

''You will help, Cahill?'' Manuela's eyes matched her hopeful voice.

Help? How could he help? What did he know about taking on the powerful to help the weak? The last time he'd tried— He shut off the thought swiftly. After eighteen years he'd grown good at that. The muscles in his thighs bunched, preparing to raise him to his feet so he could walk away. But he didn't move.

''I don't know what I could do, Manuela,'' he said with the impatience of desperation. He stood abruptly but still didn't move away.

''You are a good man. A strong man. These people are frightened. Too frightened to come forward, but you are not frightened of Franklin Britt. I think you will try to help. You understand so much about how the Immigration Service works, but you also know what it's like to be an immigrant. If you would just try…''

''I'll think about it. If I come up with something…but I can't promise,'' he heard himself saying. And that satisfied her. She quickly thanked him and returned inside before he could take back those tentative words.

So he was free to walk away now. Only he couldn't walk away from this fight he'd promised to take on. A vague promise couched in words like ''try'' and ''think'' didn't change the fact that he'd said he'd help. But how?

What would Eleanor do? A smile almost reached his eyes at the thought. She would consider the problem carefully, then develop a levelheaded, sensible plan of action, and follow it through.

The smile died. Palms resting on the deck's railing, he leaned forward. Manuela hadn't asked for his promise not to go to Eleanor, but she'd been too careful in explaining why she hadn't gone to Eleanor. He'd recognized the implicit request, but even without that, the way things were between himself and Eleanor...

Then there was the matter of Franklin Britt. If Eleanor knew what the man was doing, how he was using people, she would surely try to fight him. But there was danger in trying to stop a man like Britt, a man who would stop at little himself. Cahill's right palm came down hard against the wooden railing. No. He wouldn't see Eleanor in such a vulnerable position.

That left just him.

And what did he know about stopping Franklin Britt? What did he know about fighting someone with all the power? What did he know about fighting through a system? What did he know about finding a way to help people that didn't end up getting them hurt worse?

Chapter Ten

"**P**erhaps there's a language barrier here, Eleanor."

"What do you mean?" She didn't turn from dusting the floor lamp by the sofa.

"You know, words that mean something different in American English than they do in Irish English. I thought we'd planned a picnic this afternoon since we're not needed at The Fishwife. This isn't my definition of a picnic."

She smiled despite herself, but she didn't let him see that he'd won the smile. "We'll save the picnic for a nice day. Since it's drizzling, we might as well do the cleaning now. That's more—"

"Practical," he supplied. Her smile faded at the edge in his voice.

"And logical," she added, moving to the mantel without looking to where he sorted magazines and newspapers. Cahill McCrea easily coaxed smiles out of her. But she wouldn't let the coaxing or the smiles take her good sense away from her.

Just as she wouldn't let the fact that he'd charmed her heart away alter her determination to keep her eyes firmly focused on reality.

She loved him. Entirely. With every fiber of her sensible, practical, levelheaded self. Against all reason. She wouldn't even try to deny it. At least not to herself.

He'd said he loved her. But the kind of love she had in mind, the kind that made a full life and commitment of a marriage, required more. All his talk didn't change what he was—a dreamer. She couldn't bear to believe in this marriage and then have it collapse while he went on to another bit of fantasy.

So she would love him, and she would take every wonderful, warm, sensual moment he cared to give her in their two years. But she wouldn't be seduced away from her logical, practical reality.

"It makes more sense this way than picnicking in the rain and having to clean on a nice day," she said, still not turning around as she moved on to the bookshelves.

Behind her, Cahill said nothing, just watched.

She stretched to dust the topmost shelf, and he felt the familiar tightening in the base of his stomach. She twisted to get into the corner, and the swell of her breasts shifted under her T-shirt. She bent over for the can of polish to add a spritz to her cloth. The material of her sweatpants caressed the curves he'd come to know. Heat drummed through him.

"I can't be cleaning if you're dressed like that."

She turned to him with her gray eyes wide and unsuspecting and her bottom lip between her teeth as she concentrated on her task.

"Dressed like what?"

"Like that, Eleanor Thalston McCrea."

Before she looked down, he glimpsed a layer that slid across her eyes at his use of the last name, but he couldn't tell if it was warmth or chill.

"Sweatpants and a T-shirt?" She pulled on the loose fabric of the baggy sweatpants with a bemused little smile. "Not exactly black satin."

He moved to her, not touching her, but close enough to stand over her and watch her shifting expressions. He wouldn't touch her, not unless she wanted his touch. He'd promised himself that.

"There's no need of black satin for you."

Her eyes were wide but not with innocence. He breathed a prayer of thanks. He'd scared her with his talk of love, but the feelings had survived the scare. He saw them, there, in her eyes, heating their color to molten silver. If he could just be patient enough...

Neither seemed to move, yet they came nearer and nearer until her breasts brushed his chest and his thighs rested against hers. Their bodies drew together until they touched and merged.

"I see you covered all up like that from head to toe, and there's no black satin could make me feel the same." Desire roughened his voice.

Go slow, he ordered a body already tight and throbbing with need for her. She moved against him, so subtly he was unsure at first that he wasn't just imagining it. But she was coming to him. She wanted him. He saw it in her eyes. Heard it in the long, shallow breath that parted her lips.

He rested his hands on her hips, letting his thumbs work under the loose bottom of her T-shirt until they met the soft skin at her waist. Her small, sharp intake of breath at his first touch stoked the fire consuming his gut.

"I see you covered all up like that from head to toe, and I've got to be touching what I know lies underneath." He spread his hands to span her rib cage. His palms absorbed the erratic rhythm of her breathing as he bent to drop kisses across her cheeks, her chin, down her throat.

He pushed her T-shirt away, then loosened her bra so he could claim her breasts. Her taste drove him, and in touching her, he drove her. He peeled the shirt and bra over her head and dropped them, then freely explored what he'd revealed with mouth and tongue.

A short gasp pushed through her lips, cut off by instinctive arching to give him better access. He lowered her to the floor as he pushed down the elastic waist of her pants and snatched at his own clothing.

There wasn't time for subtlety. There wasn't time for anything but this urgent need. There wasn't time to climb the stairs to the bedroom. There wasn't even time to remove all their clothes before the fire consumed them.

He heard her cry when she reached completion. He heard in her voice the surprise and the awe he felt as he joined her.

She felt it, too, he knew she did. She couldn't hold off his love forever. If he could just be patient enough…

Later, they laughed a little as they gathered the scattered clothes and went upstairs. After another firestorm of loving, they lay naked in the bed, while the rain licked down the windowpane. Propped up by two pillows under his head, he held her, his chest a cushion for her back, her head resting in the hollow of his shoulder.

He touched her for the sheer joy of having her skin under his hand. Long, light strokes from her shoulders, over her breasts, her ribs, her belly, her thighs, to her bent knee, and back up. Again and again, invisibly branding her.

"When you touch me like that…" Her breath came out in a sigh that melded into a moan as his palms trailed over the tips of her breasts. He watched them peak and harden as his hands continued their journey.

"…I can't think.…"

He didn't want her to think. He wanted her to love the relentless, gentle rhythm of his hands. To love him.

"I feel…I…"

She felt of woman. Rounded and smooth. Full, rich curves of breasts and hips. His hands skimmed her belly and he felt a quickening in his own body at the thought of her carrying his child. Of her woman's body changing shape with his child inside her. Their child.

"How do you feel, Noreen?" He could tell the tension was growing in her. The coiling deep in her gave her body little, unstillable movements.

"I...if I tell you, don't say anything, Cahill. No words, please."

"No words, Noreen." He whispered the promise, bending to touch his tongue to the rim of her ear. He stroked the skin that shimmered under his touch with the nerves of desire.

"I feel...almost beautiful...."

"God! Noreen..." He'd promised no words. No words to tell her how beautiful she was to him. So he let his hands tell her, demand of her, *Don't you know how beautiful you are? Can't you feel how beautiful? Don't you know what you are to me?*

He finally had the answer he wanted as she arched against him in a long, shuddering sigh.

Eleanor crouched in the pantry, hoping Police Officer Mannon had a better view of the freezer from his position behind the meeting-room door than she did. If he couldn't see, they might have to go through this all over again.

Whatever time she spared from that hope she devoted to wishing that Tom Hustine wouldn't walk into the trap because he really wasn't the one responsible for all this, and then hoping he would be caught so it would all be over.

She'd been riding that teeter-totter for three days now, ever since two more pieces of evidence came into her hands. Not evidence sufficient for a court of law, but enough finally to take to the police.

The first started with a casual comment from Hillary that the "friend" who'd given her and Sandy those last-minute concert tickets back in June had been Tom Hustine. He'd offered them more since, always at the last minute and always with the waitressing staff already thin. That, Hillary had told her with great virtue, was why she'd withstood the temptation. Eleanor suspected the young woman also knew that another last-minute cancellation would cost her the job.

The day after that conversation, she'd gotten the phone call that prompted her to contact the police again. The manager of the liquor store had called. Since the incident back in the first week of June, there'd been no trouble with their liquor orders. Cahill said she still had the manager under her "evil eye."

She didn't mind the teasing if that was what prompted the man to call. Because he not only said that someone had called to change the order, cutting it so low The Fishwife would almost certainly run out over the weekend, but that he recognized the voice. Tom Hustine had worked at enough local bars for the liquor-store manager to know his voice. And he'd testify to that if need be.

That had been enough for the police to agree to Eleanor's plan. She let it be known that she'd taken advantage of a sale to stock the freezer with expensive meat. Then she arranged to leave the usually hectic kitchen ostensibly empty for an hour on this Monday afternoon.

Actually, only Val, Manuela and Cahill had to be kept away. She considered taking them into her confidence, but the police encouraged her to tell as few people as possible. "Of course," Officer Mannon had said with a magnanimous air, "if you want to tell your partner or your husband..."

But Val couldn't hide her feelings. And Cahill, yes, she wanted to tell Cahill. She wanted to ask him what he thought. She wanted to confide in him.

That was why she didn't.

She already loved him. She already wanted him. She couldn't rely on his judgment, too. She couldn't share that part of herself with him. She had to save something of herself, some core that would remain when he left. Something she could use to rebuild herself.

So, she urged Val and Manuela to enjoy a rare shopping trip. Cahill had been harder to shake. He said he'd hoped they could spend the day together. Each of her no's had been greeted by another way to fill the afternoon—a picnic, sailing, whale watching, haunting the art galleries, a movie, going in to Boston.

Finally, she'd resorted to sharpness. "Cahill, I need some time alone. I'm not used to having someone around all the time."

He'd gone utterly still for a moment. "I'll get myself out of the house then, and you can stay here."

"No. You stay here. I have a few things to clear up at The Fishwife."

"You shouldn't be there alone."

She let irritation flow through her words. "Cahill, I managed to take care of myself quite well thirty-one years before you showed up. I still can."

He backed off then, which was what she wanted. So why did she still feel so miserably guilty now, sitting in the pantry, waiting for some noise to indicate something was happening out there in the kitchen?

Some noise like that scrape. Eleanor stretched forward to catch the sound more clearly.

She widened the door's opening from a sliver to a crack. By pressing her forehead to the door frame and closing one eye, she could make out a man's figure at the freezer. Hustine. Dismay and triumph lurched through her.

She could tell that he was reaching into the freezer, but she couldn't *see*. She prayed Officer Mannon had a better view.

They'd checked the freezer before taking their places—the thermostat's setting, the security of the plug, the tuneful hum of the motor. Would that be enough?

Hustine's back disappeared farther into the freezer. He had to be reaching for the thermostat, which was lodged in the lower right-hand corner of the big upright freezer.

She ventured to make a larger crack, hoping to see more. And hoping she'd have enough warning to close the door before Hustine turned around.

She needn't have worried. By the time Hustine spun and faced the half-open door that betrayed her presence, all hell had broken loose.

Sounds erupted not from Officer Mannon, but from the dining room. Before she could react, a figure hurtled into her narrow view.

She gasped as she saw Cahill yank Hustine out of the freezer by the collar of his shirt. A strangled sound escaped Hustine's throat as the front of the shirt cut into his windpipe. She pushed open the door to see Hustine twist around. His mouth contorted in shock and hate when he recognized his foe. He cursed as he tried to maneuver out of Cahill's hold and land a punch.

"Where is she, Hustine?" Cahill easily eluded Hustine's wild throw, giving him a shake and wedging him against the door to the meeting room, their combined weight shutting it more effectively than any lock.

"I don't know what you're talking about, you damned foreigner. Get your filthy Mick hands off me."

Cahill ignored the insults and repeated his demand. "Where is she? So help me, if you've hurt her—"

Eleanor didn't hesitate. If this attempt to trap Hustine didn't work, so be it. But she couldn't bear the pain in Cahill's voice as he tried to control his anger.

"Not enough. I couldn't ever hurt her enough for a bitch who treats all you damn foreigners like damn gold."

"It's all right, Cahill! I'm here. I'm all right."

Eleanor couldn't be sure he heard her. Hustine added a crude suggestion of what the two of them could do just then, and with a rough sound in the back of his throat, Cahill slammed Hustine against the door.

"Cahill, please!" At last her voice seemed to penetrate to him. He half turned to her, taking his eyes off the other man.

"Damn foreigner," Hustine raged as he landed a vicious punch on Cahill's ribs, followed by a glancing hit to the jaw.

Eleanor thought she felt the blow to her own body. She rushed toward Cahill as he started to double over. But he uncoiled a punch to Hustine's stomach. The smaller man let out a whoosh of air and sagged against the door.

Cahill pulled back for a second blow, but Officer Mannon, barreling in through the dining-room door, shouted an order and caught his arm. Eleanor realized with dull wonderment that the whole scene had taken only a minute, just the time it took Mannon to realize his door was blocked and race through the front hall and dining room.

"All right, that's enough. Both of you." Mannon pulled

Cahill back and twisted Hustine, still breathless, to face the wall. As he efficiently crossed Hustine's hands behind his back and clipped on handcuffs, he recited rights.

Concerned about Cahill's ribs, Eleanor controlled her urge to throw herself into his arms. But she needed to touch him. She reached out to stroke his sleeve. His imperative palm-out gesture stopped her as abruptly as his punch had stopped Hustine.

He didn't need her. He didn't want her. She'd been right to hold back a part of herself, because he didn't want all of her. Not forever. Maybe not even for now.

"Now," started Officer Mannon, turning from his prisoner to Cahill, "who the hell are you?"

His green eyes rested on her a second before he answered, but the pain she felt was too strong for her to try to interpret the look.

Cahill explained who he was and how concern about Eleanor being alone in the building had brought him to The Fishwife. He'd heard a sound in the kitchen and, well, Mannon saw the rest.

"No, I didn't see the rest. You blocked that door like a half ton of granite."

As it had so many times, practicality came to Eleanor's rescue. She heard herself asking if what Mannon did see and hear would be enough.

"Might," he said noncommittally. "Depends what else we've got."

He had his head in the freezer, checking the thermostat, when Val and Manuela came in the back door. After a motionless moment of gaping, they gushed questions about finding Hustine in handcuffs, Cahill with a bruise starting to show on his jaw, Eleanor looking disheveled and a policeman apparently judging the frozen foods.

"It's well above the setting we left it on," Mannon said with satisfaction. "That'll help. Let's get you down to the station." He steered Hustine toward the door, then turned back.

"You better follow us to the station so we can get this all taken care of Ms. Thalston, er, Mrs. McCrea."

"All right. I'll be right there."

"Not until you answer a few questions, you won't," said Val as the policeman and Hustine disappeared out the back door. "Now, give us the whole story."

Eleanor complied. As she detailed her efforts to pin down who was responsible for the incidents at The Fishwife, she tried not to watch Cahill. He leaned against the sink, staring out the window across the marshes. She wondered what he thought and was glad she didn't know.

"So, when I had the evidence the police needed, I went back to them and we set up this little trap," she finished.

"That's great, Ellie! My cousin the undercover cop, I love it!" Val's exultation and Manuela's words of praise didn't drown out Cahill's silence.

"You better get going, El, before they let that rat free. He'll probably be out on bail before the day's over, anyhow. I hope they can get him to admit Britt's behind this. It'd be great to get rid of him once and for all."

"I wouldn't count on it, Valerie." Uncharacteristic skepticism laced Manuela's voice. "Men like Britt hide in the darkness behind their acts. They don't come out in the daylight."

"I'm afraid you're right," said Eleanor. "Franklin Britt is not the kind to make himself vulnerable like that. I doubt there's any provable link between him and Tom Hustine. We'll just have to be glad we've stopped Hustine for now." She took her purse from the desk drawer and drew out her keys. "I'll be back as soon as I can."

"Don't worry about us, we'll be fine," said Val. "Just take care of that worm."

Eleanor reached the door before Cahill's voice stopped her. "Eleanor."

The light from the window behind him shadowed his face so she couldn't see his expression.

"I am sorry if my interference hurt your efforts in any way. All your hard work."

The formal words matched the voice, which was even and devoid of emotion. She answered in kind.

"It's all right, Cahill. I appreciate your concern for my safety. I'm sure we'll have enough to charge Hustine." She went to her car. Only one tear escaped as she slid behind the wheel.

"Lord. What are we going to do for a bartender?"

"I wondered when you'd think about that," said Val with placid satisfaction.

Filing charges against Hustine for malicious mischief kept Eleanor so long she hadn't had time to think of anything except getting through the dinner rush. She hadn't minded, because it also meant no time to dwell on Cahill's withdrawal. Now, with the cleaning up nearly done, there was time to remember. She searched instead for practicalities to consider, and that was when she thought of the unexpected opening on The Fishwife's staff.

"We'll manage," continued Val. "We can put an ad in the paper—"

"We don't have time. The party for Roberta's cousin is to-morrow night." Roberta Cortine had directed her aunt and un-cle to The Fishwife when they started planning a homecoming for their daughter, who was returning after two years in Italy and bringing with her a new husband. "You know how im-portant this is."

Important enough for them to decide to close the dining room early. They'd planned on Hustine tending bar for the party. Eleanor would have finished in the dining room, then helped to see that the party went smoothly.

Parties like this, if they came regularly enough, could mean financial security for The Fishwife. Making a success of this one could lead to others.

"I can tend bar for the party, but then who's going to finish up in the dining room?"

"I know someone."

For a moment Eleanor didn't recognize the male voice. Then

she realized it came from Harry. He said so little, she barely knew his voice.

She saw a reflection of her surprise on Val's face. Surprise that not only had Harry voluntarily spoken words, but that he knew someone. Val encouraged him.

"You do, Harry? Who?"

"My wife."

"Your wife!" Astonishment colored Eleanor's voice. Val only managed to mouth the words.

"She's very good," Harry said with a mixture of defensiveness and pride. "She'll need a sitter for the kids, but I know she'll do it. She knows how much I like The Fishwife because I talk about it all the time. She's often said she wished she could help out somehow. She was bartender at a hotel in Boston. That's how we met."

The shocks came too fast to be fully assimilated. Harry not only had a wife but children. A family man. And more surprising, he talked all the time about how much he liked his job.

"That...that sounds great, Harry." Val got the words out, and Eleanor nodded. "Maybe you could have her stop by in the morning and we could talk about it. Get her acquainted with the layout here, things like that."

"Sure."

"And Harry—"

At Eleanor's words, he turned back from hanging up his apron.

"—thank you. We appreciate your helping us out of this jam, you and your wife."

Harry seemed to have used up his stock of words, because he responded with his customary good-night wave, though tonight he added a rather shy smile.

The outside door closed behind him, and Eleanor and Val stared at each other.

"Harry has a wife," Val told her in an awed whisper.

"And children," came her reply.

"And loves his job here." Val giggled.

"And talks…" Laughter shook Eleanor's voice along with her shoulders. Laughter that owed as much to tension as it did to amusement. "All the time," she added as the cousins collapsed together.

Cahill finished the last set and sought out the solitude he needed in his old room above The Fishwife.

She hadn't confided in him. She hadn't trusted him to help her. She hadn't come any nearer to loving him.

And maybe she had cause not to love him. Look at the way his anger had nearly ruined her plan to catch Hustine. He'd sworn he'd never again lose his hold on his anger, never again let someone he cared for be hurt by it the way Patsy had been. He'd nearly let history repeat itself, nearly let his anger rule him so completely that he hurt the person he most wanted to help.

For eighteen years he'd walked away from anger. But he couldn't walk away from Eleanor, from the urge—no, the need—to protect her. And he couldn't walk away from his promise to Manuela.

If he could find a way to fight without letting the anger and frustration take over. If he could prove to Eleanor, and to himself, that he could do that, maybe…

He stared a long time at the shadows on the white wall opposite him. He saw nothing he looked at. But inside his mind, images formed a vivid kaleidoscope, with sound and smell as well as sight. Eleanor talking about her mother. An eighteen-year-old memory of Patsy's frightened cries. His mother's lavender scent as she took his face between her hands and said, "You have to find the way to forgive yourself for something you never caused, Cahill. You won't find your new world until you do. Find a new way, then you'll find your new world." Noreen reaching to him in the faint glow of night. Franklin Britt. Officer Mannon's pleasure at noting the evidence this afternoon. Manuela's story. Hustine's hate. Eleanor's patient building of a case, working with the authorities.

An idea formed. A hope. Maybe a dream. Maybe a practical
key to a dream. Maybe a way to pay some portion of his debt
to Patsy.

The immigrants Franklin Britt was exploiting were too
frightened to come forward to testify, to put themselves on the
line and gamble that Britt would be stopped. But if he could
get inside Britt's operation somehow…

She knew Cahill wouldn't leave her to walk home alone.
But his instruments were stowed away and he wasn't in the
dining room. Or the meeting room. She looked outside to see
if he'd gone to stare at the ocean as he so often did, but he
wasn't there, either.

She found him upstairs, sitting on the edge of the narrow
bed he'd used when he lived in this room. A small dresser had
one drawer pulled out, and a box at his feet held what appeared
to be an old sweatshirt and a pair of thick socks. His hands
strangled a bulky sweater. He stared at the blank wall opposite
him.

"Cahill?"

He glanced up and seemed to focus with effort.

A smile, rueful and sad, pulled at his mouth.

She knew he, too, felt pain. She saw the lingering ache of a
nightmare in his eyes. And she longed to protect him from it,
no matter how much more it hurt when he moved on.

"How are your ribs doing now?" Val had already checked
them by the time Eleanor had returned from the police station,
and had found only bruising.

"A little sore. Not bad a'tall." He looked down at the
sweater in his hands. "I thought I'd pack up the winter things
I'd left here after the wedding. I didn't get very far."

"Leave it for now, Cahill. You won't need winter things for
a while yet."

He met her eyes. Lord, if only she could keep away the soul-
chilling cold she saw wrapped around him.

She held her hand out to him.

"Let's go home, Cahill."

* * *

"What are these?"

Cahill had gone to shower first, giving Eleanor a few extra minutes to loll in bed.

Over the weeks of their marriage, she'd come to cherish the indulgence. Especially on mornings like this, when she mentally reviewed the coming day and saw hectic activity filling every hour. With a new bartender to break in—thank heaven they had one to break in at all!—and the party to prepare for, there was plenty to worry about without Cahill McCrea standing at the foot of their bed asking questions that sounded like demands, and holding the package containing her birth control pills.

Their lovemaking the night before had carried a residue of his anger.

Not anger overtly expressed, and not, she realized, anger at her. But last night, for the first time, she'd felt how much power Cahill McCrea truly had. His anger from the confrontation with Hustine seemed to crack his control. He hadn't totally repaired the cracks when he joined their bodies. But the fierceness hadn't frightened her. The power and the passion of his loving became another memory to hold in her heart.

What frightened her now was the expression in his green eyes.

She swung her legs over the side of the bed, and sat up with the sheet covering her to face him with more dignity.

"What are these, Noreen?" he asked again.

"They are what the package says they are," she said, not faltering under his look. She knew his emotions were raw and she would save him from himself, if she could. But not at any cost. Some parts of her she had to protect. "They're birth-control pills."

"You've been taking them all along."

She answered the accusation as if it had been a question. "Yes."

"I want children, Eleanor."

She felt her insides clench at the thought of bearing his child.

Then the memories came of what it meant to be the child of a dreamer.

"You can't expect a child to live on illusions. It wouldn't be fair to a child to be brought into the world that way. A child needs reality, not just dreams. After two years, when you leave, the child you fathered—"

He made a sound she didn't recognize as a word in any language. The struggle she saw ravaging his face echoed the pain inside her. But she had to think of these things. Look ahead. Stay levelheaded.

"You think I only dream. Like your mother. You think I don't see beyond what I want at the moment. You think I'd do that to you. Worse, you think I'd be that irresponsible—to purposely father a child with a woman if I didn't love her. You think I'd—" Words choked in his throat.

She couldn't reach out to him. She believed him when he said he loved her; at least she believed that *he* believed. But a belief in fairy tales wasn't enough for a child. It wasn't enough for her.

He turned and started from the room.

He was doing it already—leaving, walking out. Pain ripped through her. And with it a spark of anger. He fought his anger so hard that she feared for him. But she didn't fight her anger, and she didn't fear it. That was a form of practicality, too.

"Don't walk away from me, Cahill McCrea," she shouted at him, already halfway down the stairs. "Stay here and fight, damn it!"

The front door slammed.

With a sound she refused to allow to become a sob, she sank back, holding on to the cool iron of the bedstead. She'd said what she meant to say—practical, levelheaded, reasonable things—but now other words screamed in her head.

Don't walk away from me, Cahill. Don't leave me wanting so desperately to turn this dream into reality.

The reception for Roberta Cortine's cousin had reached that successful plateau when the organizers could relax and enjoy their creation.

Harry's voluble wife tended bar with confidence. Billie and Jean had the waitressing duties well in hand, and the laughter and talk could have drowned out a nor'easter if one had had the bad taste to try to disrupt the celebration.

"We can coast now." Val slouched in the desk chair with her back to the kitchen. She and Eleanor were alone. Roberta's exuberant uncle, the host for the evening, had insisted everyone join the party for a while. Even Harry had been swooped into the festivities.

"We can clean now," said Eleanor.

"We can clean later," corrected Val. She grabbed Eleanor's arm as she passed and maneuvered her to lean against the desk. "We'll sit here for a minute or two, and then we'll go join the party and socialize charmingly for a while so all these nice people will want to bring all their celebrations to The Fishwife. And then we'll clean."

Eleanor let the desk support her and her shoulders slump. With the busyness past, her misery had no antidote.

"You know, with all the excitement over Hustine and stuff, it seems like we haven't talked in ages. Not really talked," said Val, apparently fascinated by the tips of her toes, which she'd stretched out in front of her. "I see you all the time, but we never get a chance to talk. I haven't even told you about what Roberta told me the other day. That rat Britt was trying to talk her into suing you and Cahill for taking care of Annie when she fell, can you imagine? She kicked him out, of course."

Oh, yes, she could imagine. She'd heard of lawsuits like that. And she could believe that Britt would suggest one to Roberta. That was probably when she saw his car in the Cortines' driveway. It didn't really surprise her that he was still trying to cause her trouble, it just made her feel even more weary.

"But that's not the stuff I want to talk about," continued Val. "I want to hear about important things. Like when you and Cahill are going to start a family."

Eleanor bit her lip to stifle a sound of pain. She must have succeeded because Val went on, pausing only for a wide yawn, then a chuckle.

"Meg and Annie were here the other day and we figured that all out. I've got to admit, they seem to have all the bases covered on exactly how your baby will fit into their lives depending on when you guys have the first one. If I can get my bid in, I'd start right now. I miss being an aunt to a baby. All of Anthony's kids are practically grown. Joe's youngest is seven and even Karen's two are eight and four. Can you believe that—my godson's eight already? So I told Annie and Meg that I cast my vote for a baby now and a couple more later."

She looked up as she chuckled again. "That's another thing— El? El, what is it?" Val jumped out of her chair, her arms encircling her cousin.

"Nothing. It's nothing." But she couldn't stop the tears.

"Oh, honey. El, I'm sorry. Did I say something wrong? Is there something wrong between you and Cahill?"

"Ev-everything's wrong." The sobs that cracked her words scared her. They should have scared Val, too. Eleanor never cried. She was the strong one, the reasonable one, the practical one. It should scare Val to death that Eleanor was the one breaking down, but Val didn't act scared to death.

A gust of laughter came from the party in the meeting room. Val glanced in that direction, then shepherded her cousin toward the other door.

"C'mon. Let's go in the dining room. It's quiet in there. No one will bother us."

Val took her time settling her cousin at the back booth, pouring them each a glass of water and giving Eleanor a few added minutes to regain the poise she so valued.

"Now tell me what's the matter, El. Are you and Cahill having trouble adjusting to marriage? That's supposed to be normal, you know. They say the first year—"

The door swung a fraction, and Val stiffened. But the door opened no farther. Must be an air draft, she thought.

"Cahill and I aren't really married."

"What? What are you talking about? I was there, I saw the

whole thing, remember?'' Val tried a laugh, but it died quickly. "What do you mean, El?"

"It was a business arrangement. Getting married. The wedding. The whole thing. It was just to keep Cahill in America."

Calm settled into Eleanor. Returning to the familiar ground of business could bring such calm. So could despair.

"But—"

"All very sensible, really. See, by marrying me, Cahill would get his permanent-resident status. After two years, he'd be on his way to becoming a citizen. In return, The Fishwife would keep its star attraction. In two years, the business should be well established. The perfect business arrangement, where both parties benefited."

Val's small fist thudded against the table, jolting Eleanor. "I *knew* it, I just knew it!" Astounded, Eleanor stared at the vindication in her cousin's face. "I thought that's what you were up to. The wedding and everything, it all happened too soon after his visa problems came up. I know you, El, and I was sure it would take longer than that to get through your stubborn head that you two were in love with each other."

"I wasn't," she protested automatically, but her cousin's expression demanded a one-word, whispered confession. "Then." She sat up straighter and strengthened her voice. "But it's not that way for him. He married me because I offered him a way to stay in this country, no strings attached."

"Oh, El." The two syllables were filled with sympathy and scolding. "Did you really think Cahill would marry you just to stay here? Did you really think you married him just for that? You're not giving either one of you much credit."

"What do you mean? You're the one who said how much he wanted to stay." Her protest withered under Val's onslaught.

"Eleanor! Open your eyes. Look at the way he treats you. Look at how he helps around here to take some of the work off you. Look at how he lit into Hustine just because he thought he might have touched a hair on your head."

"He's grateful, of course. And he—"

"Grateful!" Val muttered a rude word. The door moved again, but she was too intent to give it much notice. "Grateful has nothing to do with the way he looks at you. Half the women who walk into this place would kill to have a man look at them like that. But all right, if you won't consider any of that, then look at what the man did."

Val held up her fingers. "He arranged to marry you in a church, *his* church. He arranged to have your mother and stepfather here. He arranged to have a cake and a reception and guests. He gave you a very sentimental family heirloom. All in all, the man did just about everything but hire skywriters to make your wedding the traditional, pull-out-all-the-stops-because-we're-only-going-to-do-this-once kind of wedding. Does that sound like a man who's got a business arrangement in mind?"

Eleanor opened her mouth to repeat Cahill's words about how all the flourishes made their wedding, their marriage more convincing. Slowly, she closed her lips on the lie.

She hadn't truly believed it when he said it all those times in the weeks before the wedding. But she'd pretended to. Because that made it safe to go ahead and do something wildly impractical. Like marry the man you loved, the man totally wrong for you.

"I...I don't know."

"Well, that's progress, El. At least you're not talking that junk about business arrangements. Now—" Val took a deep breath "—tell me what happened."

Haltingly, she told Val. And as she found the words to tell her fears, she faced some truths.

She'd built such fine defenses around her emotions she hadn't considered what she might be doing to his. She'd said things this morning that hurt him. She'd watched him draw back, and she couldn't blame him. She'd hurt him. He'd offered love, a marriage, a family. A future. He meant those things. That was the danger of dreamers. They always believed in the illusions they spun.

And she'd turned it all back on him. No, she couldn't blame him when his green eyes frosted and he walked away.

She was caught. She was too practical not to see the danger of loving him. And too much in love with him not to risk the danger. But now it might be too late for him to accept whatever help she could give him. Too late to open herself to him, to give him all she had. To be his wife, his true wife, as long as the dream lasted.

"I've held so much back from him, Val. I haven't made this a real marriage at all. I said things this morning—"

"Valerie, Eleanor! There you are!" Roberta's uncle poked his head around the edge of the door. "Here they are," he announced over his shoulder. "Come out of that dark place. We want you two lovely ladies to come join us. Two more lovely ladies always help a party. Come! Come!"

Valerie pressed Eleanor's hand a moment and gave her an encouraging smile before she shepherded the party enthusiast back through the swinging door.

"Of course, I'll come, Mr. Maggio. But I'm afraid Eleanor has some more work to do." She turned to give a final order to her cousin. "Go home and talk to him."

Eleanor found herself alone in the empty kitchen, standing at her desk. Yes, perhaps work could stop this insistent beat in her head. *Too late. Too late.*

She shuffled the disordered papers on the desk. Disordered. Not the way she left them. The drawer they kept locked was ajar. The paychecks... Against the dull thudding in her head, she forced herself to check for anything missing. But everything was there. Everything except Tom Hustine's final check, and Val had said something about mailing that.

Too late. Too late. It was no good. The beat pounded too strong. Work couldn't block it out.

Impulsively, she opened the door to the meeting room. Maybe the wave of music and laughter that met her would drown out the fear.

"Come join us in a toast, Eleanor." Mr. Maggio handed her a glass of red wine, and one to her cousin. "Valerie."

"Thanks, I'd love some," said Val. "But Eleanor doesn't drink red wine. It doesn't agree—"

"Thank you, Mr. Maggio," interrupted Eleanor, taking a healthy drink from the brimming glass.

"El! You know what that does to you. You react just like Aunt Connie does."

"That was years ago. This is a night for wine," she said in defiance of her cousin, her history and her own common sense. "For once I'm going to live dangerously. Take a risk."

Chapter Eleven

Cahill was asleep when she came home.

She hadn't drunk a lot of the rich, hearty red wine. But even that first healthy swallow was enough to unsettle her stomach. And she'd nearly finished the glass before heeding the queasiness. Adding to her headache was Billie's discovery that the portable tape recorder-player she used on her beach runs was missing from the closet where the waitresses kept their things. With a sinking feeling that matched the one in her stomach, Eleanor wondered if the problems would ever stop.

By the time Val, uncharacteristically subdued, dropped her off, her stomach bordered on open rebellion. She managed a fairly cheerful good-night to her cousin, but she knew it wouldn't be a good night. The only other time in her life that she'd had red wine was in a burst of collegiate rebellion. Still she remembered the feeling.

Though her head hammered and her stomach took fitful tosses, she avoided the creaking bottom step and passed the open bedroom door without any noise. But in the bathroom, urgency overcame caution as the first paroxysm took over.

Later, she sat on the cool tile floor, trying to take off her clothes with as little movement as possible. She had her jacket laid across the side of the tub and one shoe off when the bathroom door opened.

"No! Go away, Cahill!" The abrupt move to her knees was a mistake. Her stomach rolled.

"I'm not going away." His tone made her think that if the Rock of Gibraltar had a voice, that was what it would sound like. He knelt next to her, removing her other shoe.

"I don't want you here."

"And isn't that too bad?"

Frustration and the humiliating realization that she was about to disgrace herself in front of him brought tears to her eyes. "Go away," she repeated, but with no strength to the words. She tried to push him, but had to abort the movement to grab the side of the toilet.

For a while only her own misery existed. Then from somewhere far away, she heard his voice crooning nonsense syllables. No, not from far away. From very near, but so softly. He handed her a cool, damp cloth to wipe her face. Gradually, she became aware of him removing her clothes so efficiently, so smoothly even her stomach couldn't object, though she tried to tell him no. He ignored her, easily shifting her to remove her panty hose, all the while crooning in that guttural but oddly soft voice. Gaelic. He was talking Gaelic. *"A mhuirnín."*

"What does that mean?"

"My sweetheart."

"Oh." Obediently, unthinkingly, she lifted her arms so he could remove her slip.

"Aren't you going to tell me how stupid and un-sensible I was?"

"No."

When she shivered, he drew a bath towel around her shoulders. "But I knew I could get sick if I drank the red wine and I did it anyhow," she told him defiantly. "My mother has the same reaction, but I don't want to be like my mother, so I drank the wine. So what do you think of practical Eleanor now?''

''I told you a long time ago—you're a complicated lady.''

He gathered her clothes and left. For good? Tears came into her eyes. Just as well, she tried to tell herself. She was stupid. Stupid and not sensible at all.

Again, a damp cloth materialized in her hand.

''I thought you'd left,'' she said after a while, not sure if she'd meant to sound disgusted or pleased that he hadn't.

He took the cloth from her and guided her hand into a sleeve of something soft and warm and large. One of his flannel shirts, she realized as he maneuvered her other arm in, than began buttoning it.

''I'll not leave you, Noreen.''

And he didn't. Each time she dozed, she woke to find him awake, soothing her, warming her. Long into the dark hours of that night, she fell asleep huddled against his broad chest.

She woke to the lulling rhythm of his chest rising and falling under her cheek, her body cradled in the V of his legs. At least he'd gotten some sleep finally. She stayed still a long time, not wanting to disturb him, not wanting to test the delicate balance of her stomach. Finally she quietly disengaged the arm he'd thrown across her. Shakily, she stood by bracing herself against the sink, and reached for her toothbrush. If she passed the toothpaste test, she'd be okay.

''What are you doing?''

Other than half raising black eyelashes and moving his lips, he didn't stir.

''I have to wash.'' Under her eyes were dark mascara tracks. Long dried, her tears still showed their paths. Her body felt gritty, her hair lifeless. ''I want a shower.''

''You're too weak.''

She looked from the mirror to him, and felt a lurch inside her. But this time it was her heart, not her stomach. Stubble shadowed the bold lines of his jaw and chin. His hair showed signs of impatient hands having shoved it back. Dark lashes and tired shadows made his eyes into smudgy caverns with mysterious lights at their depths. "I *need* a shower," she said with more force than she'd mustered in six hours.

He uncoiled from the floor with one powerful movement. "All right, Eleanor girl. We'll take a shower."

"We?" Her forcefulness proved fleeting as she watched him peel his shirt off over his head and start on his pants.

"You're too weak to be left alone. Haven't you read of all the accidents that happen in the home? And I'll be needing a shower, too."

"But…" Protest seemed useless with him already stripped, and working on the buttons of the shirt she wore. And what would she base a protest on? Pride? She didn't have much left after the night. Modesty? They'd been sharing a bed for weeks now. Practicality? Two sharing the water of one won out there. Besides, he was right—she was too weak.

So she let him guide a soapy cloth over her. The soft friction made her skin tingle and the familiar pressure of his touch aroused her nerves. He washed her hair, then tipped her forehead against his chest to stroke away the tiredness in her back. Desire and exhaustion lapped over each other like waves of an incoming tide on the sand, each one a little higher, a little harder until it was swallowed by the next wave.

Exhaustion rose, a final, cresting wave, as she was wrapped in a soft towel and transported in some magic manner between cool, crisp sheets.

Wearing only a pair of jeans, Cahill slept in the chair pulled up beside the foot of the bed. His left hand curled around her fingers. His legs stretched out to rest on the edge of the mattress. He'd been crowding her so hard, so long. It only seemed fair to give her some space. But not to let go entirely.

He opened his eyes to find her watching him warily.

"My father and sister died when I was fourteen." He saw her wariness instantly turn to compassion at his abrupt words.

He'd meant to tell her someday, not now. So why was he doing it now?

"My father hadn't been well. Doctor after doctor couldn't say why. Finally, a specialist in Dublin said he had this rare kind of heart condition. He was born with it and from that day it had been getting worse. He worried he'd passed it to his children, but he hadn't. Just a fluke in the way his heart developed. A fluke. A one-in-a-million fluke."

He could almost convince himself that desire to be near him made her sit up, holding the sheet around her breasts with one hand. The other he still held captive, in case she tried to pull away.

"There was this doctor in England who specialized in my father's kind of condition. Dad said he'd go, if Mom promised to stay with Patsy and me at home so we wouldn't have to miss any school. He said we'd need education for when we went to America. As soon as the term finished for the summer, she took us to London to see him. Later, I found out the doctor had told her he couldn't do anything for Dad. I think she wanted to be sure we said goodbye.

"As we were leaving after seeing him, Mother took ill. She was barely pregnant with Kiernan and didn't know it. They rushed her away. They didn't tell us what was wrong with her. They wouldn't let us see her. They wouldn't let us talk to her. We didn't know what was happening to her—"

He broke off. Those hours of waiting helplessly still gnawed at him.

"We'd gone straight to hospital, so we didn't have any place to stay. I had a few English pounds, that's all. They wouldn't let us stay overnight in the waiting room, couldn't break their regulations. They called the authorities like we were left luggage. I tried to tell them that if they'd just let me talk to my mother, I'd find out what she wanted us to do. But they wouldn't. The doctors had said no visitors. That rule they wouldn't break. They wouldn't listen to anything I said. They wouldn't even answer me. We spent most of the night on benches in the police station. They'd leave us there the night but not at hospital. I could hear them arguing on the phone with different agencies about who had the responsibility for the two of us."

Shifting in the chair, he broke contact with her. But she reached for him, grasping his fingers in hers. That eased his next words, he knew, but he didn't know why. Or he refused to know why.

"Finally, they contacted an uncle of ours in Dublin. They decided they'd put us on the ferry, and he'd drive down for us. Then it would be his problem what to do with us."

Though years had passed, bitterness still echoed in his voice.

"Patsy was frantic. She was only a little girl and she wanted to stay with her mother. I tried to tell them." He swallowed and clenched his jaw. "They wouldn't listen. At the ferry, Patsy started crying and screaming, begging me to take her back to Mother. I...I'm not proud of what happened then." He looked down at his hand around hers. Consciously, he eased his grip. "I try...to hold on to my temper now. Then, I didn't. The anger never lasted long, but while it did... That's how I got this nose. That was my solution to everything."

He stared at the delicate pale flowers on the wallpaper, but in his mind he saw a big policeman placing his sister on the ferry. He saw her eyes, red with tears and terror, pleading with him. "Don't let them hurt me, Cahill. Don't let them." He knew the policeman meant no harm to Patsy, but she didn't. She only knew she was being taken farther and farther away from her mother. And her brother wasn't helping her.

"I don't remember what happened. In the charges against me, they said I knocked out one policeman and fought off two. More police and security guards came. The ferry left while they tried to subdue me." He shook his head, as if trying to clear a misty picture. "I've tried to remember. I only see the ferry pulling away, and Patsy at the railing, crying for me to help her. I don't even know if that really happened."

His silence stretched long and deep. His fingers, usually so generous with their warmth and strength, felt clammy against her skin. Eleanor twisted her hand to gain more contact. She'd give him her warmth this time without losing its insistence.

"What happened, Cahill?" She made the question as soft as she could.

Hollow and uninflected, his words came: "There was rough weather. The ferry capsized. More than a hundred saved. The rescue was considered miraculous. Only eleven drowned. One of them was Patsy."

Eleanor closed her eyes against a pain so deep he wouldn't allow it in his voice. She leaned toward him, pulling his hand to draw him closer.

"An accident."

"No! You don't understand. I should have been there. If I'd been there, I could have saved her."

"Cahill, it was an accident. If you had been there, you probably would have drowned, too."

"I was supposed to take care of her. I couldn't get the damned officials with all their damned rules to let us stay with our parents, but I should at least have stayed with her. I lost my temper and I deserted her. Left her to drown—"

"No! Cahill, don't do this to yourself."

"Do you understand? I can't let that anger go again. Ever. I can't take that risk. When I do, it's always wrong, like the way I nearly ruined all your work to catch Hustine. That's why I walk away. That's why I don't stay and fight."

The words she'd shouted after him the morning before returned to her. *Don't walk away from me, Cahill McCrea. Stay here and fight.* What those words must have meant to him, what memories they must have reopened.

She'd been wrong then; he was wrong now. This man *was* a fighter. He'd been fighting this weight of tragedy since he was fourteen years old, carrying it all these years without bowing under it. Still dreaming his dreams, still fighting for his dreams. Not walking away from the hope of a new country and a new life. He had to be made to see that in himself.

"Cahill…"

"Don't say anything, Noreen." She heard the tears in his voice, but his face hardened. "Just let me hold you."

She opened her arms. She'd give him what he needed now. Later, she'd show him how wrong he was.

He moved from the chair to the bed, sitting beside her as she went into arms that circled her with a desperate kind of gentleness. Through the sheet between them, she felt the rise and fall of his chest. She spread her hands wide on his back, holding him closer and trying to smooth away the hurt.

"Just let me hold you," he murmured, as he laid back on the bed.

She felt his lips, gentle amid the prickle of his morning beard, touch her temple and the crown of her head.

During the long moments they lay there, she thought a kind of peace eased into him. It didn't take away the loss, nothing would ever do that, but it made it more bearable now that he'd shared the burden.

His hold tightened a little as she rose to look into his face. She kissed the corner of his eye, his beard-stubbled cheek, the bump on his nose. The tightness eased from his face.

She kissed him again, this time fully on the lips, with her tongue boldly seeking his. Making promises. Offering healing.

He tasted the promises and the healing, and knew that with them, she gave him a glimpse of a new world. One that was his and hers alone. The new world of his dreaming.

She pulled the sheet from between their bodies and skimmed her hands down his sides. When she encountered his jeans, she made a sound of impatience. He started to remove them, but she silently ordered, "Let me."

The competent hands he'd so often admired proved maddeningly inefficient at their task, tantalizingly inefficient. Whispers of touches. Brushes against his need. Drags of denim against his sensitized need. A film of sweat broke out on his body, and his breathing came fast.

He wouldn't have traded those moments for anything.

As she at last slid his jeans and briefs away and dropped them to the floor, he watched her concentration with a heart that marveled at its own ability to love. And its ability to continue beating through an ache of not knowing if its love was returned.

He'd told her about Dad and Patsy because he'd wanted her understanding, he saw that now. But he wanted more—her love. And still more. Her trust and respect, the trust and respect a woman like Noreen must feel before giving the kind of commitment he wanted from her.

She trailed damp fire across his skin with kisses that returned to his mouth. He was there for her, ready, but this was her world to explore, her world to take.

"Cahill. I want...I want..."

"Want it all. Noreen."

Want me, Noreen. Want a home, babies, a business, growing old together.... Want it all, Noreen. Come dream with me....

"Yes."

"My Noreen. Everything. I'll give you everything."

And he did. He gave her all of himself. All his dreams. All his charm. All his anguish. All his joy. All his love.

He felt Eleanor's fingers stroke his shoulder and upper arm as she lay curled against him.

"Cahill."

He managed a deep-throated purr. "Hmm."

"I have to tell you..." His muscles tightened involuntarily and he thought her fingers took on a reassuring touch.

"I love you, Cahill."

He stilled completely for an instant. When he moved it was sudden and sure, so she couldn't have stopped him if she'd wanted to. He pulled her firmly underneath him and searched her face in the light of sunrise pouring in through the window.

He smiled at her, slowly, sadly.

He saw the love there. And he saw more she didn't know she revealed.

She loved him, despite her sense and reason and caution. She didn't want to. She didn't trust her love, nor him. Not to give her what she wanted of this life, not even to give her what she thought she wanted.

There was a journey yet to complete, to reach what he wanted of her, what she deserved of him. He'd see they completed that journey to their new world. With every bit of his stubborn, dogged heart, he made that vow.

He lowered himself to touch all of her, to absorb her through every cell of his body.

"Don't answer."

"I've got to answer the phone, Cahill. Val's probably wondering what in the world's happened to me."

He tightened his hold on her. That thrilled her, at the same time she tried to slip free. Something about his possessiveness struck her as endearing. Something that would have been missing if he hadn't tried so hard to hide it.

"Be reasonable, Cahill. As much as I'd like to spend all day in bed with you—"

"Now that sounds a good plan."

"But there's a business to run, remember?"

His mumbles about taking the phone off the hook and never letting her out of the bedroom from November to May had her answering the phone with a smile.

But the smile disappeared when she turned back to him, and was replaced by a frown of puzzlement, concern and, yes, a thin veil of fear.

"That was Val. She said Britt just left The Fishwife. He's on his way here. He wants to talk to both of us."

"Nice place you have here, Eleanor. Nice place for a young couple just starting out on married life, isn't it, McCrea?"

"Get to your point, Franklin," Eleanor said.

For an irrational moment, she had considered refusing to let him in the house. Some instinct warned her to keep his contaminating presence far away from her and Cahill. Superstition, she thought with an inner grimace.

She let him in the house. But she didn't invite him to sit, and she certainly wouldn't tolerate his dithering about their home.

She glanced at where Cahill had his hips propped up on the back of the couch. His shadowed eyes rested on Britt. She'd told him in the few minutes before Britt's arrival that this was her fight, but she was still a little surprised he let her take the lead in the conversation.

"But that *is* the point," said Britt with a slicing smile. "Your married life. The marriage of Eleanor Thalston and Cahill McCrea."

Breathing became her enemy. Every breath brought fear, cold and raw, into her body, robbing her of the ability to think, to be levelheaded, practical and sensible.

"Or," continued Britt with a kind of twisted pleasure in his voice, "should I say the business arrangement between Eleanor Thalston and Cahill McCrea?"

She could feel the tightening of Cahill's muscles as if they were her own. His anger flamed through her veins. She had to take the lead in this. She had to, for his sake.

Sheer willpower produced words. "What do you mean, Franklin?"

"Oh, come now, Eleanor. You're much too intelligent for that sort of ploy. Let us be honest and aboveboard, at least here, amongst the three of us. Surely it would be easier to just acknowledge the truth of what I've said."

"If you have ever said anything honest and aboveboard, it certainly has escaped my notice."

He answered her implacable stare with a heavy sigh. "Very well, Eleanor. If you want it that way…" From the pocket of a jacket distended by his rotund stomach, he withdrew a miniature tape player. "This is one of those contraptions people use to provide themselves with music while they run up and down the beach. It happened to come into my possession. It has some interesting features. In addition to playing tapes, this one also records. And oddly enough, it had a recorded tape in it when I purchased it from a young man I know who suddenly found himself in need of ready cash.''

Billie's recorder. It had to be. And the young man in sudden need of cash—Hustine and his bond on the malicious-mischief charge. But what could be on the tape that would tell Britt of her ridiculous ''arrangement'' with Cahill?

''A most interesting tape. Shall I play it for you?''

Before the tape responded to the thick finger pressing the Play button, she knew what the words would be. Last night. The Maggio party. Billie's tape player missing. Papers messed up on her desk. Hustine's final check gone from the drawer. Her telling Val everything.

''All very sensible, really. See, by marrying me, Cahill would get his permanent-resident status. After two years, he'd be on his way to becoming a citizen. In return, The Fishwife would keep its star attraction. In two years, the business should be well established. The perfect business arrangement where both parties benefited.''

Then Val's voice. *''I knew it, I just knew it!''*

Britt flicked the tape off. ''Of course I was very shocked to discover this tape. And as much as I tried to find another explanation for it, I could only assume a conspiracy to mislead the Immigration and Naturalization Service and—''

''What do you want, Britt?''

Cahill's voice cut across the other man's words with the same efficiency that Eleanor imagined his powerful arms could have connected with Britt's jaw.

But Cahill wouldn't let his anger go enough to hit Britt. It was wrong for her to wish he would; no, she couldn't wish for that because of what it would do to Cahill. He had to see that he now fought with other weapons.

Still, Cahill's tone and presence seemed to bring Britt to his point. The unbelievable smile faded. ''I'd think it's obvious what I want. I want you to sing at The Old Salt. A doubly advantageous arrangement from my point of view, since it should improve my business at The Old Salt and stop The Fishwife from taking business away from Sand Witches.''

"And if I don't?"

"I'll have you deported. As for your *wife*..." At the leer in Britt's voice, Eleanor sensed Cahill's tensing. For a single second she thought his control would break. Then the moment passed. "The immigration laws may not punish her this time since the INS didn't do anything even when I had it brought to their attention that The Fishwife was employing an immigrant without the right visa."

Eleanor should have suspected that Cahill's file being reviewed so carefully by Jeffrey Hanson had been more than routine. Why hadn't she seen Britt's hand in it?

"But surely," he was continuing, "the liquor board would not continue to grant a license to someone who showed herself willing to participate in such a fraud."

Britt looked from one to the other. Apparently satisfied with what he saw, he nodded once and turned to the door. "I'll give you thirty minutes to think it over, McCrea. If you're not at the Sand Witches by then, I'll call the INS."

The door closed behind him, and with jerky steps Cahill moved to the picture window facing the beach.

Cahill wasn't sure when Eleanor spoke. It didn't really matter. He'd known her thoughts before she said them. Her outrage. As if Cahill would go and sing at The Old Salt. Her determination to smash Britt. They'd explain the tape. And if that didn't work, they'd appeal. As long as they stuck out two years together, he'd be on his way to citizenship.

He winced a little at the term "stuck out two years together," but didn't take his eyes from the distant swell of waves. He'd asked for his chance to get inside Britt's operation, his chance to help Manuela's nephew and all the others, his chance to maybe pay some penance for failing Patsy. His chance to prove to himself that he could do this. So he had no right to kick because his chance arrived at the wrong moment.

No, he knew what he was going to do. Working at The Old Salt, he could search for documentation of what Britt had been doing. That way, the frightened people Britt had been exploiting wouldn't have to put themselves on the line. With that kind of proof he could go directly to the authorities himself. So he had to work for Britt. That decision came easily. He had to take this opportunity. The second decision was much harder. He wouldn't tell Eleanor.

Because this was also a chance of another kind. A chance with her.

If his plan worked, he'd have cause to hope the INS would reward his efforts with immigration in his own right. With the pretense stripped away, maybe Eleanor would see their love for what it truly was. If his plan worked, perhaps she'd see him for the man he wanted to be.

And if it failed...well, the thought of failure convinced him not to tell her. He didn't want her exposed any more than necessary to Britt's vengeance. Not knowing might be some protection there.

Without turning from the window, he said, "I'm going, Eleanor."

After one quick look at her stunned face, a look that squeezed his chest like a weight of granite, he went upstairs. He heard her come into the room as he tossed a pair of socks into a satchel.

"Cahill, you don't have to go. We'll fight it. We'll find a way." Through her tight voice, he heard the determination to remain reasonable. Damn her reason.

"What way, Eleanor? What weapon are you going to use to fight Britt?"

"I don't know yet, but—"

He turned, his eyes intent on her face. "Can you trust me, Noreen? Can you be trusting me enough to believe me when I say this is the right way?"

"How can it be right to give in to a man like that?" Her frown deepened as she seemed to read something of the thoughts he tried to keep hidden. "Of course I trust you, Cahill, but I don't think you realize there are ways to fight things like this. I know that together we can—"

He laughed harshly, trying to push away her hope. Before

he took her in his arms. "Sometimes you Americans are entirely naive."

"Naive!"

"You think just because you want something, it'll come. With no trouble, no obstacles. That's not the way of the world. You of all people should know that, practical Eleanor." He threw a shirt in the bag. "I'll get the rest another time." He started to look at her, then jerked his head away.

The movement caught Eleanor like a blow to her heart. He couldn't bear to look at her.

"And us? What about us?" *Wasn't that a dream of yours, too, Cahill? To have a real marriage? To make a life together? Wasn't that the dream you've been weaving all along? I thought we were weaving it together this morning. Weren't we?*

"What about us?" he repeated, the words spaced and even, neutral. He didn't look at her, his eyes staring into space.

Sadness weighed at her, dragging her until she felt only weariness. *I thought you were different, Cahill. I thought that beneath the charm, I'd found more—strength and determination and…as much love for me, as I feel for you.* Just another dreamer…

"Is it because of what I said to Val on the tape? Is that it, Cahill? I thought I meant it then. At least I tried to believe I meant it, but…" Her voice thickened around unshed tears. "If you're angry at me for saying that—"

"No!" The explosive word made her jump. Still, he didn't look at her. "I'm not angry at you, Eleanor."

"People will think we've broken up." Heavy and listless, her voice sounded odd to her own ears.

"What people will think? Is that what you're worried about, Eleanor?" The words came quick and harsh. "That sounds like a Thalston concern, like something your grandmother would have worried about."

"I am not my grandmother." The spurt of anger was as surprising as it was welcome. At least she could feel something other than misery.

"No. And I'm not your mother. I'm not feckless and irre-

sponsible. You should know that by now. You should trust me
by now. If you could trust me, Eleanor...but you don't.''

He strode from the room. The bottom stair creaked under
his weight as he left.

Chapter Twelve

"**M**orning, Eleanor."

Eamon Dougherty took a seat on the stool, smiling across the bar at her the same way he had the first time they met. No, not the same way. His smile was strained today, and sadness tinged his eyes.

"Good morning, Eamon. I didn't know you were on Cape Ann."

"I came out yesterday to see Cahill." He hesitated, glancing up at her.

"How is he?" The question came out soft with concern and tight with the effort not to reveal too much.

"He *says* he's fine," came the disgusted mutter. From under his red bushy brows, he looked at her. "How's business these days, Eleanor?"

"We're holding our own." He stared at her, and as she continued, she ruefully realized he was using her own tactic on her. "Not as good as...before."

"You mean since Cahill left to go to that other place," Eamon said bluntly. She nodded, determined that this time his stare would draw no more words from her.

He leaned forward with the air of a man who'd reached a decision. "Well, since you asked how he is, I'll tell you. He sounds like death and looks worse. He's snarling and snapping like a bear. He near as told me to get lost last night. But I decided it was high time I found out what's going on. So I thought I'd look in on you this morning. And here I find you looking no better than him. So, I'm asking you, Eleanor, what's happened between you and Cahill?"

Eleanor swallowed and pulled in a long, steadying breath. "Cahill and I made a mistake in getting married. Franklin Britt found out about it and exploited it. That's all."

"But there's no sense in that. I've known Cahill all his life. Good times and bad. He loves you. Don't you love him?"

"I..." Eleanor searched for words to push Eamon away without hurting him. There were none. "Yes. I love him."

Slapping his palms on the bar in frustration, he demanded, "Then what are the two of you doing apart, making each other miserable?"

"There were, uh, problems. Problems we couldn't sort out."

Eamon's blue eyes pierced into hers. "His temper?" He took her silence as confirmation. "That's a battle he's waged since he was a lad. But I thought he had it nearly won. I never thought he'd do anything to hurt you."

Horrified, she reached across to touch his hand. "No! You don't understand. Cahill would never—"

"Don't be daft, girl. He's *tintrí, teasí,* but I know that Cahill would never lay a hand on *you* in anger."

He mitigated the scolding by turning his hand over and clasping hers. "I didn't mean that. I meant his ways of coping. As a boy, he fought with his fists. *Tintrí, teasí*—hotheaded. After a while, he changed. He'd try to talk away the problem. And he succeeded more often than not. He could be a marvel at making men see reason."

The Cahill McCrea charm. Eleanor felt her lips move, the closest she'd come to a smile in fifteen days. But it didn't last.

"But if he couldn't, he'd walk away rather than use his fists," continued Eamon. "A man like Cahill doesn't stomach walking away from the things he cares about. He wouldn't let himself care about much, then. Just his mother and brother and providing for them. And the dream of coming to America. Then he met you."

His free hand patted their joined hands. "I've never seen a man more in love than Cahill. And with your sensible head, I thought you'd help him see that he *could* care about things, that—"

"That you don't have to walk away. That there are other ways to fight than with your fists," she finished. Her voice rasped. "I thought so, too, Eamon. I thought he was learning that. The whole experience with the INS and some things here at The Fishwife. But it's hard. And with the things that happened to him…"

If he'd had more time to build his belief in his ability to handle it… But he didn't trust himself enough. He'd said he could never let his anger go again. "I can't take that risk." Not even for her. She wasn't worth fighting for. In the end, their marriage wasn't worth fighting for.

"Eamon, tell me about the ferry accident. That's when it all started, isn't it?"

Eamon searched her face, then nodded, apparently satisfied. "Yes, it is." He told her the story Cahill had told her, but he told her more. He told her of a boy hearing the dream of America all his life from a father he adored. Of his confusion and despair over his father's illness. Of his grieving guilt after his sister's death.

"There was no cause, no cause at all for him to blame himself. There was nothing he could have done. All the people who drowned were in the same part of the ferry. It wasn't that they couldn't swim. Huge crates fell across the passage and trapped them."

Eleanor closed her eyes, feeling the panic the young girl must have felt, and then, more strongly, the guilt and grief of the brother who'd blamed himself for eighteen years for something he couldn't have prevented. *Oh, Cahill...*

Suddenly the kitchen door swung open violently.

"El!" Val burst in, clutching her keys in one hand. She looked quickly from her cousin to Eamon and back.

"Val, I thought you'd gone to the bank and then for those supplies."

"I had the bank door open when I saw this commotion down the street. I went to find out what it was about, and when I heard—"

Eleanor watched her cousin glance again to Eamon, and back to her. "Cahill," she whispered. "It's Cahill, isn't it? What's happened?"

"It's all right, Eleanor." Val's hands on her arms stopped her as she rounded the bar. "I mean he's all right. He's not hurt or anything. But they're arresting people at The Old Salt."

"Arresting?" What could arrests have to do with Cahill?

"It's the INS, Eleanor. I got close enough to hear someone talking."

The INS. Britt had turned Cahill in for fraud. He'd used his knowledge to blackmail Cahill, and then he'd turned him in anyhow. Deportation.

Eleanor ran into the kitchen, hardly pausing to grab her purse before she was out the door and in her car. Val raced after her and jumped in.

"Tell me," Eleanor demanded as she backed up.

"There were unmarked cars all over and Gloucester police," Val started when she had breath for words. "I could see somebody in a three-piece suit talking to Britt, and I heard him yelling for his lawyer. His face was all red and—El, slow down!"

Eleanor ignored the plea as the car screeched around a curve in the narrow streets.

"They had the front and part of the parking lot cordoned off and wouldn't let people in or out."

"Did you see him?"

Val, clutching the door handle, didn't have to ask who she

meant. "No. But I heard—ahhhhhh." She squeezed her eyes shut and let out a long breath as they raced down a hill and took another curve without slowing.

"What did you hear?" A last turn, and the parking lot of The Old Salt came into view. Cars rested helter-skelter across the neatly painted lines. Police cars. Bland sedans that were certainly the unmarked cars of some agency or another. A crowd milled among the cars, trying to maneuver closer to the wooden sawhorses that separated them from a smaller group of people closer to the building. Police stood by the only gap in the barrier.

"I heard his voice inside and—"

Eleanor never knew if Val finished the sentence, because as soon as she brought the car to a stop, she was out the door and moving through the crowd.

Let Val turn off the engine. Let her take the keys. Let her close the doors. Or let someone steal the damn car. She didn't care. She didn't care about anything but getting to Cahill.

They couldn't send him away. It would be so unjust. But he wouldn't fight it. He didn't believe in fighting. To him, it meant only one thing and brought only one result. Before he'd risk another tragedy like the one that haunted his past, he'd walk away, let go of his dream of citizenship.

But she wouldn't let him. If he wouldn't fight for himself, she'd fight for him. If he didn't have the means to secure this dream, she'd secure it for him. Because his dreams were part of him. And she loved him.

She hesitated as she scanned the people. Two three-piece-suited men took notes as an excited Asian man in a waiter's uniform talked. Identifiable by their clothing, more waiters, waitresses, busboys, chefs and dishwashers gathered in anxious pockets, apparently waiting their turns with the three-piece suits. None of them was Cahill. More plainclothes officials milled with uniformed Gloucester police on the wide front porch. Through the huge picture window, Eleanor saw Franklin Britt gesturing wildly, his face red with the strain of shouting.

The front door opened for a moment, and she heard a snatch of indecipherable sound.

Cahill came through the door, escorted by a police officer. Eleanor tensed as one of the plainclothesmen joined them, flashed a credential at Cahill and led him toward the steps.

The INS. It had to be. They'd accuse him of marrying a U.S. citizen just to stay in America. They'd send him back to Ireland. Send him away from America forever. Away from his dream. Away from her.

She didn't realize she'd made a sound, and that the sound was his name, until she saw Cahill's head come up. He searched the crowd, and she felt the moment his eyes met hers.

Joy washed across his face, along with longing and need. He needed her. That surprised her a little. She knew that right now he needed her help, her practicality, her determination, maybe even her protection. But she hadn't expected to see it so clearly in his eyes.

She strode past the pair of policemen who guarded the opening between the sawhorses.

"Hey, lady. You gotta stay back. Lady!"

He caught her arm and stopped her progress. She spared him only a glare. "I'm on official business."

"Then I gotta see some identification, lady."

"It's all right, officer," Val's voice came smoothly and convincingly from behind the policeman. "I can explain everything to you."

The young policeman looked from the determination on Eleanor's face to the cooperativeness of Val's and quickly decided who would be more reasonable to deal with. "Okay, lady, explain," he said, setting arms akimbo and turning to Val.

Free of the policeman, Eleanor reached Cahill in four steps. The INS agent was talking. She heard only the final word of his sentence: "problem." It slashed into her. But she smiled brightly as she slid one arm around Cahill's waist.

"It's all right. There's no problem. He's my husband. It's all very legal, I can assure you." She pressed her other hand, fingers extended wide, against Cahill's chest. She told herself it would appear like a normal gesture of affection between a married couple. In the back of her mind she acknowledged she was stopping herself from curling into his arms and dropping her head to his shoulder.

She caught the confusion in the official's face. Good, at least she had him enough off balance to be confused. She'd add a quick, affectionate smile at Cahill and that should complete the image of a secure, serene married couple she wanted to project.

She'd miscalculated. She knew it the moment she gazed up at Cahill, and by then it was too late. There was nothing serene in his face. He looked fierce. Possessive. Satisfied. Claiming. Demanding. Yes, all those, but not serene.

She couldn't take her eyes away.

"You should be very proud of your husband, Mrs. McCrea," the official said. She had the feeling he'd said other things, but she didn't hear anything before this. "His help has been invaluable to us. When he first proposed the idea, there were doubts, but it's worked out great."

"I—I'm not sure I understand."

"Cahill!" Val erupted into the group, reaching up to plant a kiss on Cahill's cheek. "My hero! I've been hoping somebody would step on that worm for years. I can't think of anybody I'd rather see do it than you!"

Jeffrey Hanson, who'd followed Val more sedately, said hello to Eleanor, shook hands with Cahill and dismissed the other official.

"Well, Cahill, it couldn't have turned out any better than it did. You're in the clear now with your extended visa, and I'm sure we can work out sponsorship with the Rhode Island resort before this one expires. And thanks to you, my supervisors are very pleased with the whole operation. And with me," Hanson said with a self-deprecating grin. "We've even had good co-operation with the Labor Department guys. Hell, after this, they owe us one. It's great PR, too. I can see the headlines—INS Helps Downtrodden Immigrants."

"Thanks, Jeffrey." Cahill glanced at Eleanor. "Could you give us a minute?"

"What?" Hanson followed the direction of Cahill's eyes. "Oh, sure. Sure."

In the crowded area, Cahill could only pivot Eleanor away from the others to gain some privacy for themselves. Excited voices in a variety of accents still surrounded them.

"Everyone seems to think I know what's going on," she said stiffly. "Would you care to tell me?"

He considered her straight back and the chill of pride in her gray eyes for long minutes. "Eleanor..." he started, then stopped.

When he started again, he told her how he had first heard of Britt's treatment of immigrants from Manuela. How the blackmail scheme had given him the chance to expose Britt's operation from inside. How he had contacted Jeffrey Hanson and told him the whole situation. How, in exchange for gathering information needed to stop Britt's exploitation, the INS had agreed to extend his visa until he could be sponsored by an employer he'd had lined up for months, long before he knew her. That had been another secret.

"But..." No words came that wouldn't give her away, so she let the single word trail off.

"But you thought I'd run away rather than fight again."

She couldn't deny it.

"I would have before I met you, Noreen. Don't you know yet that you've taught me there're other ways to fight? I can't say I'm fond of the system, with the rules and regulations, but you've taught me to work with—"

"Excuse me, Cahill." It was Jeffrey Hanson. "Sorry, Eleanor, but this husband of yours is going to have to go back to the office with us."

Eleanor's arms tightened around Cahill.

"To make a final statement."

Cahill took her hands and held them between their bodies.

"I'll be back to The Fishwife later and explain it all. We'll talk."

But when he arrived more than three hours later, they couldn't talk. Not about what she most needed to talk about:

them. Not with all the people around demanding to know what had happened. They could only talk about what had happened at The Old Salt that morning.

Eamon, Val, Manuela, Rae, Harry and his wife, Billie, Jean and Hillary all exulted at Franklin Britt's downfall and Cahill's role in it. Eleanor listened from the far edge of the group, gathering in the details of Cahill's undercover work. All the while, one question pounded in her head. *Why didn't you tell me?* He'd said he loved her, he'd asked her to trust him, but he hadn't trusted her.

When she slipped away from the group, she thought Cahill's gaze followed her, but that could have been wishful thinking because he certainly didn't come after her.

For more than an hour she walked the beaches, not sure if she had anything in her mind coherent enough to call a thought. Gradually, the habits of a lifetime began to impose some order on the chaos of her emotions.

Levelheaded and sensible, she looked at her reactions. When it came right down to it, she couldn't bear the idea of his being sent away. When Val's words about arrests had conjured up the image of Cahill being sent back to Ireland for good, she'd finally faced her true feelings. He'd needed her. And with that need he claimed every bit of her heart. There was no possibility of self-preservation. She loved him. With no reservations. No qualifications. No pieces of herself held back.

In that moment at The Old Salt, she'd seen just how unimportant everything else was compared to her love for him. She'd seen exactly what she wanted.

A real marriage.

She knew Aidan Padraic Cahill McCrea would put every fiber of himself into making that dream come true. If he still wanted it.

He no longer needed marriage to stay in America. There was no cause for them to be together. Unless they wanted to be. God knew, that was what she wanted. Now she had to convince Cahill, and pray he still felt the same.

When she returned, The Fishwife was quiet, almost hushed,

as if the building itself had been waiting for her. Or as if it held its breath along with her.

A slight sound cut into the silence. Upstairs. In Cahill's old room.

She'd reached the fourth step when Cahill appeared at the head of the stairs. He didn't say anything, just stood there looking down at her with his eyes shadowed so she couldn't tell if he intended to bar her way or welcome her.

"You said we'd talk," she reminded him.

"Come up, then." As she followed him, she wondered at the grimness she'd heard in his voice. She tried to remember the look on his face when he first saw her at The Old Salt. The longing and the need. And the look when she had her arms around him. The possessiveness and desire.

Surely, that proved he loved her.

Her heart stopped with the first step into the small room. An empty drawer rested on the narrow bed, its contents folded into a cardboard box on the floor. A second drawer, nearly empty, hung open.

"Where are you going?" How did the words ever get past the constriction of her throat?

"Home."

The single word pushed her away from him, to stare sightlessly out the window. With every ounce of discipline she possessed, she tried to summon practicality, levelheadedness.

Sometimes practicality meant seeing things clearly enough to know the time had come to gamble. She had to try for this dream. For him.

Without time for fear, she turned back to him, grabbing his forearm between her hands. "You can't go back there. It's not right for you, Cahill. You belong here, not in Ireland anymore. I won't let you go back. It's right for you to stay here, with me."

His green eyes glinted with a new light; almost as if her words had given him hope. But before she could consider that, he wrapped his hands around her upper arms, holding her in front of him and demanding: "Why did you come?"

The hardness of his words had her so off balance she might have stumbled if he hadn't held her. "What do you mean?" Was he sending her away? Telling her he'd wanted to slip away from The Fishwife without this final, painful scene?

"This morning, at The Old Salt, why did you come?"

Telling the truth required no decision; she couldn't give him any less than that. "Val said they were arresting people. The INS. I thought they'd send you away."

"And wouldn't that have been the best for you? You'd have been clear of me then."

"I don't want to be clear of you."

"You don't?"

"No."

"Even though you think I'm a dreamer, like your mother."

She searched his eyes, trying to understand the emotion in his voice. "You *are* a dreamer *and* a charmer." She felt his tension in the tightening of his hold around her arms. "But I've learned dreams are needed, too, Cahill. We need dreams, and we need reality. I dream, too. I just cloak my dreams in practicality." That was what she'd done in proposing a business-arrangement marriage to him. She'd foolishly tried to hide her desire to keep him at The Fishwife. "The world needs dreamers. The world loves dreamers."

"And you? Do you love dreamers, Noreen!"

Her heart lurched at the name. "I love dreamers. Some. My mother. Val." She opened her eyes and her heart to him. "You."

"Love them but have no regard for their abilities."

The question in his statement couldn't have been any plainer to her. Glimpses of understanding spun through her mind—understanding of his desire to prove himself to her, and her own contribution to his belief that he had proving to do.

"You are like my mother in some ways, that's true. But not entirely. You *do* dream, but you do more. You're willing to work for what you dream of." Very deliberately, she looked at him. "I know you're not afraid to fight for your dreams."

"Not anymore," he agreed softly.

"I've never been afraid to fight, but now I see what I'm fighting for. You gave that to me, Cahill. I want you. I love you. I'll fight to keep you here. Don't leave."

He smiled, and she remembered the desire she'd first seen in his eyes at the cove, deepened now by joy and need, demand and commitment, possessiveness and giving.

"I'll not leave you, and I'll not be letting you go, Eleanor Thalston McCrea. I love you."

The words came as a whisper across her lips. Cahill swept an impatient arm out to clear the bed as he lowered himself to the mattress, holding his Noreen tightly against him.

Someday he'd tell her that when he'd said he was packing to go home he'd meant back to the house with her. She'd thought he meant Ireland. He'd tease her about that. She thought he'd go three thousand miles away from her? Never.

A sound, half laughter, half arousal, sounded in her throat. "This bed's so small. Wouldn't it be better to go back to the house?"

He slid his hands under her clothes, needing to feel her, to know her as his. It might take a thousand years of marriage and love, of walks in the rain and nights in the big bed—or a small bed if that was what came to hand—but he'd capture the dreamer in his Noreen.

He levered himself up to look into her eyes. "I want you, Noreen. Now. No practicality." He dropped a moist, heated kiss on her breast. "Come dreaming, *a mhuirnín*."

She pulled her clothes over her head and let them drop unheeded. The Celtic cross nestled between her breasts, gathering warmth from her skin.

"I love you, Cahill." She pushed a lock of hair from his forehead and traced the uneven line of his nose before cupping her hands around his strong jaw. "Take me dreaming."

And he did.

Epilogue

The couple stood on the rocky cliff at the northernmost point in Ireland. They found shelter from the raw, rough wind in each other's arms.

"It's lovely, Cahill. Do you miss it?"

"I do in a way." Lightly but with an underlying intensity, he kissed her forehead, nose, lips and chin. "It's the way I told you long ago. I miss this country the way a man misses his mother. But my wife has my heart now." This time he kissed her fully, open-mouthed and heatedly. And she responded until they were both breathless.

His breathing was still erratic when he continued. "America's my home now." He slid a hand between their bodies until it rested on the curve of her belly, discernible below the coat. "I couldn't be prouder that our baby's going to be born in America. On July the fourth. An American citizen."

"*Maybe* on the Fourth of July. The due date's no guarantee. And the child of *two* American citizens."

"As soon as they'll let me," he agreed.

She rested her cheek against the rough material of his coat and looked at the cottages strung along a winding road at the base of the cliff. "Is that why you're so anxious to get back, Cahill? You know, we could stay here until after the baby's born, so your mother and Kiernan could see it, and it would still be an American citizen—"

"Another four months? Valerie would skin the both of us if we're not back in four days. You know she wants to leave before the season. I'm thinking your cousin is in the throes of her chronic wanderlust."

His arms rose and fell with her deep sigh. "I'm afraid you're right. But I'm sure we could talk her into staying a while longer. Even though she's sold her share to you—with that money you didn't tell me about for so long."

She glared. He smiled. "I thought we settled that last summer. I'd think a woman would like knowing her husband's more than a singer of songs, but you don't act that way."

She sighed again, then snuggled closer. Leaving his prosperous inn in Ireland *hadn't* been practical. But how could she argue with a move that brought him into her life?

He'd sold enough shares to his partner in Inishowen to buy Val's half of The Fishwife, as well as put a down payment on Roberta Cortine's house for an inn, and still leave his mother and brother financially secure.

"Val has a proprietary interest in the business," she pursued. "And you know she'd do anything for you."

"And you, Noreen? Would you do anything for me?"

She looked up at the huskiness in his words. "You know I would."

"Then let's go home to Cape Ann as we planned."

The word *home* warmed her. She hugged him tightly and burrowed her cheek against the bare flesh at his open shirt collar. "All right, Cahill. I just thought your mother—"

"Will be on the first plane over to see the baby. And, who knows, maybe she'll decide a grandchild is enough reason to come to America for good."

She knew how much he wanted that. She understood his

mother's reluctance to start a new life, away from friends, extended family and the familiar landscape of her Irish world. But from the endless questions seventeen-year-old Kiernan asked about the habits and interests of American teenagers, Eleanor suspected a second McCrea might start the immigration process soon. She smiled to think of the havoc Kiernan, with his dramatic good looks, could wreak on the young female hearts of Cape Ann.

With both her sons in America, as well as a grandchild, perhaps Kathleen McCrea would follow.

Eleanor hoped so. For, in her mother-in-law, she had found the kind of woman she'd once longed for as a mother. And somehow that allowed her to view her mother's flaws with loving tolerance.

Cahill's thoughts had also gone to the growing relationship between his mother and his wife. Eleanor and Connie had reached a better understanding, but with his own mother, he knew his Noreen felt more, as though she'd come home. He saw something in his mother's eyes, too. He thought he saw her accept his wife as a daughter, but maybe it was only a reflection of his making peace at last with the loss of Patsy and his father.

"On the other hand, I've a feeling my mother might come to the conclusion that a daughter-in-law is sufficient cause to cross the Atlantic for good. Not a mere son, of course. But a daughter-in-law...."

They were a family. A growing family, he thought with the same intense stab of pleasure that came every time he thought of their child growing in Noreen.

She looked up and he saw a smile and tears in her eyes.

Gray eyes with the glitter of diamonds, with diamonds fragmenting out of them. Then deep in the center of the brilliance, a solid core, as practical, as real, as reliable as the gray flannel she'd once likened them to.

As practical, as real, as reliable as his Noreen's love.

* * * * *

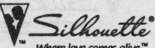